"YOU ARE SO BEAUTIFUL."

His eyes moved slowly over her face.

"I don't want to talk anymore," she said.

"At this moment, talking would be safer."

She smiled. "Only danger brings glory."

His hot, dark eyes searched hers for one long heartbeat. Then he touched one callused fingertip to the pulse beating wild at the base of her neck, trailing it out and over her collarbone onto her shoulder and down until it met the edge of her dress.

He leaned down and brushed her lips with his. Fire shot through her, fire in rainbow-colored flames.

"Ahh, Sky," he crooned.

Avon Romances by
Genell Dellin

CHEROKEE DAWN
CHEROKEE NIGHTS

Avon Romantic Treasures
COMANCHE WIND

If You've Enjoyed This Book,
Be Sure to Read These Other
AVON ROMANTIC TREASURES

CAPTIVES OF THE NIGHT *by Loretta Chase*
CHEYENNE'S SHADOW *by Deborah Camp*
FORTUNE'S BRIDE *by Judith E. French*
GABRIEL'S BRIDE *by Samantha James*
LORD OF FIRE *by Emma Merritt*

Coming Soon

WITH ONE LOOK *by Jennifer Horsman*

COMANCHE FLAME

GENELL DELLIN

An Avon Romantic Treasure

AVON BOOKS ◆ NEW YORK

COMANCHE FLAME is an original publication of Avon Books. This work has never before appeared in book form. This work is a novel. Any similarity to actual persons or events is purely coincidental.

AVON BOOKS
A division of
The Hearst Corporation
1350 Avenue of the Americas
New York, New York 10019

Copyright © 1994 by Genell Smith Dellin
Inside cover author photo by Glamour Shots
Published by arrangement with the author
Library of Congress Catalog Card Number: 93-90909
ISBN: 0-380-77524-7

First Avon Books Printing: June 1994

AVON TRADEMARK REG. U.S. PAT. OFF. AND IN OTHER COUNTRIES, MARCA REGISTRADA, HECHO EN U.S.A.

Printed in the U.S.A.

RA 10 9 8 7 6 5 4 3 2 1

For Curtiss Ann Matlock, dear friend.

Chapter 1

New Mexico Territory, 1858

"There's nothing wrong with Ysidora Pretty Sky that a good man can't cure."

Those words, flatly spoken in Grandmother Hukiyani's ancient voice, stopped Sky's breath in her chest.

Wrong. Something wrong with her.

For four moons now, she'd been hearing what was wrong with the way she behaved, but now something was wrong with her very self!

She crushed her new Spanish dress into one arm and dropped onto her knees to peer out under the rolled-up wall of the tipi. From there she could see the whole dozen or so women working at the cookfires.

They knew that. And they knew she could hear them.

"It'll take a *strong,* good man, Grandmother," her best friend, Lark, said, chuckling. "Can High Wolf persuade her not to wear that shocking Spanish dress when she defies him and goes into Council with the warriors?"

Everyone laughed.

Sky set her jaw and glared out at them, all continuing with their work, all carefully not looking her way.

Hot, rebellious fury surged through her.

She leapt to her feet, untied her elkskin skirt and let it fall, ripped the loose, beaded blouse with the long, swinging fringes up over her head, threw it across the tipi, and pulled on the soft silk dress.

Taking a long, deep breath to make her breasts fill the low neckline, she settled herself into it and fastened it at the waist.

Then she bent and stepped out through the door-opening, straightened her back, and walked out into the middle of the women working to prepare the rendezvous feast.

"I am no longer a child to be corrected with teasing and taunts," she announced. "I do not *care* whether I get the approval and praise of the band."

Every woman stopped working and turned to look at her.

She swept her gaze around to each of them as if she were Chief. Like her father, Windrider.

"You might as well save your breath," she told them. "Nothing any of you can say will make me return this dress to the trader."

They all looked at her, but no one replied.

"I like this dress and I will wear it wherever I want."

Then her mother, the Fire Flower, answered.

"I am sure you will!" she said, in her spirit-ed way. "Would you please wear it over here to the pemmican, since you are now a woman, not a child, and cut us off some slices for the feast?"

Everyone burst out laughing, then, louder than ever.

The fury flared higher in Sky, just for a moment, but her mother twinkled her green eyes at her and winked, and then she couldn't help laughing, too.

Sky knew her mother had embraced all the ways of the Comanche when she had given up her white name, Jennie O'Bannion, to marry Windrider.

She walked, with all the dignity she could muster, across the open, grassy area that was the center of this new camp on Don Diego's *rancho*, sat down, and began to work at the task her mother had given her. Soon, though, her resentment came flooding back.

Because they kept up their barrage of advice.

Even the Fire Flower.

"Sky, as a wife, I hope you'll take more interest in keeping your lodge neat than in horses and clothes," she said, when someone mentioned the need for some new parfleches to hang on their lodgepoles.

"Yes," Grandmother Hukiyani agreed. "And, also, granddaughter, you must stop that talk about not cutting your hair after you marry—it could drive High Wolf away!"

"Oh?" Sky flared, and slashed the knife down on the pemmican loaf. "Is that what is *wrong* with me? Long hair and horses and clothes? You have waited for many seasons to tell me this! All my life I thought you liked me the way I am!"

"We *love* you!" her mother said.

"But you want me to change! You let Grandmother say something is wrong with me and you don't disagree!"

"When you were a child you could gather flowers and herbs instead of berries, you could ride and raid for horses, although most girls didn't," Grandmother Hukiyani said, in her most patient tone. "You could hunt instead of scraping hides. But now you have eighteen summers."

Helpless rage boiled up in Sky for the hundredth time in the four moons since she had given High Wolf her promise to marry him.

"You betray me!" she cried, glaring from her mother to her grandmother. "Something is *wrong* with me now—yet I am the same person I always was!"

"You said it, yourself, when you were talking about your new dress," the Fire Flower told her. "Then you were a child. Now you are a woman."

"So the freedom of my childhood was only playacting? From what I've been hearing, ever since I gave High Wolf my promise to marry, the life of a woman is nothing but restrictions!"

Grandmother Hukiyani spoke again in a hard, sure tone that made Sky's temper rise even higher.

"You have no choice but to accept that."

Tears blurred Sky's vision as she brought the

knife down and made a slice of pemmican fly away from the loaf. All she saw was the bright, autumn sunlight flashing off its blade.

"I hope you won't speak English or Spanish to your husband much," Good Crier called to her. "High Wolf puts much store in keeping the customs of The People."

Slope said, with a chuckle, "You are right, Sister. But she could use English when she is angry with him. He knows very little of it."

The general murmuring of laughter rose up again, swirled around the whole circle of cook-fires.

Sky jumped to her feet and threw down the knife.

"Why don't all of you just put robes over your heads and give me a ghost scare?" she cried, glaring at their smiling faces. "Or tell me some tales of Big Cannibal Owl? You remember—he lives in a cave on the south side of the Wichita Mountains and eats bad children at night! Is he coming to get me?"

"My sweet colleen, we are only trying to help you," her mother said, and stopped stirring the stew on her cook rack to come put her arm around Sky.

"I don't *need* help! I am myself. I must *be* myself! I cannot change into someone else just because I marry!"

"We are only trying to help you live peacefully with your husband," Grandmother Hukiyani said.

The Fire Flower hugged Sky tight.

"All we want is for you to stay with us for

your whole life and be happy, my darling."

Sky's throat tightened as if she had bitten into a green persimmon. She hugged her mother back, held onto her and burrowed her face into the Fire Flower's fragrant cloud of curly red hair.

"I want that, too," she whispered.

Really and truly, she did.

But the familiar guilt surged through her. Guilt about sometimes wanting to leave them, about saying sometimes that she would go and find her mother's people. That always made Jennie turn pale and tell Sky that if she did such a thing, she would find out what restrictions really were.

She sighed. She didn't know where she wanted to go or what kind of life she wanted to live; the only thing she knew for sure was that she was different from all the other women in her band.

Nothing was wrong with her. She was just different.

"Yes, dear Sky," Grandmother Hukiyani said, giving her that sharp glance again. "We don't want to hear any more talk of you going to live with your mother's people. That will drive High Wolf away for sure."

Sky dropped her arms, stepped out of her mother's embrace.

"Then *let* it!" she snapped, fighting to keep her tone sufficiently respectful. She shook her fist in the air for emphasis. "*Let* him run away! I don't need a cure and I don't need a man!"

They all laughed again.

"Oh, yes, you do," Hukiyani said, with a lusty, rasping chuckle. "I learned on my wedding night that a woman needs a man, and so will you, dear Sky."

Meadowlark, who was *supposed* to be Sky's best friend, laughed loudest.

She said, "After one moon of sharing the bedrobes with her handsome High Wolf, we will hear no more of this talk!"

Everybody laughed some more, several made bawdy remarks, and several more looked at Lark and murmured strong agreement.

Meddlers!

Lark pressed on.

"Grandmother, do you think that, after a moon full of nights with High Wolf, Sky will stop her talk of sitting in Council?"

"Of course! Husband and lodge and babies will keep her too busy to meddle in the men's affairs."

Sweat popped out in Sky's palms.

Such duty would crush her. Somehow, she had known that all her life.

But what else would she do?

While they bantered and chuckled among themselves, while her mother went back to stirring the food bubbling over her fire, Sky walked slowly to a backrest beside the roasting pits and sat down.

Grandmother Hukiyani smiled at her.

Then she smiled at the Fire Flower, her adopted daughter.

"Fire Flower, do not worry," Hukiyani said, comfortingly. "This girl loves you and her father and her brother—she loves all of us too much to ever leave us. Remember that, dear Jen-nie."

Sudden tears stung Sky like sharp thorns.

She *did* love them all too much to go away! She *loved* them.

Yet, how could she stay and live the rest of her life as a Comanche wife?

But what else would she do? All her friends, Lark included, had had husbands for three or four summers, husbands and babies.

And where else would there be so many people who loved her?

Her throat tightened into one huge knot at the thought.

Plus, she *had* given her promise to High Wolf. She had chosen him herself, had given him her solemn word of honor. Then, Windrider, her father, had given him his.

Soon High Wolf would bring many horses to Windrider.

And he would take Sky to his lodge in exchange.

She let out her breath in a long, shaky sigh.

The sweet, homey smell of burning wood, the delicious fragrances of the wild onions and roots in the stew, the honeyed scent of the pemmican, all drifted in and filled up her body. Her people had gone hungry, sometimes, during this droughty summer, but now, with all this meat the don had given them, the old feeling of peace and plenty hung over the camp.

The dark heads of her grandmother and her friends and the bright flame of her mother's red

hair were all bent to their tasks of stirring the
stew and rolling the hackberry balls, keeping
the cookfires at just the right heat, unwrapping
the dried buffalo meat and the pounded prickly
pear cakes that would be Windrider's band's
contribution to the *rancho*'s rendezvous feast,
and stacking the stiff pieces of hides that would
be used to hold the food. Stirring the drink
made from corn traded from the Wichitas.
Boiling the berries to serve to their guests.

Preparing to nourish their visitors and their
families.

Their words and their motions flowed together like the chanting of a song that they
had all learned at birth.

All these women whom she loved and who
loved her.

The familiar yearning, the lonely longing for
something she couldn't name, fell around Sky's
heart.

The soft voices of the women, murmuring
quietly among themselves while they let her
decide whether to heed their advice, filled her
ears.

The lump in her throat grew so large she
couldn't swallow. She wrapped her arms
around herself and gazed at them, feeling
the familiarity of the camp surround her.

But a high, keening wail rose inside her.

Hadn't any of them, even one single one of
them ever felt the way she did?

Finally, Hukiyani lifted her round, wrinkled, old face from her task and spoke to Sky
again.

"You will see," she said, and now her ancient voice was gentle, openly filled with love. "You will be happy married to High Wolf, my granddaughter Pretty Sky. You will listen to him play his flute and you will help him prepare his medicine. You will do much good, you will help our people as wife of our medicine man."

Sky sat up straight; she leapt to her feet.

"Can I not do much good, can I not help my people as *myself*, Ysidora Pretty Sky?" she cried. "Can I not *be* Ysidora Pretty Sky and be a grown-up woman, too?"

She clutched up the long, satin skirt of her new dress and ran into her lodge, started jerking it off to get into her elkskins again.

A ride. She only needed a good ride, away from disapproving faces and eyes full of love.

No one called to her when she burst out of her door opening and ran between the scattered fires to reach the grassy path winding between the tipis. She ran away from them, ran toward Don Diego's racetrack on the other side of the cottonwood trees that grew along the bank of the chattering creek called Mucha Que.

Dodging dogs, children, cookfires, and halfgrown boys playing games of skill in the pathways, she ran for her mare, tethered at the edge of the camp. Ran toward the raucous rendezvous trading grounds filled with Comanches and Comancheros and their women from their village of Chaparito, sheepherders and a few Santa Fe traders, Don Diego's friends and Spanish neighbors, his vaqueros and the ones from nearby *ranchos*.

A race. She only needed a wild, fast race to clear her head and then she would know what to do.

So she jerked Far Girl loose and turned her head toward the track, knowing as she did so that her father and brother and High Wolf were in the crowd of men there. Knowing that not one of them would approve of her appearing among them.

Well, let them disapprove! She would ride into that noisy, swirling crowd and shout out a challenge for a race. She wasn't a wife yet, she was still herself!

And she had to do *something*.

She hit the flat at a gallop and didn't slow down until she'd reached the edge of the crowd pressing around the racetrack, which was a long straightaway marked out on the grass. She rode into the yelling mob, mostly men who were all howling at once, in Spanish and in Comanche, waving objects they wanted to wager high above their heads. Guns, shirts, knives, parfleches, and off to her right, even a fine bow with a swinging feather ornament. Eagle feathers.

Frowning, Sky stared at the bow until the bodies shifted and she saw who held it.

Buffalo Robe. He was staggering drunk, from liquor he'd traded for from the Comancheros, no doubt.

If he lost that bow, he would hate himself tomorrow, and so would the old man Isawuro, whose skilled handiwork it was.

She had just decided to try to push into the

crowd and talk to him when Far Girl jumped sideways. Sky turned to see why.

Something silver was flashing in the sunlight right at the young mare's nose, something in the fist of a Comanchero who wore a dirty, pink-and-brown-striped serape thrown diagonally across his stocky body. He stood directly in her way.

He waved his hand again. Far Girl danced backwards.

Sky tightened her seat and her grip on the one rein.

"Stop that!" she yelled in Spanish. "Make way for my horse!"

"Wouldn't you like to have these genuine silver combs to wear in your beautiful hair?"

"No, thank you!"

She tried to get around him.

He caught hold of her stirrup, wrapped his hand around her moccasined foot.

"I'll make you a wager—the combs against your mare," he shouted up at her over all the noise. "The next race is a Don Rafael Montoya purebred against Old Owl's black pony. You take the pony!"

"I don't want to make a wager with you. Get your hand off me!"

He ignored that and stared up at her, demanding with his close-set, bloodshot eyes that she agree to his plan, holding her stirrup in an unrelenting grip. This time he waved the silver in *her* face.

Then he smiled. "Come down off of there and let's talk about it. I can persuade you—

the women always give in to my charms."

"Get away from me!"

He kept on smiling. He didn't move a muscle.

Sky picked up the end of her braided horsehair rein and lashed it down on him.

"Pedro!" a woman's voice screamed.

He turned Sky loose and whirled away from her.

The woman was fighting her way through the crowd, her wild, burning eyes fastened to the silver that he still held high in the air.

"Don't wager my combs!" she shrieked. "Pedro! My combs!"

The crowd fell apart as if shattered by the quick throw of a lance. The noise of the shouted wagers lessened, then faded still more.

For an instant Sky thought it was for the sake of the screaming woman, but then she looked toward the racetrack.

The sight of the Spanish horseman struck her like a hawk diving.

She could not take her eyes off him.

He was dressed in black and white, resplendent as an eagle in the bright sunlight. His broad shoulders stayed straight and still while he loped the high-headed gray Andalusian through the crowd. Like many of the Spanish, he was a natural horseman.

And so naturally handsome that not even the wonderful, purebred horse or the heavily carved silver-trimmed saddle he rode could pull her gaze away from him. His hat hung down his back, from silver-threaded strings that lay along his stiff white collar.

She could not take her eyes off him.

His hair was as black as his waist-length coat and tight pants; it was drawn back and tied at the nape of his muscular neck. His skin was a deep reddish brown that met the white of his collar in a stark line like the edge of the earth meeting the sky.

He was darker than most of the Spanish she'd seen, from riding in the sun, no doubt. But he was dressed much too richly to be a vaquero. He must be a ranchero, perhaps a neighbor of Don Diego.

He stood out from all the other men there like a bright star in a black night.

Her fascinated gaze clung to him, even after the struggle erupted again at Far Girl's head.

"Give me the combs!" the woman screamed. "They are mine! They were my mother's! Pedro, if you wager them, you will lose them, you thief!"

"Thief!" the man roared. "How can you call me a thief? I am your *husband*! What is yours is mine."

A terrible, smacking sound followed. It sent Far Girl into a wild, dizzying spin that tore Sky's gaze from the Spaniard and her hand from the rein.

When the mare stopped, the woman lay on the ground, shrieking, with the dirty man looming over her. She looked up at him with eyes full of despairing tears.

And terror. She was obviously afraid of him. Yet, beneath the terror, in her eyes and in the set of her mouth, lay an unflinching determination. That woman was not going to lose her mother's combs.

Sky's pulse stopped for a moment out of fear for her. If she got up and hit Pedro back, if she tried again to get the combs, he might kill her—his face was twisted and dark with enough hateful anger to destroy everybody at the rendezvous.

She would have to help the woman.

Sky stood in the stirrup.

But, before she could step down, the gray Andalusian thundered into the space between her and the couple, slid to a stop, and the Spanish horseman swung off onto the ground, moving like sparkling lightning.

Tiny, round silver conchos ran down the outside seams of his tight black pants, winking in the sun all the way down his long legs. He had saddle-muscled thighs so strong they strained against the covering cloth as he strode toward the Comanchero.

This man possessed much *puha*, and he knew it.

She could not take her eyes off him.

The crowd grew more silent still, straining to see what he would do.

The grimy Comanchero hurriedly stuffed the combs into his clothing beneath the serape, set his heels, and raised his fists to fight.

But the Spaniard moved past him as if he were not even there and bent over the woman.

He lifted her to her feet. She glanced once

into his face with a quick, staring look of shock and then hung her head.

"Are you hurt?" the Spanish horseman asked her.

The low, rich sound of his voice sent a thrill running over Sky's skin.

"Shall I call someone to help you?"

The poor woman shook her head mutely and fixed her eyes on the ground.

The Spaniard held one huge, brown hand around her arm to steady her and turned to look at her husband.

Pedro was still waiting to fight.

But, already, while the Spaniard's back was turned, he easily could have sent a bullet or a knife into him. The handsome horseman had helped the woman without stopping to think of the consequences.

Just as Sky had almost done. She tried to see a flash of his eyes, to get a glimpse of his soul. He was her kindred spirit.

"The combs," the horseman ordered.

He held out his free hand.

"The silver has nothing to do with you," Pedro snarled, dropping his fists to his sides. "Who do you think you are to interfere? *Madre de Dios*, man, she is my *wife*!"

"I am Don Rafael Romero Montoya y Teran. I am ranchero here," the horseman replied, in a tone so hard and cold that Sky could not believe this was the same voice that had spoken to the woman. "Give her her property. Then leave my land."

His strong brown hand hung steady in the

air, like a stone suspended. Palm up. For any
other person, that gesture would be a plea.

But for this man of much *puha*, somehow, it
was a command.

Sky's heart swelled with joy that he was
doing such a thing. No man she knew, no
Comanche man, would've interfered between
a husband and wife, no matter what the injus-
tice. She wanted to raise her fist high in the air
and let out a thrilling cry.

Don Rafael Romero Montoya Y Teran calmly
waited.

Reluctantly, stiffly, as if his arm moved
against his will, the Comanchero reached in
and pulled out the combs. He gave them
up.

Then he stared at the Spanish ranchero, hate
gleaming like a torch in his bloodshot eyes.

But Don Rafael didn't spare him so much as
a glance. He took the woman's hand, folded
her treasure into it, and strode back to his
horse.

Pedro, roaring incoherently, started to lunge
at him, but a man right behind him, wearing
a yellow cloth shirt the color of buffalo grass
stepped out of the crowd, caught his shoulders, and held him.

Pedro twisted around to see who it was.

"Let me go, Jaime!" he roared, and struggled
like a wild man.

But Jaime was the stronger.

"You will get yourself killed, Pedro," he said,
coaxingly. "Don Rafael said to leave his *rancho*
and you must do so now. Think about our

trade, man! Don't get us both run off from this rendezvous!"

Pedro surged forward, Jaime held him back.

But Don Rafael seemed not to care in the least which of them won. He never paused, never glanced back at them.

He stuck the shining, polished toe of his boot into his silver stirrup and stepped up into the saddle. Only then did he look at Pedro the Comanchero.

One look, sharp as an arrow's point.

It told the man, as clearly as his words had done, to leave his land.

Pedro turned his back and pushed his way into the crowd with Jaime following.

The Spaniard wheeled his mount. His gaze met Sky's.

A flame leapt between them.

Some part of her she had not known existed, something at the very core of her deepest self, contracted.

His eyes flashed hard and bright, like dark suns.

He made a slight bow in the saddle.

"*Señorita!*" he said, his sensual lips lifting at the corners in the ghost of a smile. "The Comanchero will not bother *you* again, I am sure."

His nose was strong, slightly hooked, very arrogant, his cheekbones high and hard-chiseled. He looked almost Indian, but she had never seen an Indian man as handsome as he.

His hot black eyes swept over her, over all of her, as a man looks at a woman.

A strange feeling danced down her spine.

Then the moment was gone.

The gray stallion swung in a circle that pointed him toward the track again and the Spanish horseman galloped away.

Sky could not take her eyes from him.

His silver trimmings caught the light from Father Sun and threw its brightness everywhere, sparkling like the crispness that filled the cool air here on the higher plains, closer to the mountains.

Blazing like the brilliant, boundless blue above them.

Leaving her alone.

Chapter 2

Rafael knew that his father could not let him enter Windrider's tipi without repeating his instructions, and he was right. Just outside the door-opening, Don Diego stopped and gestured for Rafael to listen.

"Remember, *mi hijo*," he said, "our Comanche friends do not know yet about Waters's new *rancho*. Let me tell them that news—I will choose the right time."

The old, resentful irritation ran through Rafael.

The hidalgo trusted him with managing a huge *rancho* with the thousands of animals and hundreds of people that lived on it, but not with making an alliance with Don Diego's Comanche friends. Would he never trust him to grow up?

"*Sí*," he said, abruptly.

"And move to the right around the circle when we go in. Never step across the fire, nor between someone else and the fire."

"You have told me that already, Don Diego."

"I only want you to behave properly," the older man said, testily.

Rafael permitted himself one small flare-up.

"You sound as if I am ten years old!"

He bent his back, ducked his head, and stepped into the dim lodge full of people.

Immediately, the sweet smell of the smoke from the fire filled his nose and his lungs. It made his eyes sting.

He blinked and exhaled, trying to blow it away as Don Diego entered and they began moving around the circle toward Windrider, who sat directly across from the door.

"*Ahó!*" he said, raising his hand in greeting.

He gestured toward the empty backrests on either side of him.

That was when Rafael saw the girl.

She sat behind Windrider, in the shadows slightly to one side of him, as still at this moment as she had been vibrantly in motion when he'd seen her by the racetrack. But it was she—the heavily beaded blouse was the same, and so was the flash of her huge, dark eyes.

So was the swift rush of sensation that surged through him.

He tried to ignore it.

The don and he sat down in the places Windrider had indicated. That made them part of a large circle of Comanches who sat cross-legged on the ground around the fire.

The silence became more complete. Nothing moved except the skillful hands of one warrior, who was preparing the pipe.

Rafael kept his eyes straight ahead, refused to let himself even try to get a glimpse of the girl. Spirited wild beauty or no, he had enough on his mind without thinking of her.

What was she doing here, anyway? She was the only woman in the lodge.

At last, Windrider spoke, in Spanish as good as Rafael's.

"My friends, Don Diego and Don Rafael! I, Windrider, welcome you!"

Rafael wished, suddenly, that the chief had spoken in the tongue of the *Nermernuh*, even though he could not have understood it.

That would have seemed more right, somehow, here in this Council lodge filled with smells of men's sweat, tobacco, burning pine and sage, with the softness of a buffalo robe under him and the sunlight coming in through the translucent walls.

This was a different world.

The world of the girl who would've stepped off her horse in defense of a helpless woman if he hadn't done so instead.

Windrider raised his hand and gestured toward the people he named as he spoke.

"My son, Nokona. My brother, Ten Bears. My nephew, Eagle Tail Feather. My daughter, Ysidora Pretty Sky. Our medicine man, High Wolf. We and all of the Council of our band of the Antelope Comanche welcome you."

So. The girl was Windrider's daughter.

He smiled to himself. Of course. The War Chief's daughter, whipping an insolent lout away from her horse with her rein. The War Chief's daughter, ready to leap into the dangerous fray for the sake of fairness—not for herself, but for a stranger.

That willingness and the look of contempt

she'd been giving the Comanchero were partly what had made Rafael do what he'd done. Usually he didn't act on impulse or follow his feelings that way.

"We thank you for the beef we eat," Windrider was saying. "Tonight, at the feast, we will present you with gifts."

Don Diego cleared his throat.

"My friend, Windrider," he replied. "We thank you and your band for the gifts. We welcome you to our *rancho. Bienvenido*."

After several more such formalities, the two men made polite talk of the weather, the scarcity of buffalo and of rain, the condition of the *rancho*'s cattle, the speed of the horses that had been raced that day, and they compared this rendezvous with others from the past. Rafael joined in once or twice, when directly spoken to, but he had trouble keeping his mind on the conversation.

The fragrance of the smoke was becoming stronger again. A curl of it, full of the smell of burning sage, drifted his way.

He could feel the presence of the girl sitting behind him. Ysidora Pretty Sky.

"My friends and brothers!" Windrider said, in a compelling tone, and Rafael began to listen again. "You remember the events of the past fall and spring. In the time before the last Big Cold, an Anglo intruder called Waters settled his man in Comancheria to make a ranch."

He stopped and accepted the pipe that the medicine man, High Wolf, leaned forward to hand to him. Windrider lifted it to his lips and took a long draw from it.

Then he said, "The foolish white-eyed one did this thing after the *Nermernuh* had warned the Anglos many, many times not to make any permanent settlement east of the Río Gallinas!"

His measured, angry words boomed up from the bottom of his powerful chest. They filled the tipi.

Every eye in the lodge turned to him. His face became fierce as a panther's in the glow from the fire.

"In the Cottonball Moon, March, the *Nermernuh* attacked and destroyed that ranch!"

A great cheer went up. Windrider waited for the sounds of the voices to die away, then he expelled the smoke from the ceremonial pipe.

"In the Flower Moon of May," he said, and his tone grew soft, calm—dangerous—"the Texian Rangers rode deep into Comancheria to take revenge, deeper into our own places than they had ever come before, all the way to the Big Sandy River."

His words became slow, hard, as full of menace as a gathering storm. "Those Texans slaughtered many men, women, and children of the Kotsoteka Band."

Don Diego made a clucking sound of sympathy.

"The Anglos," he said, "will do anything for more land."

Windrider passed the pipe to him.

"You speak truth, My Friend," he said. "Their

forts and their settlements that they call Texas have already forced us far to the west of where we normally range. Now others of them have made New Mexico."

He waited until the don had taken a pull on the pipe.

"We need the help of the Spanish to keep them from pushing at us from the west side, as they already push from the east," Windrider said.

Don Diego's dark, slender fingers tightened around the carved stem of the pipe.

"I have much to tell you, *mi amigo*," he said, and his voice wavered a bit under the weight of the words that Rafael knew were coming. "The Anglos are not only hungry for land, but for gold. The long-ago legend of the treasure of the *Conquistadores* is traveling on the wind again—these white men have heard it for the first time."

"That old story!" Windrider said, derisively. "Everyone knows there's nothing to that."

"I agree," Don Diego said. "But those greedy ones don't want to hear our opinion, which most people share. They listen only to the words of the legend."

"What legend, *Señor*?"

The velvet murmur vibrated into the air from behind him. A woman's voice. Ysidora Pretty Sky, whose voice was misty and warm, like smoke.

The medicine man, High Wolf, looked up, stared past Rafael's shoulder at her, and frowned fiercely. He made a sharp gesture as if to signal that she should not speak again.

"Mesa Rica got its name because of an old story," Don Diego answered her, "only a legend, a myth, that says some exhausted *Conquistadores* cached gold and silver somewhere in its north wall."

He drew on the pipe.

The words hung in the air, hovered over everyone there, for the length of two heartbeats.

"The legend is true!"

The words burst from Ysidora Pretty Sky with the suddenness of a ripe fruit splitting its skin.

"That is more than just a story, *Señor!*" she cried. "The treasure is there! I know that—my medicine tells me—it hasn't been moved in all these many seasons!"

Her low-pitched voice was filled with such faith that it brought a stunned silence sweeping through the lodge.

And made the hair stand up on the back of Rafael's neck.

He wanted to turn and see her face, but somehow he couldn't look away from the fire.

It crackled and hissed, it called to him, and sent its flames leaping up. He watched them.

Two tall, yellow-orange flames curved outward and met at the top. That shimmering point, for one long, airless moment, held a pile of glittering coins, gold, and silver, too. And a gold cross.

All of them, the coins and the cross, grew larger and larger until they filled the lodge, shining and flashing nearly bright enough to blind him.

Dimly, as if from a long way off, he heard the bitter bark of Windrider's voice.

"Daughter, don't be as foolish as the white-eyes! No one will ever find that treasure. It does not exist."

Rafael felt a sound of dissent rip itself loose from his throat, but he didn't recognize the voice. It was unfamiliar to him, as if it belonged to someone else.

The coins melted all together and ran down the curving flames to disappear into the fire.

Then his father spoke and Rafael heard him at his elbow.

Close. As he really was, not far away, as Windrider had sounded.

Don Diego gave Rafael a frowning, curious glance and their eyes met.

To Rafael, suddenly, he looked like a stranger.

Sky stared at Rafael's broad back. He held himself even straighter now, as if the noise that had rushed out of him a few minutes ago had stiffened his body as well as his voice.

His spirit-medicine voice, coming, with the same truth as hers, out of a vision in the fire!

Did the Spanish also have medicine visions? Like the Cheyenne and the Shoshone, perhaps, without first going on a quest for them?

She shivered, ran her hands up beneath the long fringes of her blouse, and tried to rub away the goose bumps on her arms.

This man had spiritual power as well as every other kind.

From the moment he had entered the tipi he was drawn to her as to a fire in winter.

Exactly as he had done the first time she saw him.

"The treasure may be there or it may not . . ." Don Diego said, and the rising new note of anxiety in his voice caught Sky's ears.

But her eyes stayed on Rafael. He turned and looked at her.

His dark gaze burned into hers.

And, with no words, he spoke to her.

He knew that she knew he'd seen a vision.

A vision that validated her own medicine.

The two of them knew that the treasure was there.

An instant later, he had turned back to stare straight ahead of him into the fire.

She shivered, but inside her blood ran warm.

He truly *was* her kindred spirit!

Don Diego cleared his throat and went on.

". . . however, it is certain that the Anglos are there. I have the sad duty to tell you, Windrider, *mi amigo*, that Charlie Waters has started another ranch on the east side of the Gallinas."

That incredible news tore a gasp from Sky's lips and whipped her head around so she could look at her father.

Windrider's face went still as stone. His eyes glittered as he searched his friend's lined face.

"Are you sure?"

"With my own eyes I saw it—about half-way between the river and the mesa—before I came to tell you."

Then Don Diego, speaking even more gently, added, "This time, Waters himself is at that *rancho*, too. I believe it is because he has heard the legend and he is searching for the old treasure."

Windrider made a noise rough enough to tear out his throat.

"Why don't the white soldiers who have set up the fort at Hatch's Ranch stop him?" he cried. "That is why they are there—to hold the boundaries and keep the peace!"

"Sometimes they look the other way," Don Diego said, with a shrug. "I heard that General Sykes warned Waters not to go back across the river, but did nothing when he disobeyed."

"Why *wouldn't* he stop him?" Windrider growled. "Is this agreement we made with the Americans also no good, like so many of the others? Didn't you tell me that Sykes is a good, honest man?"

"He is. But I heard that the men who give orders to Sykes, perhaps even his *presidente*, have told him to let Waters test you again," Don Diego said. "They want to see if the time is right to take another slice of Comancheria and add it to the Territory of New Mexico."

Sky tried to draw in some air to calm her thundering heart, but an awful fear filled her chest, a fear that would not let her breathe.

The same fear she had heard in Windrider's words.

Her whole body went numb.

Fear. Never before had she known it could touch Windrider.

Was this threat of the white-eyes that enormous? Was it actually too big for Windrider?

Windrider, War Chief, best warrior, best horseman of all the *Nermernuh*, was afraid.

Her adored father who could face any foe, fight and win any battle.

He could not win this one. She had heard that truth in his voice.

She could see it in his face, which was still turned, almost in pleading, to his old friend, Don Diego. A terrible truth.

And a dark fear.

A sudden burning spread over her scalp at the back of her head, a chill shivering chased along her skin.

Windrider clenched his fists, brought them down hard on his bare, muscular thighs.

"The *Nermernuh* will do more than raid *Señor* Waters's ranch now! We will destroy *all* the Anglos and their ranches and their worthless soldiers—we will ride the warpath before the Big Cold!"

Shouts of angry agreement filled the tipi.

They filled Sky's ears, then her whole head, they boomed off her bones like the echo of doom.

Sheer panic rose in her stomach and chest, bubbled up into her throat in a tearing, ripping scream. She clamped her lips shut to hold it in.

The warpath! Against the *soldiers*?

The soldiers at Hatch's Ranch, which her people had ridden past on the way to Don Diego's *rancho*? The soldiers with the enormous guns?

And only another day or two away there were many, many more soldiers at Fort Union.

Stiff with terror for their lives, she looked around the circle from one hard face to another. Her wonderful father, whom she could not bear to see in such pain.

Her brother, her darling brother, Nokona, who had fought the other boys when she was little to make them let her ride with them and learn the games of war and raiding instead of playing the boring girls' games.

And Eagle Tail Feather. Her precious cousin, almost as close to her heart as Nokona.

Her old, grouchy uncle, Ten Bears, gruff and sour so much of the time, yet sweet sometimes with her, his favorite.

And High Wolf. Even though she dreaded to live in his lodge and let him direct her life, she loved him in a way. High Wolf, who played on his flute songs so high and sweet that the birds fluttered helplessly around in circles of jealousy. High Wolf, who was so proud to say that Sky was his promised one, even though he *did* want to change her.

Only a few suns from now, a very few, they would all be gone from her, gone fighting the white-eyes.

Fighting the white-eyes who had guns so huge they rolled them about on wagons.

The scream erupted from her lips as a shout.

"No!" she cried. "We cannot fight them. If it's treasure Waters wants, if that is why he's in Comancheria, let's give it to him so he'll go! If his ranch is not there, east of the Gallinas, we will not have to fight!"

Once again, because she had spoken, all noise left the lodge.

This time, dozens of dark eyes turned on her, glittering in the firelight and the dim sunlight that came through the walls.

High Wolf's eyes scorched her face worse than all the others. His voice thundered into the silence.

"Do not say another word! You have already contradicted your father and his honored guest about the treasure and now you try to stop a war after Windrider, our *War Chief* has called for it! No woman should speak in Council!"

She scrambled for her courage among the ruins that panic had made inside her.

She found it and glared rudely back at him.

"No woman should *sit* in Council," he said. "Pretty Sky, go now to the other women."

Sky's thigh muscles flexed; she laid her knees flat against the robe on which she sat as if to stake them through it to the grassy earth beneath. High Wolf was forgetting himself, forgetting in the excitement of the coming warpath that she was not yet his woman. That he was stepping on Windrider's authority.

Her stomach tightened with a quick, sick feeling that wormed its way up into her brain beneath her fear. Soon, once he had brought horses to Windrider, the authority over her *would* be his.

She felt heat suffuse her face. Now, *now*, she had to set the limits of what she could bear.

"No man," she said, her throat tight with the effort it took to keep her voice steady, "*no one* will tell me when to speak and when to be silent."

The firelight melted High Wolf's face. It hardened and turned into a mask.

"Or when to go out and when to come in."

High Wolf's stiff lips opened to reply.

But Windrider spoke first.

"High Wolf holds to tradition, but he has seen only a few winters," he said, clearly irritated by the distraction, but also plainly determined to assert his authority. "Those of us who have seen many winters know that, in seasons past, women in our band have not only sat in Council, they have spoken in Council."

He swept his glance around the circle of faces. It touched Rafael.

The Spaniard took that as an invitation to speak.

"A woman may speak as much wisdom as a man," he said, in that rich, low voice, his tone firm and full.

Windrider responded with a quick nod.

He did not give so much as a glance in High Wolf's direction.

The heat in Sky's face burned hotter, spread down over her neck, throughout her cold body. It warmed her all the way to her bones.

He was defending her! Rafael, the handsome Spanish don, this man of much *puha*, her kindred spirit, was her ally!

And High Wolf was her enemy. Enemy to her real self.

Her instincts had been telling her that for four moons. She felt their truth, now, like a hand laid on her head.

She could not marry him. She *would* not, no matter what promise she had made.

But she could not stop to think about it now. The People were in danger and Nokona, like Rafael, had recognized the possibilities in her idea.

He asked, "Would finding the treasure stop the war, my father?"

Windrider barked, "Forget it. That treasure is nothing but an old *narukuyunapu*, a tale."

High Wolf glared at Nokona.

He said, "Listen to your father, Nokona. That treasure does not exist."

"We will call warriors from all the Plains Tribes," Windrider proclaimed, in a voice heavy with danger. "If all of us cannot band together, the Anglos will squeeze The People off the face of our Earth Mother and the Spanish, too."

Sky stared at him, stunned.

Bad as the threat was, she had never thought it could come to that, to the destruction of all her people!

The Anglos will squeeze The People off the face of our Earth Mother.

Her heart beating hard and deep like the

war drums that would soon be sounding, Sky searched each face again. Not one of them showed a flicker of turning back from their War Chief's vow.

Nor did he. All traces of fear had left him.

"Nokona, you will ride to the Kiowa," he said. "Eagle Tail Feather, I send you to our Kotsoteka brothers."

"I will send word to the Spanish farther west," Don Diego promised. "They live under the Anglo government, but they will help as much as they can."

"Remember! All of you!" Windrider said. "Be quiet at this rendezvous. We must keep this plan from the Anglos and from the Comancheros until our next camp is hidden and our brothers have gathered. The fort might send soldiers down on our women and children."

This was not a bad dream—they were talking a full-scale war!

A war of bows and arrows, lances and shields plus a few long rifles against giant guns she had seen with her own eyes. The Spanish no longer had guns like that, Windrider had told her, now that the American government controlled Santa Fe and the New Mexico territory. The People had never possessed such weapons.

They would not have a chance.

Her blood rushed screaming to her head. Someone had to do something to stop this!

But who? And what?

Then her own words pierced her soul like a frantic cry from her medicine spirit, the killdeer bird. *If it's treasure they want, let's give it to them, so they'll go.*

It had to be possible. She had heard before of the white men's greed for gold. Hadn't hundreds of them worn deep trails in the earth to the south of here, traveling in herds, like buffalo, to a far place called California to look for it?

She would find the treasure and give it to the stubborn rancher named Waters! In exchange, of course, for taking himself and his men and his cattle out of Comancheria and never coming back across the Gallinas.

Sky sat up very straight and drew in a long, ragged lungful of air, pressed her trembling hands palms-down onto the soft robe. *She* would be the one to stop the war and save her people.

Another thought followed that one like thunder following lightning. If she did something *that* wonderful, wouldn't she have a special place in her tribe?

A great wave of relief flooded through her. Such a feat would bring her great honor!

Perhaps she would be named Peace Chief! Long ago, a woman called Tatseni had held that position. Then she would have a place of her own in the band, without having to be married to High Wolf!

Faintly, she heard snatches of the war plans flying around the lodge, talk of trading for more rifles and of moving camp to a hidden place and of finding buffalo to leave food with the women and children, but not one word of it really penetrated her brain. She was too busy making plans of her own.

The only thing she knew for certain was that she had no time to lose. She must find the treasure soon, within only a few suns.

During this half of this fall moon. It would take no longer than that for her father to gather warriors from every part of the plains.

That would be no time at all compared to what she needed for her task. She must ride to the Mesa Rica, search its many rocks and hills for the treasure that had lain hidden among them for hundreds of years, take it to Waters and strike the bargain with him, and get him physically back across the Gallinas before Windrider and his men took the warpath.

The thought leapt at her like a wolf attacking: she could not do all that without help.

But whose help? Nokona and Eagle Tail Feather had their tasks, Windrider did not believe the treasure existed.

However, Rafael knew it did—he'd had the vision.

No one could help her except Rafael.

Her kindred spirit.

Sky took a long, deep breath to carry the sweet woodsmoke of the fire into herself, thanking the Great Spirit, since it was a messenger between The People and Him. Of course.

Rafael would go with her.

Chapter 3

"Madre de Dios*, hombres*, get out of the way!"

Rafael sent his stallion through the narrow space that finally opened up in the crush of Comancheros and their customers crowded around the carts.

Only to skid him to a stop again because some latecomer to the rendezvous came ambling across the grassy path in front of him on a wagon pulled by four snail-slow oxen.

He pulled El Lobo's head around, started to turn him, then stopped.

He could go back, leave for home by riding down the creek, but he'd have to go through the center of the Comanche camp. Don Diego would see him and call to him to come and sit down at the feast—if he hadn't been so absorbed in talking to Windrider right after the Council broke up, Rafael would never have gotten away from him without his making a scene.

As it was now, he wouldn't have to face his fury until tonight when Don Diego rode back to *la casa grande.*

And he would have a right to be furious. Rafael's rude behavior in running out on the feast without taking leave of anyone would insult Don Diego's Comanche friends, and he hated to do that, but he had to get out, now.

Visions in the fire! God in Heaven, what was *happening* to him?

At last the ox-wagon passed and he picked up his reins, put his heels to El Lobo to tell him to move on.

Something bumped his foot, pulled on his tapadero, pressed against his thigh.

He looked down. At his stirrup, in the middle of the busy barterers, her beautiful face flushed from running, stood Ysidora Pretty Sky.

Her huge brown eyes blazing, she kept her hand on him to hold him there until she could recover enough breath to speak.

It burned its shape into his skin.

"I have to talk to you!" she shouted, over the noises of the greaseless wagon and the yelling traders.

She brushed her blowing hair out of her face with her free hand.

"We must go and find it, you and I—the treasure of the Mesa Rica! To stop the war!"

The tingling ran down his spine again.

God help him, here she was, the cause of the vision, or whatever it was he'd been racing out of this camp to escape.

He had to resist her. If he didn't, he'd be lost.

"No! I cannot!"

She snatched her hand away, but she laid it against her own thigh and held it there, making him feel, somehow, that he'd touched her.

Or that he wanted to touch her.

Well, he did, damn it! He'd wanted to touch her from the moment he'd seen her looking at him from the back of the splendid paint mare.

"You must! You are the *only* one who can help me!" she yelled, her face turned up to him like an open, fresh flower.

If a flower could be desperate and hopeful and incredibly determined.

"Did your vision show you *where* the treasure is?"

His gut constricted.

He could *not* let himself be drawn into this.

"I deeply regret, *Señorita*," he said, firmly, in as formal a way as possible over the noise that surrounded them, "that I know nothing of any treasure. Nothing at all."

He cursed himself for a liar the minute he spoke.

His words bruised the hope in her face and turned her eyes to huge pools of dark hurt.

He took a turn around each hand with the reins to keep from reaching down to comfort her.

"That is not what your eyes told me in Council!" she challenged, her voice breaking. "You know that I saw you have a medicine vision!"

Sweat broke out on his palms.

"I *imagined* I saw something in the fire because my head was filled with smoke! The

tipi was crowded. I meant nothing by that
look."

"You lie!" she shouted. "You saw a vision
and it told you the treasure is real, just as my
medicine told me! We are destined to find it
because you had an Indian vision and I have
a Spanish name—Ysidora, after Ysidore Oñate,
friend of my parents."

The sudden unexpectedness of that information tore a laugh from his tight throat.

"You have a Spanish name because your
parents had a friend they wanted to honor,"
he said, dryly.

"And because you and I together are meant
by the All-Father to stop this war!"

She stepped closer to the restless stallion,
fixed Rafael with her dark, blazing eyes.

"It means that together we can do anything.
Rafael, listen to me. My father is sending for
warriors from all the Plains Tribes. They will
raid Waters's new ranch and every town, every
Anglo ranch."

Her voice caught; he thought she was going
to burst into tears.

But she swallowed hard and went on.

"Finally, the soldiers will go out from their
forts and slaughter them. Windrider and his
band will be destroyed. Many, many people
will die!"

Her whole body quivered with passion.

Her eyes shone with hope.

A flame of admiration flared inside him.
She was so brave. So incredibly strong that
she wasn't afraid to feel such depths.

The depths of emotion that terrified him, that he had spent years learning to lock away from his heart.

"All of the Mesa Rica could be made of silver and gold," he said, as gently as he could, "and we could find it tomorrow, but it could not be enough to stop the Anglos. If Waters goes away, more, many more, will come."

She shook her head as if to fling those awful words out of her ears.

"No!"

She stepped back, away from him, and a hardening came into her beautiful face and her eyes.

Suddenly, it struck him that she would try it alone. She was obsessed with this plan that had fallen into her head during Council, and having no help would not deter her. Truly, she had much courage.

It was none of his business, but the thought made him cold with fear for her.

"Forget this whole idea about the Mesa Rica," he said, harshly, wanting to get down and shake her to make sure she heard him.

"It is a dangerous place these days, the Mesa Rica," he said, putting all the warning he could into his voice. "I rode there with my father to see Waters and his ranch. His hired hands are many."

She did not even blink.

"They will not see me until I am ready to bargain with their chief."

Exasperation flooded through him.

Desperation, to get away from this awful pull

of feeling he should go with her.

"Go back to your mother's lodge!" he shouted. "Let your father take care of your people!"

"He is a man! He looks to his lance and his arrows; he looks to his pride. He will not admit that this is a fight that will take everything from him."

A sudden calmness came over her, then. She spoke her plea once more with a gallantry that broke his heart.

"The Mesa Rica is too big for me, alone, to search every cave, every rock in seven suns' time," she said. "It will take no longer than that for the war parties to gather. Your vision will guide us. Come with me."

Goose bumps stood out on him, all up and down the flesh of his arms, holding the sleeves of his shirt and his coat away from his skin. The hot life-force in this woman was an incredible lure.

God knew he *wanted* to go with her. She had made him crazy. He *wanted* to go.

But if he did that, he was lost.

He didn't know why, but knew he would be lost. Perhaps because he'd always known it wasn't safe to follow his feelings the way she tempted him to do.

"I must stay with my *rancho*," he said.

The shine of her huge, dark eyes glazed over to become a glittering shell. She would never forgive him for this, they promised.

Good, he thought, even as he felt the sharp stab of regret.

Good. Maybe now she would let him alone. But he could not set his horse in motion.

"Don't go," he said, hoarsely, and thought he would strangle on the words. "There are bad men roaming the Mesa Rica. You'll get yourself killed. Or worse."

She answered only with a look, a scornful glance so sharp with hurt and disgust that it hit him like a blow.

Then she whirled away from him, her hair flying out into a huge, dark auburn fan that covered her shoulders with fire in the sunlight, and ran into the shouting, shifting crowd of animals and Comancheros and Indians.

"You'd rather take the warpath than have peace! You're no different from all the rest of the men!" she turned and yelled at him. "*I'll* go! I'll go alone before Father Sun comes up again!"

Rafael sat still and watched her until she disappeared.

Jaime jerked on Pedro's serape and pulled him back behind his cart.

"Montoya will see you!" he hissed. "He might shoot you for not leaving his *rancho*."

"*I* will shoot *him*!" Pedro snarled, and hit his friend's hand away. "I will catch him out alone without no vaqueros, and I will make him sad for the day he insulted me and caused my woman to run away!"

"He has no vaqueros riding at his back this minute!" Jaime taunted, slapping back at him. "Why don't you follow and kill him now?"

"Because this is rendezvous! There are too many people between here and his *casa grande*. I will watch and bide my time."

"While you are biding it, ride to Chaparito and bring the ammunition we cached there."

"*Porque?*"

"*Why?* Didn't you hear what the girl said? Windrider's going on the warpath! I'll sell the ammunition to Windrider and then ride out to sell the information to *Señor* Waters. Don't tell *anyone*—he must hear it first from me or he will not pay."

"That cheap one! He will pay nothing!" Pedro scoffed.

"Keep your mouth shut. He might at least forgive me my debt."

Sky slipped into the darkness of Grandmother Hukiyani's lodge while the camp filled with sounds of drums, flutes, and dancing songs. The familiar smell of the place brought tears to her eyes.

She hated to run off without saying goodbye, to Grandmother and to her parents, but there was no other way—if they knew, they'd find some way to prevent her from going. Blinking to try to help her see in what dim light there was, she felt for the second lodgepole on the right.

Her fingertips ran over one full parfleche and then another hanging slightly beneath it. They touched beaded trim that was broken and sparse and bulges where the hide was worn thin.

This one.

Letting her own traveling bags slide off her shoulder to rest on the ground, she pushed the top parfleche aside and lifted the one she wanted off its peg. She sat down in the darkness, cross-legged, to take what she needed.

Grandmother would understand why she had not asked first. And it wasn't stealing. Many times Hukiyani had told her she could have all of her extra-sweet pemmican that she wanted.

"*Hukaru*?"

Sky jumped, alarmed for an instant by the sudden challenge, then more so by the fact that it was her grandmother's voice coming from the door-opening.

Wildly she considered escape beneath the rolled-up walls, but Hukiyani would raise a hue and cry.

"It is Sky, Grandmother," she answered, abruptly.

Frustration set her teeth on edge. Now she would be delayed by arguments and lectures because her grandmother would notice her packed bags. Hukiyani might even send for Windrider!

"Grandmother Hukiyani, why are you not at the feasting?"

"Why are you in my lodge?"

Hukiyani bent stiffly and came in.

"I am taking some of your pemmican," Sky said.

"As I thought," said the old woman, as she made her slow, rustling way around the firepit toward her granddaughter. "Your love for my extra-sweet pemmican is so great that they sing of it now at the fire."

Sky laughed in spite of her irritation. Hukiyani dropped heavily down to sit beside her.

"So," she said. "You are going?"

"You know?"

"Yes."

Sky stared at her through the darkness, shocked by the calm acceptance in her voice. She reached for Hukiyani's dry, weathered hand.

"I saw it clearly that you would go when Nokona told your mother what you said during Council."

The dry, delicate fingers squeezed Sky's.

"I will help you."

Sky leaned forward to try to see Hukiyani's face in the trace of light filtering through the walls from the big dance fire. Her heart beat hard, as loud as the drums.

There would be no arguing? Hukiyani would not try to stop her?

She would *help*?

"You? But, Grandmother, there will be much hard, fast riding and much danger."

"Ha! And you think I am too old for such?"

"No-o-o, but . . ."

Hukiyani chuckled. Her hand moved over Sky's, patted it gently.

"I am not going with you. I will help you in another way," she said. "I have come to give you a song, dear daughter Pretty Sky. It is one that my grandmother gave to me."

She reached for Sky's other hand, then, and held them both in her papery palms.

"This song tells the way to that Mesa Rica treasure."

In a high, thin voice, she began to sing.

I see a lodge made of rainbows.
I see a lodge made of flaming rainbows.

The melody was beautiful. It sent a thrill all through Sky.

Father Sun's rays are traveling. Father Sun's rays are traveling to find his heart in the Earth Mother's breast.
The rocks run back racing, the trees turn into arrows that fly.
The Eagle dives through the wind to strike flame from the coals of the fire.
He'yay, He'yo, He'yo, yoyo!
Eya, yo, yoyo!
Eya, yo!

They sat very still after Hukiyani's song had died away into the swirling sounds of the drums and the voices in the center of the village. Sky clung to the echo of it, trying to lock the wild, quavering tones and each of the precious words away in her heart.

Then she threw her arms around Hukiyani and pressed her wet cheek to her grandmother's leathery one, also covered with tears.

"Thank you," she whispered.

Hukiyani made an incoherent, throaty sound, then, patting Sky's back, she muttered, "Foolish girl. Your parents worry. You should stay in camp, marry High Wolf, ease the minds of Windrider and my Jen-nie."

Sky pulled back.

"If that is what you believe, Grandmother, then why do you give me the song? Why don't you call them now to stop me?"

Hukiyani shook her head, and her short, black hair swung back and forth on her cheeks with a tiny brushing sound.

"Because I want you to stop the war. To help your people as you wanted—as Ysidora Pretty Sky, not as the wife of High Wolf."

She chuckled again, softly.

"But mostly because I was a girl once. And I would have loved to go on such an adventure as this."

Sky's throat choked with tears as she hugged her again.

Hukiyani pushed her arms away.

"Hurry," she said. "Go, now."

In the long, dark hour just before dawn, Rafael strode down the wide corridor that led to his father's bedroom, his bootheels striking the tiled floor and his spurs jingling in a rhythm that taunted, over and over again, *Tu es loco, tu es loco.*

And he was. Papa would tell him so, too, a thousand times.

He reached the door, stopped, and knocked.

A bolt of panic shot through him. Why did he have to do this? Don Diego was getting old and Rafael's riding off alone on a whim would be a terrible upset to him. Don Diego didn't believe in whims.

He knocked again, remembering their last conversation, only a few hours ago. To Rafael's shock, his father had seemed scared, not angry, because Rafael had rushed away from the Comanche camp without a word.

But, of course, he hadn't explained his feelings and Rafael had not asked him to do so.

Rafael clenched his jaw and knocked again. This time the door's latch clicked and Alfredo, Don Diego's body servant, stuck his head out, his bright eyes as alert as if he'd never gone to sleep. Rafael pushed the heavy slab of oak all the way open and strode into the room.

His father sat stiffly upright in bed, the silver in his tousled hair shining in the moonlight slanting low through the window. Alfredo went to the bedside table, lit a candle, set it into the sconce above.

As it began to burn, it threw shadows on the wall.

"I'm sorry to wake you, Father," Rafael said.

"I was not asleep."

The don's narrow eyes swept over Rafael, from the leather hat hanging down his back to his toughest, most comfortable boots.

"You have changed into fresh traveling clothes to visit my room?" he demanded, his light tone brittle and uneven. "In the middle of the night?"

Rafael smiled, in spite of the dread sitting heavy as a stone in his stomach.

"The vaqueros always say that your busy eyes miss nothing," he said.

"*Es verdad*," the old man said. "And I can see at this moment that you are leaving your mother and me."

Rafael stared at him, stunned.

"Why would you say that? I am merely riding up into the Mesa Rica again for a few days," he said. "I may be gone for two weeks."

Don Diego's whole body stiffened even more. He bored his eyes into Rafael's.

"When war is about to break out and the fall roundup is not done, you are going away for two weeks?"

"I have decided to look for the treasure."

"Why now? Not a fortnight has passed since you and I rode the Mesa Rica. You saw how many Anglos roam the hills looking for the gold, yet you showed no interest in looking for it."

"A thought has come to me. If I had that much money in hard currency, I could easily buy Beck's ranch to the south."

"Once you're married to Marquez's daughter, you'll have his whole land grant to the north," the old man snapped at him. "That's enough for one man to oversee."

The very thought made Rafael's heart heavy as a rock.

"*I* won't be overseeing it as long as Marquez can climb into a saddle," he said. "I want a place of my own."

"You *have* a place! And cattle to separate and market, horses to race and to sell. Your place is here, not in the Mesa Rica, for the love of the Saints!"

"You can manage while I'm gone."

"I'll be organizing the Spanish to help the Indians. I can't do both."

"I won't be gone long."

Don Diego's lined face flushed red. He threw back the covers and got out of bed.

"You don't *need* that treasure, even if you could find it! Even if it existed! Why are you doing this *loco* thing?"

"Your Comanche friends need it."

The hidalgo's face lost all color.

"I thought you were old enough, settled into the *rancho* enough . . ." he said, in a strange, cracking voice that trembled.

He broke off, staring up at Rafael with hard, hot eyes.

"What are you talking about, Papa?"

The old man waved the question away.

"I cannot believe you would leave me now!"

"I'm not *leaving* you! Why do you keep saying such a thing?" Rafael thundered.

Don Diego squinted at him in the candle-light.

"Who is going with you?"

"No one!"

Rafael snapped his mouth closed.

"You are going alone to look for the treasure to help 'my Comanche friends,' " Don Diego said, tightly. "To my best recollection, that idea comes from Windrider's beautiful daughter."

He slammed one of his fists into the other palm.

"The *muy loco* idea of finding a treasure which does not exist and using it to bribe the Anglo Charlie Waters to go away so the war will not happen!"

Rafael's gut tightened. He stared straight ahead and said nothing.

"Is this not true? You are going into the Mesa Rica with that girl, are you not?"

"I refused to go *with* her. She is already gone, no doubt."

"But you will find her."

The older man's jaw set hard, his eyes burned beneath a sheen that had to be tears.

A terrible guilt ran through Rafael, but he clamped his heart closed against it. And against the realization that the hidalgo truly was getting old—that must be why he was taking this news so strangely.

"Remember, Rafael, that you will soon make the arrangements to marry the Marquez girl."

"I will make those arrangements when I please!" Rafael roared. "So far I have made no promises to Marquez. This journey has nothing to do with that—I'm sure I will marry Elena—I might as well. One woman is much like another."

Except for the Comanche girl.

He pushed that thought away.

"I may disinherit you for this," Don Diego cried, "for going off on this wild-goose chase and leaving this *rancho* to fend for itself!"

"You and the vaqueros can do everything

that needs to be done. I won't be gone more than a few days."

Rafael clenched his jaw until the bones popped.

"I'll come back with the treasure, I'll buy Beck's *rancho* and our position will be stronger than ever. You just wait and see!"

"Rafael, the practical one, always the realist!" Don Diego snorted, and advanced on Rafael as if he would strike him. "Bah! You have become the dreamer, now!"

"*You* are the dreamer, bringing nightmares on yourself!" Rafael said, roughly. "Saying, for no reason, that I am leaving you! Can't you ever trust me? I'll come back soon, I tell you!"

"Let me just tell *you* one thing," the older man said, glaring up into his face. "Friend or no, Windrider is one War Chief who will take your scalp and burn this *rancho* if you dally with his daughter."

"I have no such intention!"

Rafael turned on his heel and left the room, sick to his stomach at parting from his father in this way.

The heavy door slammed behind him.

He struck out down the corridor at a pace faster, much faster than when he came in, his heart full to overflowing—with guilt for the sorrow and pain he was causing, with terror that the don might, indeed, disinherit him and take away this land that he loved, with resentful resignation that when he returned he would marry Elena and be forever related to her obnoxious father, with a faint hope that he might be led to the treasure and, therefore, to a ranch of his own.

Yet it pounded with a fierce, wild excitement, too.

Chapter 4

Sky turned Far Girl off the path and stopped her, facing back the way they had come. Her eyes patiently searched the back-trail, even though her hands and her feet itched to whirl the horse around and keep pushing up the trail. She had so little time to do what she had to do!

But if she was dead, she could do nothing at all, and dead she might be if she didn't discover who was following her. She pulled Pabo around, too, so close that the pack mare carried bumped against Sky's leg.

"Puhkai!"

Both horses stood obediently quiet except for the faint, rhythmic sounds of their breathing. They pricked their ears and helped her look and listen.

The rays of Father Sun glinted off their gleaming hides and off the red beads of Sky's largest parfleche. They glowed in the dark green needles of the pines at the top of this hill and glistened off the silver of the narrow creek that wound through the valley below. The water ran swift.

Nothing else moved.

Sky's breathing stopped. She stood in her stirrups and sent her narrowed gaze searching in earnest, swinging in a slow half circle back and forth across the half-moon–shaped valley.

No one.

Yet she *had* heard it: the ringing noise of an iron-shod hoof against stone.

Father Sun dropped a strong beam of heat down over her, like an invisible tipi, but his warmth went no deeper than her skin. The chill in her bones grew.

Whoever it was had stopped when she stopped. Someone *was* following her.

"Kill-deeah! Kill-deeah! Dee-ee, dee, dee!"

The bird's loud call sent a tremor racing down Sky's spine. She didn't move.

Quickly, though, she decided it wasn't a human imitation, it really was a bird, and that gave her comfort. A rocky hill was a strange place for her medicine spirit bird—mostly they lived on the plains—so that meant her medicine spirit was protecting her.

Clink.

The hot breeze carried it to her again, that small, peculiar sound, from only a short distance away. Her pursuer was on the move. He was closer than she had thought.

Her heart thudding, she turned her horses around and walked them farther off the path, then headed them upward over the hard ground, moving fast, but quietly, weaving in and out among the scattered pine trees. Then, at the top of the hill, the Earth Mother gave her the perfect place to hide: a bend in the trail caused by two massive, dun-colored rocks.

She dropped the packhorse's lead, whispering the command for her to stand, then side-passed Far Girl to a spot behind one rock where she could see whoever was coming. She pulled her bow from the case and an arrow from the quiver on her back.

"Kill-deeah!"

The pealing cry rose higher. "Dee-ee! Dee, dee!"

Then the bird, even the breeze, fell silent.

Hoofbeats, coming toward her at a long trot.

Sky strained to see the faint path below. It still lay empty.

Whoever was following wasn't her father or High Wolf or anyone sent by them. Their horses were not shod.

Besides, once she had left camp to look for it, The People would let her learn for herself whether the treasure existed or not. If she didn't return in a few days, they might send someone to look for her, but not now.

She nocked the arrow.

More than one horse. She could hear two horses. Both shod.

She pulled the string of her bow and fixed her gaze on the spot where the riders would pass in front of her before they vanished behind the rock.

Her hands were completely steady. Amazing, for her insides were trembling.

Never before had she been in danger, alone, far from camp.

With the fate of her people at stake.

The weight of that thought made her heart sink.

But she was not alone. The killdeer bird was here. Her medicine spirit would protect her.

She tightened the pull of the bow.

The black-tipped ears of a gray horse appeared, then its head, heavily carved leather brow band shining.

The gray Andalusian? Could it be?

Rafael!

The taut bow wavered back and forth in her hands, her tired, tense muscles fought to hold the arrow, to keep it from flying at him.

Her whole body started to shake. She could have killed him!

"*Tu es loco!*" she yelled, and sent Far Girl leaping out of her hiding place. "*Poo?sa?!*"

Rafael whipped the gray and his packhorse around with a wild, noisy scraping of feet.

When they stopped, Sky was looking straight into the small, evil eye of his rifle.

She held the sharp arrowhead pointed at him, her arms still frozen by shock.

"I almost shot you!" she shouted. "What do you mean, sneaking up on me like this?"

He reined the stallion in.

"And I didn't come within a heartbeat of shooting *you*?" he yelled back. "You jump out behind me screaming like a horse with a mountain lion on his back and you accuse *me*?"

His dark eyes blazed at her from beneath the shadow of his hat brim.

She answered, "I never said I wouldn't, but you did!"

He glared at her in surprise, frowning.

"What's that supposed to mean? That you're justified in leaping at me from hiding, squealing at the top of your lungs, calling me a crazy person?"

"Yes! Because you said you wouldn't come with me and then you did! How could I know it was you?"

He shook his head.

"I would never have thought of it in quite that way," he said, dryly.

Deliberately, slowly, in the same rhythm as he spoke, he lowered the rifle and laid it across his lap.

His long, brown fingers rested on it gently.

He took off his hat, let it hang from its silver-threaded strings.

His hot, black gaze held hers captive.

All her strength left her. The bow dropped to hang over the fringed horn of the saddle. The arrow dangled awkwardly from her fingers.

She said, weakly, "Oh, Rafael! I almost let this arrow go!"

"I would've called out to you a long way back there," he said, the wry shadow of a smile playing on his sensuous mouth, "but I was afraid."

"*Afraid*? Of me?"

He nodded, still not quite really smiling. But his dark eyes held a humorous glint.

"You bet. Judging by the way you left me at the rendezvous, I thought you really *would* shoot me if you knew who I was."

Sky burst out laughing.

Then his smile became wide and real and magically wonderful. He laughed, too, with such a rich, warm sound that it was like a caress.

Joy rose in Sky's veins, singing a melody pleasing as a bird's song, climbing high and sweet.

Rafael had come with her, after all!

The breeze blew cool around Jennie's legs the instant the door-flap lifted. She whirled, digging her fingers anxiously into the soft buffalo robes she was folding.

"Was she there?"

Windrider waited to answer until he had dropped the flap closed behind him.

"No," he snapped, striding straight to her. "And the boys watching the horses say neither Far Girl nor Pabo has been in the herd all night."

His voice and his eyes held a hot undercurrent of anger.

Jennie's temper flared to answer it.

"Well, you don't have to look at *me* that way! I didn't give her permission to go!"

"You never taught her to ask for it! Sky doesn't know what that word means—you gave her too much freedom for a girl because *you*, as a child, had none!"

"While *you*, as a child, were headstrong as a bull and daring as a loco wolf!"

Jennie let the robes fall to her feet and raised both hands to tick off her points on her fingers.

"Your daughter not only got the dark in her hair and eyes from you, Windrider, but also her too-strong will and her foolhardiness! Did you ever think that *that*, and not the way she was raised, is the reason she has run off alone to go hunting for a treasure that is only a legend?"

She drew in a ragged breath and took a step closer to him, tilting her chin so she could look up into his set, handsome face.

"Don't misunderstand me, though," she said, hotly. "Even after sharing with both your son *and* your daughter, you still have plenty of stubbornness left!"

They glared at each other.

"And you still have plenty of quick temper," Windrider said. "Now *that's* one trait she gets from you."

But this time he spoke with the crooked grin she loved.

He was trying to distract her, she realized, from the pain that was gnawing her insides into shreds. The same pain that was devouring the anger in his eyes.

"Oh, Windrider!"

Jennie threw herself into his arms, wailing.

"What are we going to do?"

"Nothing. She'll have to learn for herself that there is no treasure."

"But we have to do *something*! No telling how many greedy, *evil* Anglos are on the Mesa Rica. There are mountain lions and bears and wolves and God only knows what else lurking in the hills up there!"

"It's the way of The People for parents to let their children learn through their own experiences."

"I don't care! She's in danger! We must go to her!"

Helpless against them, she gave in and let the sobs come.

Windrider folded her closer, cradled her head where it rested in the middle of his chest, and rocked from one foot to the other, back and forth.

"She has grown up into a beautiful woman," he murmured into her hair, "but, remember, my Fire Flower, we are talking of Ysidora Pretty Sky. She is a match for . . . what? A dozen mountain lions, fifty Anglos, a mother bear with cubs . . ."

Jennie made a strangled sound and wrapped her arms tighter around him, trying to absorb the familiar feel of the powerful muscles that roped across his back, trying to take into herself the rocklike steadiness of his dear body.

"I know," she said, with a small, rueful laugh, "but what if she runs into all of those at once?"

Windrider gave an angry grunt. "Then she'll learn for herself how foolish this is. I told her the treasure didn't exist and she didn't believe her own father!"

"By the time she learns for herself it might be too late!"

Jennie raised her face to look at him, not even trying to stem the tears pouring down her cheeks.

"You know how much some Anglos hate The People! What if men like that capture her and . . ."

He stepped back, but he kept holding her by the waist with both hands as if she steadied him. Wretched worry filled his eyes.

She spoke quickly, to take advantage of it.

"I know it's the custom of The People not to dictate to their children, to let them learn for themselves," she said, her words falling over each other between her sobbing and her haste, "but our stubborn daughter doesn't realize the dangers she rides into. Bear and mountain lions, maybe, but not the white men!"

The misery deepened in his dark face.

"I can't go," he said, "and I can't let you go without me. I must lead the band to one more herd of buffalo before the snow flies. I have to gather warriors and prepare for the war trail. My brother is too old for such tasks."

"And Nokona has already ridden out to the Kiowa," she said, leaping at his tacit consent to her plea. "Eagle Tail Feather has gone to the Kotsoteka . . ."

She thought hard and fast.

"I know!" she said, grasping his muscular arms although she could reach only halfway around them. "High Wolf!"

Startled, he stared at her.

"They are not married, remember?" he said. "The two of them would be making camp alone."

"But they are promised! And Sky herself chose him out of all the young warriors! She's only putting off the ceremony because she's reluctant to actually give up all the freedoms of her girlhood."

Windrider narrowed his eyes, thinking.

At last he said, "Fine. This will give High Wolf a chance to show Sky how to be a wife without the whole village watching and wagging their tongues about how she hates to be told what to do."

"Yes! And High Wolf can give you the horses to seal the wedding agreement after they come back to us. We'll have a celebration then."

"He's a good warrior," Windrider mused, nodding. "And a good hunter. He has much medicine. He can protect our daughter and provide for her."

Jennie squeezed his arms.

"Windrider, when you send High Wolf, tell him not to try to force her to come back now. For the sake of their marriage. She's so stubborn, she would resent him forever if she didn't see for herself that the treasure isn't there."

He smiled at her as he turned to go.

"I'll tell him. Also, I'll tell him to ride straight for the Mesa Rica and meet her there. But High Wolf is stubborn, too—probably stubborn enough to try to pick up her trail just to prove that he can."

Relief, pure and simple, surged through Jennie. With High Wolf's protection, Sky would be all right. Her daughter would be safe.

That was one joyful thought to cling to in the midst of all this talk of war.

"Ysidora Pretty Sky and High Wolf," she called after her husband. "Marriage of the *sutenapus*. It will be interesting."

He stopped at the door and turned.

"*Ours* is the marriage of the stubborn ones," he said, and flashed her the sexy smile that still, after all these years, picked up her heart and turned it over. "And I have just realized that, once again, you've talked me into a compromise, even into going against custom."

"You were going against custom long before *I* ever met you," she retorted, deliberately teasing him with her voice and her eyes.

His grin grew bolder.

"So *you* say. Twenty of the Big Cold Seasons we have lived together and the matter of who is chief in this lodge, it is still a draw."

Jennie laughed. "Come back to me when you have talked to your son-in-law and we will try once more to resolve that question."

Rafael rode out a little ahead of Sky, scanning the horizon, pretending to be looking for the trail ahead. Pretending not to hear her latest question.

Trying his best to hold on to his meticulous courtesy.

Madre de Dios, had the woman no shame?

Next thing he knew, she'd be asking the size of his *rancho* and the number of his cattle and telling him all her deepest feelings about her parents and every other subject under the sun! Never, ever, had he seen someone so openly comfortable with a virtual stranger.

Especially not a woman so comfortable with a man! Never, ever, would a Spanish woman behave so informally, speak so familiarly.

It was beginning to make him extremely uncomfortable.

She trotted her horses faster to catch up with him. And, as he expected, she repeated the question.

"Rafael, where have you been during all the other rendezvous that my people have camped at your *rancho*?"

None of your business. Leave me alone with my thoughts for awhile. We don't know each other well enough to ask such questions. Why do you care?

But he said none of those rude things.

Her trusting face was turned up to him with the greatest of goodwill and a beautiful smile. And his unbending Spanish rules of good behavior had been ingrained in him ever since before he could remember.

However, he did assume his stiffest, most formal manner.

"Why do you ask?"

"I was just thinking about it," she said, guiding her mare to trot along companionably exactly beside and in step with El Lobo. "Since my tenth summer—and now I have my eighteenth summer—Windrider's band has come to visit Don Diego, yet I've never seen you before this time."

"At this time of year I'm usually driving cattle down from our high mountain pastures."

"But you have many vaqueros to do such work! Don't you hate always to miss the feasting and the talking and the trading and the horse racing?"

The question stabbed him with a little knife of regret.

"I've never thought of it in that way. It is my duty to oversee the vaqueros; the cattle drives are my responsibility. It never occurred to me to try to shirk it."

She tilted her head and looked at him.

"Never? Not even when you had an especially fast horse who could beat all the Indian ponies and the Comancheros' mounts? Do you always go by the rules and not think about having fun?"

A flare of anger flamed hot in his belly.

"Do you always bombard strangers with personal questions?"

Her smile vanished.

But instead of taking offense at his remark or falling into an angry silence, she protested— something he would never have expected.

"Rafael, we aren't strangers!" she cried. "We're friends, long destined! Why, we are kindred spirits!"

He stared at her.

"I don't think so. I go by the rules. You think about having fun. I keep my feelings to myself. You tell yours to the world."

She tossed her head angrily, her magnificent mane of auburn hair rippled like a waterfall of flames.

"*I* start to step off my horse and help a poor woman in trouble. *You* do it before I can move. *I* have medicine that tells me the treasure is real. *You* have a vision that tells you the same."

Her huge dark eyes challenged him to refute that.

He couldn't.

She smiled, in victory, and triumphantly added her final proof.

"And you knew that I knew you'd had the vision!"

But you know nothing, absolutely nothing of the agony I went through to make this decision to come with you!

He touched his spurs to El Lobo.

"The way narrows here," he snapped at her over his shoulder. "And gets rough and rocky. We need to ride hard and cross the Gallinas before dark."

As soon as the stallion had gone three lengths ahead of her, Rafael knew that his ploy was useless. The questions still beat at his brain, even though Sky's voice was silent.

He set his jaw and silently answered them.

It had *not* been a vision, it'd been an hallucination in the fire.

He had helped the woman at the rendezvous because he didn't countenance such behavior on his land.

And he had come on this journey, not because some supernatural force had made that his destiny, but because he wanted the money to buy Beck's *rancho*.

He and the open, emotional, destiny-believing Sky were *not* kindred spirits. There was no way that that could be true.

He kept them moving fast along the narrow way through the hills that forced them to ride single file. Thank God, with her behind him like this, they could talk very little. The trail wouldn't widen for most of the afternoon.

By evening, without her sultry voice murmuring insanities into his ear, he should have his thinking straightened out again. By then, he would be in control of his riotous feelings and of the relationship with her. He would put it on a much more formal footing and keep it there.

When the sun began to slide down and down toward the line of the blue mountains far behind them and they came out onto the flat plain dotted with mesquite that stretched toward the river, Rafael dropped back to ride beside her.

"On the other side of the Gallinas, to the north a little, a creek runs down into the *río*," he said. "We could camp there."

She nodded, then glanced at his pack, which had been bobbing ahead of her all afternoon.

"I have seen guitars at traders' wagons and the rendezvous," she said. "Is that what you carry wrapped on top of your pack?"

"Yes."

She looked from it to him and back again, giving him a teasing smile.

"A guitar. And two awkward wooden buckets which won't collapse out of the way like skin water bags would do, buckets which bang around on your pack all day."

She shook her head. "Strange things to bring on a treasure hunt."

He slanted a glance at her. Her choice of subject was so unexpected and quirky, her smile was so pert and impish, so *contagious* somehow, that he felt his hold slipping on his resolve about his feelings toward her.

"There you go again," he said, as the horses moved side by side through the clouds of dust they were making. "Don't you think it's a bit personal for you to criticize the equipment I choose to bring?"

But he had lost the bite in his voice; he couldn't find his resentment this time.

"No more personal than the remarks you made to me at the rendezvous, criticizing my decision to hunt for the treasure."

That is certainly true! What is it about her that made me blurt out such things?

"I forgive you, though," she said, smiling at him. "Because you've changed your mind and admitted that you're destined to help me find it."

"I admit only that you need help," he said, dryly.

He held her gaze from the corner of his eye, then looked away, looked ahead to see the trail.

"I'm so happy that you came, Rafael!" she said, and suddenly her voice shook with the weight of her gratitude. "Thank you, from me and from my people."

His heart expanded, then contracted and fell. God in Heaven! What had he gotten himself into?

"Deep down, I really trusted you to do the right thing," she confided. "Somehow, although my mind didn't know it, my heart knew you would come, Rafael."

The warmth of her trust and the fact that she was so at home with him that she could share it, swelled his heart again, and this time it stayed so full that it filled his chest.

He tried to deflect the strong emotion.

Lightly, he answered, "That's better. For a while, there, it seemed that threats to shoot me and ridiculing remarks over my buckets and my guitar would be all the thanks I'd get."

"The buckets I might understand, since every camp has to have water," she said, following his lead and going back to her old, teasing tone. "But the guitar?"

He shrugged.

"Everybody likes music."

She laughed.

"So. If some Anglo has found the treasure already, you plan to charm it away from him with music? Perhaps persuade him to trade the treasure for a song?"

"That is my plan," he said, solemnly.

Then they laughed together and he turned and looked full into her face again. Their eyes met and held for a long time, in spite of the motion of the trotting horses and the curtain of blowing dust.

Then he surprised himself.

Just as Sky began to grow uncomfortable under the scrutiny of his dark gaze, Rafael's next words surprised her.

"Just so you can no longer accuse me of never thinking of fun," he drawled, still looking into her wide brown eyes, "how fast is that mare?"

"Fast," she said, quickly, and lifted Far Girl into a lope. "Fast enough to leave your poor, worn out, spavined, Andalusian stallion eating her dust!"

"Never! We will race you to the river ahead—and win!"

"Leave the packhorses!" she yelled. "Winner names a prize!"

Sky dropped Pabo's leadrope, her heart racing ahead faster than the horses. Rafael *wasn't* stiff as a stick, after all!

She bent over Far Girl's neck and kicked her into a gallop. The mare was delighted to stretch her legs, in spite of all the distance she had traveled that day, and she shot like an arrow across the slightly rolling incline.

In the next heartbeat, Sky heard the gray's hoofbeats.

A thrill of excitement surged through her. He would never be able to catch her!

Laughter bubbled to her lips. She raised her face from Far Girl's fast-whipping mane and shouted toward her small, laid-back ears, listening for Sky's next command.

"We will outrun them, my Fast Spotted One! The two Spanish stallions, they cannot touch us!"

She tried to grin against the great force of the wind. Rafael might be a good rider, but he could never be as good as she was. He was not of the *Nermernuh*, he had not been trained by warriors of The People!

Far Girl flattened out into a dead run.

Yet the hoofbeats behind them sounded louder.

Sky threw a glance back over her shoulder, peering through the mass of her flying hair that lashed across her face. The gray stallion was floating like a thistle on the wind, his nose coming up to Far Girl's rump, his master sitting him as easily as if they were standing still.

The shock of that sight opened her eyes wide, into the onslaught of rushing air that whipped at her face when she looked ahead again. *Dear Merciful Saints, as my mother would say, what will he demand for a prize if he does win?*

She squeezed with her thighs and pushed Far Girl with her hands, urging the mare on. But the sound of the Andalusian stayed right behind her.

No, he was moving up. She knew it, she could tell without looking.

And then, to her horror, she felt, then saw, the stallion moving ahead, moving past her. Rafael stayed with him without showing one glimmering of light between his seat and the saddle.

In spite of her fearful shock, a burst of pure admiration shattered in Sky. The man could ride. Spaniard or no, he could ride like a Comanche.

Far Girl, like Sky, hated nothing worse than having another horse running in front of her. She added more speed while Sky leaned forward, buried her cheek in her mare's mane, and pressed her free hand against the other side of her sweating neck.

They caught Rafael on the gray Andalusian; they roared along beside them side by side, forcing a path through the chaos of swirling wind. By the time Sky glimpsed the blurred green of the cottonwoods that marked the edge of the river and they dashed the last few lengths leading down into the shaded space along the bank, the mare's nose was locked into the air exactly even with the stallion's. Their hooves rang on the rocks and they splashed into the shallow river together.

Water drops flew up in every direction and into Sky's face. She tossed her hair back over her shoulder and tried to pull a long, healing breath into her burning lungs as she reined Far Girl in and turned in the saddle.

Rafael pushed his hat off again to hang down his back. His face looked like a boy's, lit by the same excitement that pounded in her veins.

"We hit the bank this much ahead of you!" she called, holding up one hand with her forefinger and thumb only a tiny space apart.

"*No es verdad!*" he boomed. "El Lobo and I, we won!"

Laughing, they eyed each other, as the horses slowed, circling in the water, blowing and shaking their heads.

"No! Yes!" they shouted in unison.

His glinting black eyes never left hers.

That strange feeling that wasn't so new anymore stirred deep in her core. A tingling, arousing sensation caused by his smile.

The gray horse circled closer.

"I demand the ornament in your hair as my prize," Rafael said. "The beads and feathers."

She cocked her head to one side and looked at him, trying to stop the feelings long enough to think.

"The ornament is yours if I, too, can claim a prize," she said, pushing the words breathlessly past the weight in her chest. "That's only fair since the race ended in a tie. You must admit that."

He kneed El Lobo closer to her.

"I admit nothing," he said, teasing her with his rich voice, laughter bubbling deep in his throat, dancing in his dark eyes. "But I would be less than generous if I did not offer you something."

"Done," she said, still having trouble speaking. "The ornament is yours."

She reached up and felt for it. When she had worked it loose from the tangles created by the wind in the speed of the race, she untied it and slipped it out of her hair.

She held out the feathers to him, and in that first, reddening moment when Father Sun started to slip down behind the Earth Mother and the sunset began, he reached for his prize.

They leaned from the backs of their horses to touch hands over the water rushing below.

His fingers had calluses on the tips that rubbed against hers. A sudden flame leaped to life in her belly.

Firesticks they were, his fingers and hers.

She squeezed her thighs closed against Far Girl.

Then she laid the rein against her neck, and the mare turned away from El Lobo.

But that proved useless, too.

Rafael's piercing look would not let go of her.

The gray horse circled still closer. Without warning, he hit a deep spot in the riverbed and kicked out in fear, throwing water up and out in a giant arc that caught the reds and golds of the sun. It wet Sky to her waist with its coldness; she could not feel it.

Her blood pulsed so high and so hot in her veins that not even a blizzard could cool it.

Chapter 5

Rafael settled his horse onto a shallower spot, pulled the strings of his hat over his head, dropped it onto his saddle horn, and fastened the beaded ornament to the plain, gray horsehair hatband. Its five feathers moved like soft breaths in his palm as he worked.

Once tied, they lifted in the sunset wind and fluttered, red and white, against the black brim of his hat, trying to break free. He looped the rawhide thong around the braided horsehair one more time.

They kept holding his eye. The wild, deep red color and the dazzling white, the rakish movement of the feathers in the breeze, brought a lilting lift to his blood.

"You're supposed to wear them in your hair," Sky called to him from the back of the mare.

"My hat would then crush them!"

He set the hat on his head and turned to look full at her. Then, for a moment, he let his eyes linger on the pure features of her face, luminous in the light of the setting sun.

"What do you think?" he asked, turning his head so she could see the feathers.

"I think they brighten your plain clothes which have no silver," she said. "And I think that the members of my band would be very happy to see them on you instead of me."

"Why?"

Even in the dusky light, he could see the flush of color rise into her face and the stubborn set come into her jaw.

"Because custom says a woman does not wear them, only a man. To show his brave deeds."

She rode the mare closer to El Lobo.

"But *I* wear them sometimes to show *my* brave deeds. To show that I have counted coup on a sleeping enemy twice and that I have raided three times for his horses."

She nodded her head for emphasis; her waterfall of auburn hair caught fire from the sky.

"Then it is only right that you should wear feathers," he agreed, firmly.

"As it is only right that I keep my hair long all my whole life if I want!"

Sudden determination came into her face and set it into a beautiful mask.

"Why shouldn't you?" he asked, as the horses danced closer together.

"Married women cut theirs. To chin-length or shorter."

The word stirred a strange feeling in him.

A strange sinking.

"You are to be married?"

"No! And I will never be!" she struck her thigh with her fist for emphasis. "I will find this treasure, stop the war, save Comancheria, and my people will make me their Peace Chief!"

The wave of color deepened beneath her skin which was the exact color of the Manzano peaches that grew in Don Diego's orchards. She looked so *hopeful*, sitting there on her horse, making her preposterous claim with such passion.

So vulnerable.

A heavy knot formed in his throat.

How could she touch him so, how could her desires have so much power to stir the ones he had spent years and years keeping locked in his chest?

Why, *why* had he followed her all the way out here?

And what if they didn't find the treasure? What would happen to all her passion and optimism, then?

It would turn to an equal amount of pain and he could not bear to see it.

She would not be able to bear the shock. He needed to try to prepare her.

Her words interrupted his thoughts.

"You know that is true, Rafael!" she cried, happily. "Or you would not have changed your mind and come with me. You know that the two of us together can find the treasure and stop the war!"

She smiled at him so confidently that it broke his heart.

"No!" he blurted. "I don't know that . . ."

She slammed her fists onto her hips.

"Rafael! You do know it! That's why you came!"

The happiness was gone from her voice, replaced by consternation and fear.

Damn it! He hadn't meant to do that to her. But she *must* know the truth!

"How can you be so naive?" he shouted.

"How can *you* be so afraid to put faith in your feelings?" she shouted back.

"You don't know my feelings!"

"I know you're afraid to step out-of-bounds and trust in your instincts! You're afraid to believe in your visions and follow them! You're afraid to really *live,* Rafael, because you're afraid to dream!"

He slammed his heart shut against that onslaught.

"I'm afraid not to use my brain and you might at least *try* to do the same! Think, Sky! Even if we do find the treasure, Waters may not take it for a bribe. And if he does, you know that won't stop more white men who will settle in Comancheria."

She jerked as if he had slapped her.

"Then why did you come with me?" she shouted, with sudden tears in her voice. Her face had gone pale as the sandy soil along the shore.

"Go away!" she yelled. "Go back to your *rancho!*"

She whirled the mare in the water and headed back for the bank where the packhorses waited, their leadropes trailing. Drops of river water, clinging to her hair, sparkled in the last of the light.

Ysidora Pretty Sky. She held her back so straight and her head so high that he felt a terrible tumbling of his heart.

He sat still and waited.

"Lead your own packhorse," she snapped, when she returned to the middle of the shallow river.

She threw him the leadrope.

"And camp wherever you please," she said. "So long as it is not with me."

Quick anger at her unreasonableness flared in him.

"Don't be ridiculous! You can't camp alone."

She whirled around in her saddle to face him across the back of her packhorse, trotting behind her toward the east bank of the Gallinas.

"I most certainly can!"

She turned her back on him and faced forward to look for the best place to leave the river, low in its banks after the summer of little rain.

"To your right!" he ordered. "Up that slanting gully!"

For a moment he thought she would ignore his advice, but finally she angled off in the direction he'd pointed. He followed her to the edge of the water and up and out onto the steeper bank. When they reached the top of the low bluff, she pulled up and looked back at him.

"I *will* find the treasure," she said. "I can do it alone. I *will* stop the war and save our land."

Then she rode on.

He followed, furious, aching to tell her that she was right so she could keep her passionate hope, desperate to grab her and shake her until she stopped being such a stupid daydreamer.

He was torn between the two feelings like a calf roped head and heels.

She had made him have more different and deeper feelings in two days than he had had in years.

He would not let anyone have that power over him.

"You're a dreamer if I ever met one," he snapped. "You need to wake up."

"You sound just like my father," she shot back.

She smooched to the mare, rode out onto the top of the high ground ahead of him, and then reined in, staring ahead through the dusk toward the Mesa Rica. Her profile, lit by the falling, flaming sun, showed pure and proud against the twilight sky.

The sight sent the most piercing feeling of the whole insane day stabbing through him.

What he really wanted to do was to ride fast up beside her, reach out, and pull her into his arms.

Sky rode through the falling dark without once glancing back to see if Rafael followed. He could camp on the open prairie like a

Cheyenne for all she cared, or in the dense thicket of piñons at the foot of a hill like a Pawnee. He could go wherever he wanted, for he would never help her.

She would find the treasure alone. By the power of Father Sun, she would do it alone.

But as she turned Far Girl with her knees and headed into the scattered pine and juniper trees that grew alongside a little creek running down and down into the Gallinas, she heard the hooves of his horses striking the harder ground behind her.

She held up and waited for him.

"Don't come into my camp," she warned.

"Don't act like a stubborn simpleton," he retorted.

He passed her and rode into the rough circle made by some of the trees.

"This's the only decent place to camp around here and I'm not riding on," he announced, as he dismounted.

She followed him in.

"There'll be a big moon," she said. "You'd have enough light for traveling."

"You'd have wood for a fire," he said. "If you'd gather some while I go for water."

"I'm making a cold camp," she retorted. "I don't want every white-eyed treasure hunter in the hills to know I'm here."

"We're a day's ride from the mesa. And Waters's ranch is halfway between here and there—better make a fire, it might be your last one for a while."

"I can make camp without being bossed around!"

He stepped to his packhorse, removed his hat and his coat, untied a bundle, and then he was gone, carrying the two wooden buckets, in the direction of the creek.

Fury and amazement warring in her, Sky stared after him as he disappeared into the growing darkness.

Carrying water was the last thing she had expected him to do, the last thing a Comanche man would have done with her, a healthy woman, in the camp.

He *was* different from every other man she knew—at least in that he could continually surprise her.

The evening breeze picked up strength, touched the back of her neck and her arms with cool fingers. Autumn was coming, it was in the air at night now, every night. A fire would feel good before morning.

And hot food would taste good to her growling stomach.

Warm blankets would feel good to her limbs, tired of riding.

She would stay. *She* certainly wasn't going to ride on through the dark.

And she would build the fire, since he was getting the water. But she would not let him tell her another single thing to do. Not one.

There weren't many rocks close at hand, but she finally gathered enough to form a firepit and took out her flint and steel and the pounded buffalo chips she carried to use as tinder. She had coaxed the first spark into flame when the shot rang out behind her.

Sky leapt to her feet and ran, doubled over to make a smaller target, her hand on the knife at her waist, into the deep shadows floating among the trees. For a few heartbeats, she waited, listening. She heard nothing.

She moved toward the creek, toward the sound of the shot, feeling with the toes of her moccasins for the ground's bumps and hollows, straining her eyes to try to see through the dark.

Her breath came in shallow bursts of air, her mind whirled with questions. Had someone shot at Rafael? Or was that the sound of his gun? His rifle was still in its saddle scabbard, she had seen it when she tethered El Lobo, but he wore a pistol.

She searched the black dark ahead of her, took another step, and racked her brain for its caliber. She didn't know. It didn't matter—she didn't know enough about guns to be able to tell the sound of one from another.

There were no other shots. No other sounds at all.

Had she imagined it, that one, sharp crack that was gone as quickly as it came?

Her blood stopped in her veins. Had it hit him? Was Rafael lying at this moment, helpless or dead on the bank of the creek?

Her stomach went sick and her heart turned over. It couldn't be. It simply couldn't be.

She started to run, straining her eyes so wide in the dark that she thought they would tear.

An instant later, new noises covered the ragged sounds of her breath and he came striding toward her—water sloshing and bootheels breaking twigs and striking rocks. She skidded to a stop almost within reach of his tall, broad form, darker by a shade or two than the night.

"Sky!" he said. "Did you hear the shot?"

"Yes! Was it yours?"

Her voice shook with delighted relief.

She wanted to shout it, but her whole body went weak.

"I was afraid someone was shooting at you."

"Hey!" he said, and set the buckets down with a gentle sloshing sound. "I didn't mean to scare you."

He laid his hand, warm as summer, on her shoulder.

"Sorry."

And he was. But there was something else in his voice—her deep concern for his safety had pleased him, somehow.

She felt a little stab of pity. Was he not accustomed to that? Didn't anyone ever care about him?

"I shot at two eyes and a mutter of a growl in the dark," he said.

"Rafael! It might've been a bear or a mountain lion, hungry because of the dry weather. Did you hit it?"

"I didn't try, since I only had the pistol. I'm just glad it scared him away."

"So am I."

Just thinking about the danger stiffened her legs, pulled them into taking a step and then another, toward him. The moonlight had strengthened enough that she could see the glitter of his eyes.

"Which way did he go?"

"West. I heard him headed down creek. I don't think he'll bother us, but we'll build the fire up big, just the same."

"There you go," she murmured, "being the boss again."

"Because I'm right," he said, chuckling.

Then, he blurted, "Sky, down there at the creek, I was thinking—I need to give your feather ornament back to you."

Astonished, she said, "No wonder you almost got eaten alive if you weren't paying any better attention than that! Why were you thinking about my feathers?"

"They have meaning for you. I didn't know that when I chose them."

Sky's heart, already open to him, filled.

Without thinking, she reached out and laid her hand on the rock of his arm.

"No," she said. "The ornament is yours, Rafael. But . . . thank you for thinking about it and for caring about my feelings."

He held his arm very still.

She didn't remove her hand.

"I only wore my feathers on this journey to give me courage and they'll do that when I see them on your hat."

The tantalizing power of his flexed muscles vibrated beneath her fingers. His skin burned them through the thin fabric of his shirt; it melted her to him and she couldn't pull away.

"Sky," he said, finally, and she knew by his voice that he was trying to distance himself, "I am not admitting to a tie in our race or anything like that, but I'd feel better about keeping your feathers if you'd choose a prize from me."

She laughed.

"Because of your guilt!" she said. "You're not admitting we tied, but you know we did. My horse is as fast as yours, Rafael Montoya!"

He laughed, too.

"What can I give you?"

"I'll decide when I see what else is in those packs of yours," she said. "Wooden buckets and a guitar might be only the beginning."

"They might," he murmured.

Sky started to answer, but somehow she had lost the thread of the conversation. The rhythm of his heart pumping his blood through his veins beat its way into her fingertips and into her own blood.

"Come on," he said, finally, and bent to pick up the water buckets again.

Her hand fell to her side.

He took a long stride toward the camp, but he didn't walk away from her or ahead of her. She stayed beside him.

His arm brushed hers.

His scent was musky, a mixture of horse and leather and sweat and dust and his own hot skin. She fought the urge to reach out and touch him again.

"I hope no one will come here because of hearing the shot," she said.

"I doubt there's another human being except us between my *rancho* and Waters's new one."

"You said you and your father saw lots of men looking for the treasure there," she mused, lost in the heady sensation of the two of them keeping pace, walking side by side through the silver slants of moonlight. "On the mesa we should use my bow and arrows to hunt so we'll be silent."

"I hope you're a crack shot, then," he said, as they entered the black, stick shadows of the taller trees. "I couldn't hit the side of the mesa itself with an arrow."

"Anybody who can pack a horse with wooden buckets and guitars can learn to shoot a bow," she teased.

"My servant, Tonio, built and tied my packs."

"But Tonio isn't here to shoot the bow for you."

"Why do I need to learn if you know how to shoot it?"

"You might not have me to protect you all the time," she said, teasing him. "I might be busy looking for the treasure when you needed to shoot."

They came out into their small camp clearing, he turned and flashed her a smile.

"I see you built the fire. Does that mean I'm welcome to camp here?"

"I suppose so. But only because you brought your guitar to play for me and the buckets to carry the water."

"Wise woman! You see how useful these are."

He bent over and set the full buckets down.

"Look at them!" he said. "They sit on their own bottoms, they offer us water whenever we need it, they are easy to carry around."

"And the spyglass you carry, that's another reason for you to stay. We can use it to look for the bear or the mountain lion when Father Sun comes up."

"He'll be across the river and onto my *rancho* by then," Rafael said. "But there *is* another reason for you to give me hospitality—I drove him away and saved your life."

Sky laughed as she walked past him to the fire she'd built, which had grown into a red glow of low flames.

"You can't be so pleased with yourself about bringing all these useful pieces of equipment. Tonio gets the praise for sending them along."

Rafael's rich chuckle sent a thrill along her spine.

"Tonio *built* the packs," he said, "but I told him what to put in them."

"Oh?" she said, glancing up at him as she knelt to set the sticks of her pot rack into the ground. "And you told him to send along your guitar?"

"Of course," he said solemnly. "As soon as I have a full stomach I'll play for you so touchingly that you'll dance with happiness. You'll never travel without music again."

They both laughed. The moonlight had grown fuller. It poured into the opening in the center of the trees, falling down to surround them like a round tipi wall made of silver.

She felt him come closer.

"You are very sure of your charms as a musician," she said.

"I have many other charms as well."

Her fingers went still on the cross-stick she was fitting, her eyes flashed up to meet his.

Again, as she had at the end of their horse race, she forgot that she had heard her father's voice saying, *they will squeeze The People off the face of our Earth Mother*. The terrible fear that had ridden and spurred her fell away.

She forgot why she was here, alone with a stranger on a hillside far from the camping place of her band, forgot her parents and her friends.

Forgot everything except the face of the Spanish ranchero, Rafael, looking at her in the moonlight. A high-cheekboned, arrogant face handsome enough to stop Father Sun in his sky path.

"I am sure you do," she said.

He took a step, then another, toward her.

"I believe," he said, and his deep voice was like the velvet that the traders sold for many skins, "now that I think about it, I know that one of my most powerful charms is a talent for the bow."

"We shall see," she said, her gaze never wavering from his.

His eyes glittered, searched her face, then they slid lower to caress her neck and her breasts. The tips tingled, then hardened, beneath her thin elkskin blouse.

She rose, wondering that her body could feel suddenly both very heavy and incredibly light. She walked toward him. He was standing between her and her horses.

Every muscle in her body, every yearning in her soul, pulled her to him, but she did not give in to it and he did not move. He only watched her, with a look like a touch.

She passed him by. Her feet moved with a will of their own until the warm flesh of her horses was there beneath her hands. The knots that held her pack closed were loosened already, otherwise, her tingling fingers would have been useless.

The small iron pot already holding the dried strips of beef and the wild onions and lily bulbs felt like a lead weight on her arm. She lifted it out and reached with her other hand for the bow case still slung from the high, fringed horn of her saddle.

As she made her way back to the fire, she saw he had moved and was now sitting on his haunches beside it. The blaze burnished his copper-colored skin stretched over the strong-chiseled bones of his face which the fire lit like a carving.

But he was not a carving; he was real, breathing the same air that she breathed.

His eyes reflected the flames glowing between them. They followed her every move.

He was real. Flesh and blood.

His flesh longed to touch hers, his blood roared in his head.

Just as hers did.

She did not know how she knew that, but she knew it.

She dipped water from his bucket into her pot and hung it over the fire from the crosspiece of her cooking rack, stirring their supper with a horn spoon so cooled by the evening air that it sent a chill up her arm.

Then she stood up and looked down into his glittering eyes while she slid the strap of her bow case from her shoulder.

"Come out of the shadow of that juniper tree," she said, "and I will teach you how to use the bow."

Without a word, he rose in one flowing motion and walked toward her with a sure tread, like that of the wild animal he had challenged.

Sky moved a few steps to the side, away from the fire, out into the full bath of the moonlight.

"Don't move," he growled. "Stand right there."

"*I* am the teacher, remember?" she said, the breath so tight in her chest that the words came out in a thin whisper that floated away on the breeze.

He laughed, made that low, rich sound, and filled the night with power.

"Of course," he said. "The sky rules over the earth."

He came to her, he let her fit the bow into his hands. He permitted her to step around behind him and draw his arm back to judge the full pull of the weapon.

And all the time she could feel his great *puha*.

The back of his iron-muscled arm brushed her breast as he pulled back the bow.

Neither of them moved.

Neither of them breathed.

Gently, very gently, he moved it forward, then, and let the string go slack.

As they both had known he would, he slowly let it fall into the deep grass. He turned around and took her into his arms.

Chapter 6

He pulled her to him as inexorably as Father Sun had slipped down behind Mother Earth. And not just with the strength in his arms.

The whole length of his body called to hers, brought her against him. His hard chest brushing her breasts, his long, muscular thighs caressing hers, had far more power than they needed to lift her arms and place them around his neck. Her lips parted.

"I have always wondered what it would be like to kiss," she murmured. "It is not our custom, but I have seen my parents . . ."

His mouth stopped her words.

Never, ever, had she known such a delicious thrill. Nor such a warmth.

The chill air of the autumn evening became a bath of hot honey, the fire in her blood turned to fever. He melted her bones.

She floated, connected to nothing but his mouth, able to stand only because it was molded to hers, able to breathe only because he shared his own breath. Colors, every color of the rainbow, sparkled against the black of her eyelids.

Her arms moved apart and lay along the wide ledges of his shoulders, her hands caressed the warm column of his neck. His pulse beat deep and steady beneath her fingers in a primal rhythm that caused a mighty throbbing to start inside her.

Another sweet shock flashed through her, zigzagging through her veins like arrowy lightning.

His tongue! He actually was trailing his tongue along the seam of her lips, parting them, touching the tip of it to hers!

What a *strange* custom!

But what a wonderful one!

After that, there were no more thoughts in her head. Her mind vanished.

She became all body and soul, a body ravaged by a glorious weakness, collapsing even closer against him. A soul twining itself into his, never to be alone again.

She heard a moan, only knew it was hers because she could feel it. Rafael wrapped her closer, deepened the kiss.

A desperate need to feel his skin against hers set her restless hands moving, pressed her palms to his neck, slid them up and thrust her fingers into his hair. His silky hair, wonderful and smooth, better feeling in her hands, even, than the Spanish dress.

She loosened the thong that tied it and cradled his head in her hands, pulled him even closer, stood on tiptoe to move her whole body against his so she could kiss him back, harder.

She pressed her breasts harder to him, tantalized his tongue with hers. Her hands slipped down to cup his cheeks, to hold his mouth to hers.

His mouth. His mouth was her sun, her fire, her only way to get warm in the winter.

Yet, somehow, she wanted more. More.

But she didn't know what.

Suddenly, he reached up and tore her hands loose, held them out away from him by the wrists. Out in the cool, sharp air.

"No," he muttered. "Sky, I . . . I'm sorry."

Shock chilled her, but her blood still raced, still pounded hot in her veins. It rushed, thundering, to her brain.

"What's wrong? Am I not very good at kissing? I can learn!"

Her hands itched to go back to him, her bruised lips ached for more, but he held her away.

He gave a strangled little laugh.

His long fingers squeezed her, hard.

"No, it is not that," he said, his voice rasping in his throat.

"Then what is it?" she demanded, and shook her hair out of her face so she could search his.

"I . . . I . . . we need to stop this. We have to stop it."

"I don't understand! I thought that a kiss meant that you cared for me and I cared for you!"

He let go of her nerveless hands and stepped back.

"Sky," he said gruffly, "Sky. You are very . . .impetuous. Very . . . young."

He looked down into her eyes for the space of three heartbeats, his face shadowed by the loose swing of his hair. Then he turned on his heel and walked away.

Stunned, Sky stood still and watched him vanish into the shadow of the trees where the horses were tied.

Very *young*?

Wasn't she a woman? Wasn't kissing what happened between a man and a woman?

Why, she had eighteen summers! Four more summers than most girls had when they married!

What was he *talking* about?

A terrible feeling, cold and lonely, swept through her, dragged her heart to the ground.

He cared nothing about her. That had to be it. Kissing meant caring and he did not care for her.

Bitter tears stung her throat, filled her eyes.

With the whole world a blur, she turned, ignoring him, and ran for her horses a short distance away in the trees.

But the tip of her treacherous tongue darted out to taste him on her lips.

Hot tears hit her cheeks. She untied the horses and led them to the opposite side of the camp to unsaddle and unload them, dumping everything heedlessly onto the ground. She got her hobbles and started to lead the horses to the creek, then stopped and went back with them trailing behind her.

She knelt and fumbled with both hands into her largest parfleche, pulled out the Spanish dress.

He would see! She would show him that she was not so very young, that she knew something about the world! After all, she had been to more rendezvous than he had ever seen!

He had to know that he could *not* kiss her and then suddenly abandon her—just throw her away like that!

Not when they had been so close. She had never before felt so close to anyone. Then he had just thrown her away!

Once the horses had drunk their fill and been hobbled, Sky knelt and washed her face in the creek. The splash of the cold water on her skin did not wash away the taste of Rafael nor the pressure of his lips, but it calmed her a little.

She looked again at the moonlit creek bank to make sure that Far Girl and Pabo had found a good spot to graze, then she stepped back into the dark trees to change into the dress. A crashing and crackling through the trees told her Rafael and his horses were coming—she froze with the soft fabric filling her hands.

But he never sensed her presence, never knew she was there. He watered his animals, then turned and led them back up the slope toward the camp. So. He wasn't even going to let his horses stay with hers.

Perhaps hers were too impetuous, too young.

She stripped out of her elkskins, stepped into the dress, and pulled it up to where its neckline clung just at the point of her shoulders. Rolling her blouse and skirt into a bundle, she went out into the moonlight, looking down at the way the dress pushed her breasts up and out.

Good. He could see that she was not so very young.

And that she could make him want to kiss her again. She would make him want to, but she wouldn't let him.

Rafael leaned back against his saddle and clutched the guitar closer to him. He struck a high, dark chord that rang through the night like a cry.

He hit it again. Then he threw himself into playing the fastest, hardest flamenco he knew, forcing his fingers to find the way, wrenching his mind from Sky and putting it into the wild, fierce melody.

He played it all the way through, then started back again, adding variations, entwining the tune with the most intricate new themes, clinging to the sound of each note so that it could fill up his memory and drive her out. Drive out her scent and her look and the sound of her smoky voice.

The fire leapt and crackled—he'd built it up to blazing—but he didn't even look at it. No more visions for him.

And no more Ysidora Pretty Sky. Kissing her was the craziest thing he had ever done.

The dumbest.

Don Diego had been right not to trust him out alone. He shouldn't let him go out of the *casa* by himself, much less off the *rancho*.

"Rafael?"

He looked up.

His fingers stopped moving on the strings.

She stood just a few steps away from the fire, her magnificent hair catching its reflection and its sparkling heat. Hair that flowed like an auburn river over one shoulder and left the other one naked.

In a dress that left her breasts almost bare, too—pushed them up into soft, wondrous mountains and hardly covered them at all.

He could not take his eyes from her.

He could hardly believe it *was* she; he could not imagine her as anything but a purely wild free one, dressed in beads and buckskins.

He forced his hands to move, he made them make music, but he barely heard the wandering song.

The dress was a bright blue, the color of her namesake, the sky. The exact color of the sky in New Mexico on the most brilliant day of October that had ever been seen.

She made the long, full skirt swirl around her feet as she walked toward him. As she came closer, she tossed her hair back over the other shoulder and flashed him a smile bright enough to blind him.

A terrible desire rose up in him.

So. That was what she was doing, making him wish he hadn't broken the kiss. He hadn't meant that as an insult, but she obviously had taken it so.

She was bent on revenge.

"You must be very much afraid of that mountain lion or bear, or whatever it was," she said. "Impetuous and young as I am, I know that this much fire, a fire big enough to drive off the wild animals, will ruin our supper."

He continued his song, with no idea at all of what he was playing.

"Your supper is safe," he said, over the music that was coming from his aching fingers. Aching to touch her again.

But he only smiled at her, coolly.

"Sit down over here on the blanket in your beautiful dress and I will serve you."

He nodded to a place between him and the fire.

"I would've dressed for dinner if I'd known what you'd wear," he said. "You look beautiful."

"Thank you. No one else approves of me when I wear this."

"Well," he said, coolly, as the song drifted to a lilting finish in his hands. "You must remember that I see you in an entirely different way than your relatives do."

He put aside the guitar and went to the dishes he'd taken from his pack, filled them from the pot he'd moved off the fire, added silver spoons, and carried one serving to Sky.

She accepted it, hesitantly.

"Is something wrong?"

She shrugged. The dress slipped off the curve of one peach-colored shoulder; her full breasts almost burst out of it.

He ought to look away. He had to.

But he couldn't.

"I've never had a man serve me food," she said. "And you went to the creek for the water."

She sighed, and, again, the dress could barely contain her.

"No matter how mad I get at you, Rafael," she said, and looked up at him with eyes so huge he could fall into them, "I must admit you're different from all the other men."

"How so?"

"I knew it when you helped the woman get her combs from Pedro at the rendezvous. And when you offered to give back my feathers. Most men wouldn't do that."

He picked up his own food and went to his place.

Sky took a small bit of food onto her spoon, leaned forward, and put it into the fire.

"How do you know you don't like the food?"

"I was only feeding the fire to give thanks," she said, tossing him a glance over her shoulder that made sweat come out on his forehead. "Now you know that I do keep *some* customs."

He laughed.

"One, " he said. "I have only seen you keep one."

"Tomorrow," she said, and she laughed, too. "When we reach the mesa. I will let you kill a deer and I'll scrape the hide. That will be two."

"Done!" he said, and they sealed the bargain by dipping into their food.

"Delicious!" she proclaimed, then laughed her velvety laugh that came curling around his heart like smoke. "*That's* my second one, already—I did cook the supper."

"I helped," he teased her. "I took it off the fire when it would've burned."

"So it's your success," she teased, in return. Then she sobered.

"It gets so tiresome, listening to them all constantly criticize what I do," she said. "Trying to make me behave as a Comanche woman should."

He looked at her, trying to imagine her in camp with her band, doing chores, being corrected and bossed around. He couldn't.

"My parents have always taught me to behave as a Spanish ranchero should," he said, thoughtfully, his heart suddenly beating harder.

Somehow, here, in some way he didn't understand, he was feeling his way into new territory.

He went on, "But isn't that what all parents do—try to prepare us for our life's work?"

"Maybe they don't know what that work will be!" she said, rebelliously. "We are who we are and the work must come to us! Rafael, sometimes don't you just want to ride away from all the rules and the restrictions and never come back?"

A deep, trembling warmth toward her, something more than the desire, shot through him.

"Do you ever *yearn* to break away and be free, to go someplace new and be only yourself as you really are?"

She was putting his feelings into words.

"Yes," he admitted. "But I push that yearning away."

He stopped. She made him open his heart as never before. If he wanted to maintain this distance between them, he must guard his feelings more.

"And you behave as they say you should," she said. "Sometimes I try that, too, but it is not worth it. If I try too hard, I might lose myself."

"You might," he blurted. "That's what I've done."

Then he clamped his treacherous mouth shut, set down his bowl, and reached for his guitar.

"You can find yourself again if you let yourself dream it," she said. "If you trust in your instincts."

A trembling shot through him, inside. What had he meant by that remark? He was who he'd always been. Who else could he be?

He tucked the instrument into the curve of his body, wrapped his arms around its familiar shape.

"I trusted my instincts to come with you," he said.

She smiled at him in the glow of the firelight.

"Trust them more," she said.

He couldn't. He couldn't even think about it—a riot of emotions was trying to burst forth from his heart. He had to keep it locked, as always.

He pulled the instrument even closer to him and reached for a melody, tried it, then remembered another. His fingers flew over the strings, sorting through the songs, searching for the first notes that would lead them into a trailing strain of sound that would be the right one.

They found it.

This melody was high and haunting, wild and sad, and it filled his eyes with tears the moment it began.

It wove itself into a song.

A song that Sky could sing.

Her sweet, husky voice came throbbing into the air to set words upon his strings.

I see a lodge made of rainbows, I see a lodge made of flaming rainbows.

Rafael played on, his fingers strong enough to pluck the moon from the sky, bringing each note ringing from the guitar on exactly the right breath to sound beneath her voice.

Father Sun's rays are traveling. Father Sun's rays are traveling to find his heart in the Earth Mother's breast.

Her dark eyes flashed auburn fire at him, their power wouldn't let him look away, wouldn't let him breathe. His lips parted and he began to sing with her.

The rocks run back racing, the trees turn into arrows that fly.

The Eagle dives through the wind to strike flame from the coals of the fire.

He kept playing and singing, but he turned away from her then and looked into the fire. Because he could hear another voice now, a voice which was giving him the words, a wispy, sweetly ancient, strangely familiar voice singing with him and Sky.

He kept staring into the fire while they all three sang the ending chant together, fervently, like a prayer.

> *He'yay, He'yo, He'yo, yoyo!*
> *Eya, yo, yoyo!*
> *Eya, yo!*

And he saw another vision, a bigger, brighter one this time, while the echoes died away into the hills.

His hands fell away from the guitar.

He turned to Sky.

She was real, flesh and blood. Suddenly, *only* she was real.

The vision, the song were gone. His old world, his old self gone with them.

"How did you know that song?" she asked, and her quiet, smoky voice evoked her presence in the night.

"An old man was singing it in my ear," he

said, surprised as he spoke that such a mystery could be put into words. "Then I saw him in the fire, standing in the lodge of rainbows."

She didn't speak, only looked at him, waiting to know more.

His voice, too, was very quiet as he went on.

"I saw a tipi with lodgepoles made of rainbows that were burning. A black eagle diving through them into the firepit full of coals."

He hesitated, then added. "The old man stood beside a spill of gold and silver coins—the ones I saw in the Council fire vision."

Sky shivered, wrapped her arms around herself."

"The silver-whites of the moonlight and the blacks of the shadows lengthened out and fell together at the top like lodgepoles," he said, remembering.

"Then they burst into colors—red, purple, orange, blue, green, everything bright, and made a tipi with a circle of glowing coals in the center of its airy floor."

He was seeing it all over again, trying to let her see it, too, wanting her to explain this magic.

"A sleek, shining bird, fast as an arrow, dived streaking between the open lodgepoles straight into the firepit, which burst into flame."

They sat silent, for four long heartbeats, with her waiting for him to tell her more.

Finally the whole truth burst from him.

"The old man was my grandfather. My Kot-soteka grandfather. I remember now. I am of the *Nermernuh*."

Suddenly, he was on his feet.

"All the Spanish rules I've fitted my life into are nothing but a lie!" he said in a strangled whisper. "I'm not what I thought I was!"

With an anguished cry he turned and left her.

Rafael stood outside the circle of trees and stared down toward the river. Toward the hills they had ridden through on the way they had come.

Moonlight and shadows rippled like water over the rolling land. But he could not move. He felt stunned, in his body and mind, in his heart, as if from the blow of a hand.

The breeze blew his hair around his face and swept over his skin with the faintest promise of winter on the wind.

Then, behind him, soft as if he had imagined it, he heard Sky's voice.

"This night is one of summer-going-away, fall-months-coming," she said. "It hovers between two seasons. It holds much *puha*."

The light sparkled silver now, dancing downward from Sister Moon, riding higher and higher.

The scents of cedars and sage and burning pine filled the air.

"Yes," he said, bitterly. "The power to destroy my life!"

"The power to give it to you."

Her flat, sure tone infuriated him.

He wheeled to glare at her.

"How can you *say* that? It'd be better if I'd never remembered! I am Spanish, raised to be more Spanish than the people in Spain, meant to live on the Rancho del Cielo!"

"You are *you*, meant to listen to your heart and live in it."

He tried not to hear that.

"You don't even seem surprised," he said.

"I must have know it all along," she answered. "From the very first I noticed that you looked different from the other Spanish. You ride like a Comanche. You had the vision in Council and spoke with the voice of your medicine spirit."

"I have no medicine spirit," he said, and a great hole opened in him. "I had not lived enough summers to go on my vision quest before I was snatched away from my band." He was sure of this knowledge that seemed to come from nowhere.

Huge pieces of him were missing.

He tried to slam the door of his heart against that thought, tried to hold it closed.

But Sky had unlocked it and, to his great distress, she held it open.

"Who took you?"

"The Osage, I think. Dimly I can see a young, painted warrior, feel him grabbing me up from the bank of a creek, hear a woman, I guess my mother, screaming for me."

"Don Diego must have bought you from them."

"*Sí*," he said, shortly. "He has often told me how much he wanted a son."

"And he loves you. I saw it in his face during Council."

"*Sí*," he said, again. "And to keep me from finding out or wanting to go back to my people, he sent me to the high pasture during rendezvous. That's why, when I told him good-bye, he kept saying that I was leaving him and my mother."

"He was afraid of losing you," she murmured.

"He was. That's why he said, *I thought you were old enough, settled in the* rancho *enough . . .*"

Rafael shook his head, wonderingly.

"And all the time I thought he didn't trust me to grow up. Instead, he didn't trust me to stay if I felt the pull of my blood and wanted to go back to The People."

Behind them, on their picket line, his horses snuffled and stamped. Far away, a coyote barked.

"Will you?"

"How can I know?" he cried, and the anguish stabbed right through him.

"I have a *rancho* to take care of—land and people and animals that I love—and here I am, leaving it all, risking it all, to search for a feather in the wind! Here I am, seeing visions in the fire!"

"Don't let it worry you so, Rafael," she soothed. "Visions are gifts from the All-Father."

"Visions are the self-serving dreams of weak people!"

"No! Sssh!" she cried, and took a step to be closer to him, close enough he could catch her scent, could imagine her taste on his lips again.

"Rafael," she said, "only strong people, favored people, see visions and hear the voices of the spirits. Our warriors fast and pray and smoke and search for them."

His eyes filled.

"I am not one of your warriors! I am a Spanish ranchero!"

"You are yourself. *Who* you are is not the same as *what* you are."

He went still as midnight, staring at her in the pale wash of the moonlight, listening, now, with his eyes as well as his ears. Listening with all of himself.

"You would be you, even if you had been raised by my mother's Irish people," she said, emphatically. "The Fire Flower is an example of this. Now she is one of the *Nermernuh*, as much as I am. More."

"More?"

"That life gives her her freedom," Sky said, trying to explain to herself as well as to him. "It puts ropes on me. But I know who I am, I know myself and I will not lose me."

He smiled at her. His heart turned over.

She was right. And she was real.

She was the only reality left to him.

"Who *you* are is a sage woman, *Señorita* Pretty Sky," he said, his voice coming hushed from the depths of his being. "A shaman. A medicine woman. You have much insight, much power to ease pain."

Sky stared at him, not comprehending at first.

No man had ever said such a thing to her, no man of her band ever would. That would be granting her too much *puha*, which was only for males.

And, rarely, perhaps, for a very old woman, one who had acquired her *puha* over a long lifetime from her medicine man husband.

Rafael truly *was* different from any man she had ever known.

Impulsively she threw her arms around his neck.

"Oh, Rafael!" she cried. "No one ever told me that before!"

He clasped her close, kissed her hair, kept one arm around her to lead her back to the blanket and the fire.

He drew her gently down to the blanket and for a long moment he just held her there, feeling as though he was as light as thistledown ready to go dancing in the wind, loose from the cusp of loneliness. Then he bent his head toward hers.

Rafael's kiss took Sky twirling into the air with the strength of the twisting tornadoes that roared across the plains. It was nimble as the lightning, triumphant as the thunder, as sweetly relentless as the rain.

When they stopped kissing, at last, they were dizzy and drunk with it.

And his lips lingered very near hers. His breath still tickled her mouth, she breathed in its cedary scent.

She let her languid gaze linger on his handsome face.

His hip burned her thigh through their clothes, the hardness of his manhood tantalized her.

She met his dark eyes.

His sensual, heavy-lidded eyes.

Eyes that drifted away from hers to caress the tops of her breasts.

For an instant, her heart lurched with the cold irony.

He was one of the *Nermernuh*, a man who was by blood Comanche. She did not want to love a Comanche man.

But his face was rich with his marvelous smile and his eyes could see nothing but her.

He had not been raised Comanche. He was different.

This moment was the reason they had been sent onto this trail by the vision and the song.

This moment was the reason they had been born.

Chapter 7

Rafael turned and stretched out beside her, propped up on one elbow to look at her.

"Ysidora Pretty Sky, Wise Woman," he said, teasing with his rich voice and his eyes.

But the lingering touch of his fingertips on her cheek was simply, indescribably tender.

"So you guessed my secret, that I am of the *Nermernuh*, before I knew it?"

He spoke lazily, as if the question was nothing, but she could feel his inner self waiting.

"Yes."

She touched his face as he had touched hers.

"You could tell by my looks?"

"Yes. I am wise woman," she said, teasing him in return.

Then she answered solemnly, tracing the line of his cheekbone and his aristocratic, slightly arched nose as she spoke.

"This face of yours. This wonderful, handsome, strong Comanche face. I noticed your skin was darker than that of the other Spanish. I looked at you and some part of me knew."

He nodded and then tilted his head so that her fingers drifted up over his brow and into his hair.

"And when you had the vision in the Council fire," she went on, dreamily, remembering, loving the feel of the silky strands in her hand. "I did not know whether that could happen to the Spanish."

"The smells of sage and pine and cedar in that lodge, just being inside a tipi with the sun coming through the walls must have begun bringing my memories to the surface of my mind," he mused. "And you. Being in the same place with you, hearing your voice speak the truth, gave me that vision."

She whispered, "So all this trouble of yours is because of me."

"Yes. Because of your awful, distressing honesty, which is so real and so true. You *know* things, Sky."

She lifted her other hand and traced his arching brow.

"So do you. You must have known you were one of us, even then, in the Council. And you knew your own truth in your own heart about the treasure—that's why you've come with me, Rafael!"

Her heart lifted to the heavens again, just with the thought.

"I know we can stop the war. I just know it, no matter what doubts you have!"

"Shh!" he said, and placed a rough finger gently across her lips. "Let's not talk about that now. I want to hear you talk about me some more."

"Vain!" she said, laughing. "You want to hear again how handsome you are!"

His eyes were laughing, too.

But he said, very seriously, "No, not that. Hearing you say that I am Comanche—it makes me feel . . . whole, somehow."

His voice had gone raw with emotion.

"Whole?" she whispered.

"I suppose that is the word."

His hand caressed her bare shoulder in a gesture almost like a plea.

"These memories are all so new to me. And so strange. How could I have forgotten?"

She was barely able to breathe now, from the pain in his voice.

And from the allure of his rhythmic touch on her skin.

She wanted to throw her arms around him, to comfort him, but the pride she sensed in him held her back. She took her hand from his hair, caressed the nape of his neck.

"You forgot because you couldn't bear to remember," she whispered. "It would have been too sad. You would have felt trapped, and, as a child, you couldn't have escaped and found your band again."

He lifted his head. His eyes looked past her now, into the darkness.

"I feel so sorry for my father," he said.

"Why?" she whispered, full of joy that he would talk to her of what was in his heart.

Gratitude and joy that he would trust her so much.

Somehow, she knew that he had never before talked of these things.

"Don't feel sorry for him—he got the best son in the world!" she said, softly, stroking his face.

He looked down at her, then, the look in his eyes so intense she thought she could not bear it.

"I hated so much to tell him I would come to look for the treasure," he said. "He thought I was running away from the home he gave me to join your band after my first time to visit in your camp."

She gave the look back to him.

"Are you?" she asked.

His hot gaze moved down over her face and throat, onto the tops of her breasts, swelling from the low, ruffled neckline of the blue silk dress.

"I am not running *from* anything."

Their bodies touched here and there, up and down the length of them. His knee burned against her thigh.

She laughed, the joy bubbling up in her.

"You are so beautiful," he murmured. "So open to life. Let's talk about you and how you are not supposed to be wearing this dress."

His eyes moved slowly over her face again.

"I don't want to talk anymore," she said.

"But I have taken your feathers away and have given you nothing in return," he said, and gave her his charming grin. "I am admitting nothing about a dead-heat ending to that race, you understand, but . . . what do you want for your prize?"

"This."

She laid both her arms around his neck and pulled his head down for another kiss.

But he only brushed her lips with his. Then he bent to bury his face between her breasts. He cupped the side of one in his hand and pressed his open mouth to her bare skin.

Her flesh melted into his, that heat suffused her whole body, made it limp and helpless and weak and warm.

And stronger than she had ever felt before.

Then he took his mouth away and she cried out in protest.

His face hovered over hers, his eyes demanding that she listen to his words.

"At this moment, talking would be safer," he said.

"Safer than what?"

She ran one hand down over the tense muscles of his back, onto his small, rounded buttocks. Slid it around toward the front.

His smile curved the corners of his sensuous mouth, caused a rakish dimple to form.

"Than what I am going to do if you keep touching me that way."

She smiled back.

"Only danger brings glory."

His smile deepened, then disappeared into a frown.

"Do you know what you are talking about?"

"Yes," she lied. "I do."

His hot, dark eyes searched hers for one long heartbeat.

Then he touched one callused fingertip to the pulse beating wildly at the base of her neck, trailed it out and over her collarbone onto her shoulder and down until it met the edge of her dress.

He pushed it off and freed one of her breasts.

"Ahh, Sky," he crooned.

Reverently, he cupped it in his hand, where it fitted perfectly into his palm, and placed his lips around its swollen tip.

Fire shot through her, fire in rainbow-colored flames. And light, brilliant as both the sun and moon, sparkling and wheeling and dancing.

Why had she never known there could be so much pleasure?

So much pleasure that it could lift her to float in the air?

Then it was gone and she was desperate, opening her eyes and reaching for him, but he had sat up and turned away to pull off his boots. Sky went onto her knees behind him, her arms around his neck to unbutton his shirt. She moved them to underneath his arms and finished as he threw away the second boot and turned to shrug out of his shirt.

She ran her hands over the muscles of his chest, gloried in it, while he reached for the other side of her dress and sent the whole top of it crumpling to her waist.

"Oh, Sky," he muttered huskily, his eyes on her breasts in the moonlight, and fumbled for the buttons among the folds of cloth.

Regretfully, she took one hand away from his sleek skin to help him.

When they were done and the dress lay in a heap around her hips, he took her hand and pulled her with him as he stood up. She stepped out it and kicked off her moccasins.

He made a sound of voluptuous admiration that she knew she would never forget.

She reached for the row of buttons that ran up the front of his tight pants, dizzy now with the power that she knew she had. She undid the fasteners, one at a time, her fingers trembling from each brush against the forceful life of his manhood beneath the cloth.

The breeches were undone at last, he peeled them off and fell onto the blanket with Sky in his arms.

The silk dress beneath her gave no delight at all compared to Rafael's skin above.

He rolled over onto her, onto both his elbows and cupped her head in his hands, taking her mouth with a passion so savage it slammed through her bones like a blow. Her lips parted beneath it, her tongue rushed, searching, to his.

To the masterful, loving laving of his. To the hot, boundless fascination, the possession of his.

Rafael. Her mind and her heart shouted his name while her mouth lost all desire ever to speak again.

Rafael. He was the reason she was not yet married, the reason she had put off all her suitors and kept High Wolf waiting so long.

She had been waiting for Rafael.

His hands left her hair, caressed her shoulders, moved down the hollow of her spine to cradle her hips closer against him. The hardness of his manhood against her skin set her on fire.

He broke the kiss to sink his mouth into her hair, his breath hot and fierce in her ear.

"I have run to you, Ysidora Pretty Sky," he rasped. "I know that, now."

Her mouth, her tongue, her throat, all were too needy for his kiss to return for her to be able to speak. She groaned and arched her body upward against him, sliding her cheek hard across his to pull his mouth back to hers.

But his knee slipped between her legs and his lips began a trail of tantalizing kisses burning down the side of her neck. Her arms, her whole body went alarmingly weak, but she managed to raise her hands and thrust them into his hair. To guide him.

No, to hold him still. To keep his mouth in one spot until it melted into her, until it satisfied the longings springing to life in every part of her body.

And her soul.

But he reached her breasts again and she lost all hope of having any kind of control over herself or him.

A trembling ecstasy took possession of the night. His face nuzzled into the hollow between her soft, welcoming breasts. He could hear the frantic beating of her heart as his hungry lips moved toward one hard, thrusting tip.

Her hands hovered helplessly over him. Her breath left her.

Teasingly, ever more slowly now, he pressed openmouthed kisses in a circle all around the base of her nipple and felt it harden in pleasure.

No, in *need*.

Tears sprang into her eyes. Every part of Sky's soul, every part of her body, wept for something more.

She would beg him for it, she would call out his name. But she could not speak.

After a lifetime of wanting, his lips reached the full, pink bud. And took it.

Then his tongue loved it gently, while his finger and his thumb, his rough callused thumb, took possession of the other nipple and teased it, sending shivers of need up Sky's spine.

"Rafael," she whispered, then gave herself up to let him melt her completely into the cradle of Mother Earth.

But the hot, raw desire for more poured anew, restless, questing strength into her veins. She pressed closer against him, pulled him nearer to her, bowed her back to put herself more fully into his mouth, rubbed her palms into the muscles and sinews of his back, his neck, his small, hard buttocks.

He cried out something incoherent, something that was not even of words, and moved both knees between her thighs. His lips left her breast and found her mouth again, his magic hands moved over all of her body.

She clung to him, held onto him for her only hope of knowing how to escape from these mounting, unquenchable flames. The air of the night, cool as it was, had no power at all against the heat of his skin. His thighs seared the insides of hers and she burned all the hotter.

Then a fresh, hard heat pushed into her and the pain it caused tore a cry from her lips.

Rafael hesitated, thrust again to bring a second sound of pain.

"You lied to me," he muttered into her hair.

"I know," she whispered, "and I am glad I did."

Her body leaped into rhythm with his. She wrapped herself around him, drew him in, held him close enough to make him a part of herself.

He buried his face in the hollow of her neck.

They fit together, moved together, as naturally as the flames danced in the firepit of their camp. They were fuel, fed by air, making elemental fire that would never burn out.

The bird's call, its notes starting low and sliding up, then down again, penetrated Sky's ears and worked itself into her dream. She was lying in her husband's arms, her legs tangled with his and her head on his shoulder, the two of them breathing with one breath. The meadowlark was singing a wedding song to them, a medicine song, like a blessing.

Her husband was not High Wolf, she knew that. He was a stranger and a strong man who had given a thousand horses to her. He did not give the horses to her father when he asked for her hand. He gave them to her.

She had more fast, beautiful horses than anyone else in her band, even the important men. All the other women were scandalized.

She felt a smile curve her lips.

The bird sang out again, closer and louder this time.

Its call sounded almost like a signal. It made her stir enough to know that she needed to listen, ought to wonder about it, but she couldn't wake up enough to think. She snuggled deeper into her husband's embrace, slid her face down from his shoulder to press her cheek into the slight indentation in the middle of his broad chest. She sighed, and drew the spicy, masculine scent of him deep into herself.

Surely that raucous bird would quiet down, tuck its head under its wing, and sleep until morning. At daylight it could wake her and she wouldn't be angry at all.

The muscular chest beneath her cheek continued to rise and fall in the same, slow rhythm. It was sweetly naked and incredibly warm. So were the arms that encircled her and the legs that wrapped around hers.

Every inch of her skin that was not touched by his, however, was standing in goose bumps, shrinking with cold. Fall Month was coming. The dry, cool air of this night carried its warning.

Ta-be Na-ni-ka! Na-nan-is-yu-ake!

The urgency in the bird's sweet tones tore Sky's eyes wide open.

She froze, listening for it to come again.

The pink light and the gray grass and the black trees listened with her while they waited for the yellow brightness of the sun.

When the echoing song sounded once more, she knew why the blood had stopped in her veins. That voice did not live inside a bird.

It belonged to a flute!

The dark limbs of the piñons melted into their darker trunks and then into the pale earth, although the blur of sleep had fled from her eyes. She was not dreaming any longer. She was awake.

Awake and turned to stone in Rafael's arms.

That voice belonged to High Wolf's flute, carved by his own hands, with six holes to represent the four directions of the wind and the earth and the sky. High Wolf had followed her!

He was here—he would find her naked in Rafael's arms!

He would kill them both before she could say that she had changed her mind about marrying him.

Trembling, shaking with the need to avert the imminent danger, she pushed at Rafael's arms, jerked her legs from their tangle with his and rolled free.

He muttered a sleeping protest and clutched at her, but she was already out of his reach, snatching up the Spanish dress and darting to her packs to put it away and throw on her elkskin clothing, watching Rafael over her shoulder one minute, scanning the thin stand of trees for High Wolf the next. The flute's song had come from the direction of the creek.

Rafael's head dropped onto his forearm and his hair fell like a curtain over his face. His breathing stayed deep and regular. Thank the All-Father!

She found her skirt, tied it on, jerked her blouse over her head so fast the long sleeve-fringes whipped at her face, then she pulled out the only blanket she had brought, dumping her buffalo robes out onto the ground as she shook out the blanket, and ran to throw it over Rafael. Then she ran toward the creek.

She had to tell High Wolf she wouldn't marry him and make him go away before Rafael even knew he was there. The flute's song had been meant to reassure her, to let her know who was approaching her camp. Only her horses grazed near the creek. High Wolf thought, naturally, that she was alone.

Every trace of sleep left her mind as it raced faster and faster with fear. She would find High Wolf, tell him that she had changed her mind, and that he had no chance of persuading her to give up her search for the treasure. He would be furious that he couldn't control her, they would argue, and finally he would storm away and go back to their people.

After all, the medicine man couldn't be away from his band too long, especially not while they were planning war.

But before she went very far into the trees, High Wolf found them both.

"Sky!" Wolf called, his voice ringing out strong against the rocks. "Come here."

She stopped where she was and whirled to see him.

He stepped out of the ring of piñons from the east, out of the growing day's light, instead of from the north, where the sound of the flute had been. His sharp gaze lingered on her for only a moment, then dropped to the man in the bed on the ground.

Rafael was sitting straight up, his heavy-lidded eyes flashing from High Wolf to Sky and back. Not three long strides separated the two men.

She ran back toward them, feeling like a child's rawhide doll, her limbs moved by an outside force, her skin shriveled by the shock of being out here in the cool morning all alone after leaving Rafael's arms so fast. All she wanted was to crawl back into them.

But High Wolf was there, with an uncased bow on his shoulder and a furious scowl on his face, his eyes glued to her lover. Rafael was unarmed, his pistol and his rifle lay with his saddle just out of his reached. He did not even glance toward them, he kept his eyes on High Wolf.

"What are *you* doing here?" High Wolf demanded.

"I don't answer to you," Rafael snapped in reply.

Sky shivered in the cold air and ran faster, hurrying to put herself between them.

"*Ahó*, High Wolf," she said.

"Stay where you are!" he answered.

He took a long step forward.

In one fast, flowing motion, Rafael stood, wrapping the blanket around his waist as he came up. He fastened it tight without looking down.

"I'm glad you are on your feet, Montoya," High Wolf said, in Spanish. "Because I intend to avenge the insult you have given me."

Rafael shifted his weight onto the balls of his feet and made loose fists of his hands. He was ready to fight, but he clearly was not worried.

He was naked and unarmed, but he wasn't afraid!

"I do not know you except for your name and that you are a shaman, *mi amigo*," he said to High Wolf, calmly. "How could I have insulted you?"

"You have made camp, all night, alone, with my woman."

His sharp eyes flicked from Rafael's blanket to the robes piled beside Sky's packs.

"I see that there are two beds here," he said, "but that makes no difference. I have Pretty Sky's promise soon to be my wife. Her father, Windrider, also, has given his word. I am holding many horses for him."

Rafael turned his back on High Wolf as if he were not even there. His blazing eyes found Sky's.

Her feet clutched the long grass, her toes curled through it, seeking the solidness of Earth Mother underneath.

"Is this man telling the truth?"

His rich voice rasped harsh in his throat. His eyes burned like torches, searching her face.

He looked like he hated, not loved, her.

"Y-Y-Yes," she stammered. "B-but I have changed my mind. I decided not to marry . . ."

High Wolf's belligerent tones overrode her words.

"How can that be when I, the husband, know nothing about this changing of mind?"

Rafael's face suddenly went pale as the ashes of their fire. She couldn't tear her eyes from it.

"In Council," she said, her tone asserting itself with High Wolf while her eyes pleaded with Rafael, "when you ordered me to be silent and then to leave. I . . . I decided never to marry you."

He gave a rough bark of a laugh. "You might have told me," he said, every word dripping with sarcasm. "A long time has passed since that Council."

"I had to *leave*, to come look for the treasure! You would have tried to stop me . . ."

He chopped a hand through the air.

"Silence, woman," he roared. "*I* will decide if we marry. I can refuse you because you

have been here all night with this man, but
you cannot refuse me. You gave your word
and Windrider gave his."

"I refuse you now!" she cried, desperate
because the still, dangerous look on Rafael's
face had not changed.

She begged him with her eyes to help her
with this, begged him to understand.

Surely, *surely* he would, after what they had
shared! She was saying now, right out, that she
didn't want High Wolf. And he knew, from
last night, that she wanted *him*!

Rafael shot her a look of cold anger, of
hatred. She felt a shocking, terrible sense
of loss.

Where was the gallantry he had shown that
woman, that Pedro's wife? Where was that
willingness to protect a woman who was
weaker than the man trying to control her?

Where was the miraculous closeness they
had felt in each other's arms? *Talking* to each
other?

He whirled on his heel to speak to High
Wolf.

"I knew of no promises between Sky and
you," he said. "She told me nothing of a
promised marriage."

His tone said her behavior had been des-
picable.

A hot fury flared in Sky. Blame it all on
her!

She had betrayed no one. When she had
lain with Rafael she had already broken her
promise to High Wolf; she simply had not

told him yet. Her heart had been free. *She* had known that.

Rafael took a step toward his adversary. "I offer you whatever satisfaction you choose."

Her fury grew.

What a noble hidalgo! He would pay the price, although the guilt all belonged to her!

Then she realized the import of what he had said and a terrible, sudden fear flowed through her.

But, to her shock, High Wolf did not raise a hand to Rafael.

Nor did he demand hundreds of horses and blankets and much tobacco in restitution. Of course not. High Wolf always respected people who played by the rules.

"For someone who is not of the *Nermernuh*, you are a man of much honor," he said. "You believe in a person keeping his word, given in faith to another."

"*Sí*," Rafael agreed. "Otherwise, there is no one to trust."

The cold words stabbed deep into Sky's heart as she recognized Rafael's reference to her betrayal of him.

High Wolf grunted approval of that bit of wisdom.

"I could not have said it better in my own tongue," he replied, with a formal gesture toward Rafael that reminded her of handing over the pipe.

Sky stared at the two men, disbelieving her eyes.

Next they *would* be smoking the sacred pipe and making blood oaths with each other! Or hugging each other's necks!

High Wolf said, "I ask no satisfaction from you. By offering it, you have proven your bravery."

Rafael inclined his head in acknowledgement. His hair, shining like a raven's wing, brushed the side of his strong neck, the top of his shoulders. The enormous breadth of them seemed doubled now that she could actually see the muscles flexing across them, rising and falling under his smooth, coppery skin.

She could remember exactly how it felt. A thin layer of sweat broke out on her palms.

She wiped them on the sides of her skirt.

High Wolf walked on into the camp and slid his bow off his shoulder, his quiver off his back. He laid them down carefully at the foot of a tree and put his flute on top.

"Windrider asked me to follow and find Pretty Sky," he said, speaking to Rafael once more, as if he should explain to him why he was moving into Sky's camp.

She walked over to the firepit, filled with ashes, glowing now with a few embers only.

"Oh?" she said. "My father sent you to help me find the treasure and stop the war?" she asked, determined to make him acknowledge her. To make *them* acknowledge her.

Neither of them paid her any more attention than they would give to a buzzing fly.

"Windrider insists that even a foolish girl should learn for herself that the treasure is only a legend," High Wolf said to Rafael. "I wanted to bring her directly back to camp."

"Talk to *me*!" Sky cried. "I am taking care of myself; I don't need to be watched over!"

But her heart sank through her body and into the ground like a stone dropping to the bottom of a lake.

Her father had sent him! She would never get rid of High Wolf now.

Even High Wolf, confident, powerful medicine man, headstrong as he was, would do exactly as Windrider said. Any young man, any member of the band, male or female, no matter how young or how old, would follow the slightest suggestion of their War Chief.

Except for her. And sometimes her mama. And old Uncle Ten Bears when he was in one of his grouchy moods.

But she had to at least *try* to send him away.

Then another thought hit her and her heart died.

If Windrider and the Fire Flower had sent High Wolf to her, alone in the hills, they would consider them married when they returned to camp.

Oh, yes! She *had* to send him away.

She tried to think. A direct confrontation would only make him stubborn. She must be clever.

"My father believes in the tradition of the *Nermernuh* that people should learn by doing," she said, kneeling down by the fire and picking up kindling to start it burning again.

She cleared her throat so her words could come out clear and steady.

"I am sure that he means for me to hunt for the treasure myself. Please return to camp and tell him and my mother that I am well. I need no one following me."

"This *Spaniard* is following you!" High Wolf said, with a trace of bitter rivalry coming into his voice.

He turned to Rafael.

"Aren't you?"

"No, I am riding with her," Rafael said, in his low, rich voice.

A trembling shock went through Sky.

At last. Finally he would tell High Wolf that he had come after her because he cared for her, that he wanted to help stop the coming war that scared her so. He would tell him that the All-Father had given them two parts of the same vision and that they were meant to do this great thing together.

He would send High Wolf on his way.

She looked at Rafael, then down at the kindling, shaking in her hands. The tip of her tongue slipped out to touch her lips, still swollen and bruised from his kisses. Her skin still openly yearned to rub against his, her body still smelled of him and the love they had made.

She would never forget one instant of that if she lived to have one hundred summers.

Her eyes lifted, went straight to Rafael again. She watched him while she waited for him to speak.

His torso gleamed in the growing dawn light, bare and beautiful. Its coppery color burned against the pale gray of the blanket, made him look very much alive and on fire.

He stood on his long, powerful legs, standing easily now, hipshot and loose, as perfectly calm and in control as he had been dressed in fine fabrics and silver atop El Lobo the first time she'd seen him.

He had much *puha*. Much more than High Wolf, even, who was a medicine man.

Rafael would send High Wolf away.

He would say, *Ysidora Pretty Sky belongs with me, now. I love her.*

But Rafael's next words were not at all what she expected. They were an arrow to her heart.

"I'm here to help Sky find the treasure," he said, in a voice cold as the blood barely moving in her veins. "Because I have need of cash money. When we find it, I will take half."

Chapter 8

Fay Nickerson was trying his lonesome best to keep a dozen cows and their great big, bawling calves bunched and pushing along when he spotted the coyote running down the low ridge of hills that ran between Waters's new ranch and the Mesa Rica.

"Dammit to hell!"

His contrary horse, Red, who was the only help he had or was likely to have in this cheapskate outfit, swiveled his ears back to ask for more information.

"Sneakin' damn coyote," Fay told him. "Soon's it's dark he's liable to scatter this gather plumb to kingdom come."

Red nodded and they both looked over the situation. Right here they were in a shallow valley, a natural little bowl and, late as it was in the season, it still had plenty of grass. That was why it was so doggone hard to keep these buttheads moving—they kept dropping off and trying to graze.

"Stands to reason they'll wait for us here, don't it?" Fay muttered, and pulled the rifle from his saddle scabbard at the same time he touched the spurs to Red's flanks.

138

One little pop of the rifle wouldn't scare them mamas into running, not if he was all the way yonder and them down here with their noses in their supper. He and Red hit it for the hills at a long lope, at an angle behind the thievin' critter, so as not to spook him out of range.

But Fay never even got off a shot.

He topped the ridge, slipped along the way the coyote had gone for a minute or two and then he saw them.

Not too far off—down on the opposite side of the hill from the cows—scooting right along at a long, all-day trot, coming right at him, were six horses and three people. Indians.

Fay's blood turned to ice water in his veins.

Maybe Comanches!

He headed for cover like a rabbit heading for a hole, shifting the rifle back and forth between the mouth of the scabbard and the ready position across his pommel. As he rode into the little thicket of aspen trees, he made up his mind and put it away.

He couldn't hit more than one man with one shot. No sense bringing the other two down on him to take his scalp and cut his heart out with him still alive.

His breath was hard to get all the time he waited with his hand over Red's nose, but when they got close enough that he could see the whites of their eyes and see the trim on their tack, he couldn't drag a drop of air into his lungs in spite of *how* hard he tried.

That was because then he was as surprised as he was scared.

Two of them was Indians, yes. Well, one of them, at least. A woman, a woman so beautiful she'd knock a man's hat in the creek was in the middle of the single file.

His eyes glued themselves to her and wouldn't let go. Now that *there* was a creature that was truly wild and free, if he ever saw one.

He guessed she was Comanche, but then he thought she wasn't. She wore beaded elkskin and rode a high-horned fringed Indian saddle on a painted horse, but her skin wasn't very dark and her long, flowing hair was dark red, downright auburn, when it was hit by the light of the sun.

Somehow, though, he didn't think she was a white captive. She sure as hell sat that paint like a Comanche.

Her big brown eyes flashed as she watched both sides of the trail, her face told the world that she was mad as a hornet about something and that she didn't give a damn who knowed it. He'd be willin' to bet she'd fight a rattlesnake with a willow stick.

She carried her head like she owned all of New Mexico Territory and the State of Texas. And, by God, her people once did. Maybe she'd be the one to take it all back for them.

The Indian man was Comanche, without a doubt. He was a half-naked, muscled-up son of a gun, bringing up the rear, watching ahead and then their backtrail with eyes so black and sharp they could cut a man to ribbons.

But it was the leader of the three that made the hackles on the back of Fay's neck stand up. He knew him!

What in the name of all that was holy was the powerful young hidalgo Don Rafael Montoya doing riding with these Comanche?

He already acted like he was the King of Spain—with the Comanche at his back he'd think he was God.

They were riding straight toward the ranch!

Sweat broke out all over him. Dammit! His old buddy, Luther, had tried to warn him not to throw in with Waters and come across the river. *Comanches done laid down the law,* Luther kept saying. *No Anglo ranches east of the Gallinas.*

But Fay hadn't had nowhere else to winter— since his drinkin' got so bad, nobody wanted to hire him. He felt his mouth twist in a grim smile while the trio came on, almost silently, toward his high hiding place. He'd get cured of that drinkin' now, if he wanted to or not. Damn boss, Waters, was too tightfisted to keep any firewater around. Didn't know what he'd do when the little stash he had hidden was gone.

But what was this unlikely combination of characters *doing* on Waters's land? Had that rich old bastard, Don Diego, thrown in with the Comanches to raid this ranch and burn it like the Injuns had done the one last year? Surely not! He couldn't be *that* afraid of a little competition in the cattle business.

And he surely would send more than two men and a girl to do the job. Maybe this was the advance scouting party.

But a *girl?* That made no sense at all.

A blur of gray, caught from the corner of his eye, turned his head around. And stopped the trio trotting toward him in their tracks. The coyote!

Why in the name of perdition it had doubled back, he didn't know, but it had. Or that was its brother.

It crossed the trail between him and the oncoming riders and streaked off to the north, vanishing as quickly as it had appeared. Quicker than that, though, faster than the crack of a whip, Montoya's rifle was in his hands and he had a bead on the critter. But for some reason, he didn't fire.

The Comanche man shouted something and all three of them stayed where they were, Don Rafael circling back to talk to the other two.

The male Comanche glanced up, toward Fay, black eyes raking the low hillside like the talons of a hawk.

That made him fade farther away from the edge of the ridge, and, after one last look at the girl, he pushed Red, backing, downhill until they were out of the trees and halfway down the slope. Then he stepped up into the saddle and set out for headquarters.

He went at a long lope, trying to stay on soft ground that was quieter and trying to make sure he kept below the line of the hill.

He pulled his flask from his saddlebag and took a healthy nip.

The rest of the boys had to know about this, and *now*. To hell with the cattle. Somebody might be trying to burn them out of their bunks before morning.

Then he grinned.

If they did, he hoped the girl was the one that got ahold of that whining coward, Jed Beeler.

When High Wolf went on ahead to scout, Sky turned and rode back into the trees on the north side of the trail, leading her own packhorse, leaving Rafael to take care of High Wolf's. He grabbed the leadrope as the medicine man passed him and nodded that he understood the silent signal. High Wolf wanted him to watch over Sky.

Well, he would, he thought, turning El Lobo to go after her. And if she gave him any trouble, he'd . . . He would . . .

That horrible hole opened up in him again, as if the ground threatened to swallow him. The first person, the *first* that he'd ever really opened up to—his deepest heart—and she couldn't be trusted.

She had brought back the memories that had destroyed his old world, only she had been real in his new one. And she had been promised to another man all the time.

He tried to close it out of his mind. The whole, horrible betrayal had cut him too deep. He couldn't think about it.

Wise woman, indeed! *Lying* woman was more like it.

He set his jaw and rode straight into the shimmering curtain of silver-yellow aspen leaves, all trembling like teardrops in the crisp breeze. Sky's horses' legs showed through the trunks of the trees directly in front of him.

Her low voice floated to him through the trees, carrying a hard undertone of anger and hurt.

That made him furious. Why should *she* be hurt? Or angry?

"We'll soon know what trouble Brother Coyote foretold," she said, sarcastically. "It can find us here with no trouble at all since you're crashing through the trees like a fort full of soldiers."

"And since you're talking loud enough to wake the dead," he retorted.

"I am *not!*"

He broke through the leaves to where he could see her.

Her huge, dark eyes blazed, her cheeks flushed rosy with passion.

Like when he had held her in his arms.

His heart constricted, in spite of the fact that, early this morning, it had turned to stone.

"I don't need you here," she said. "You should have gone with High Wolf, since he's so close to your heart and your blood brother and all."

"And you are betrothed to him," he snapped. "Of course, I realize you tend to forget that at times."

Her eyes set off sparks that threatened to set the aspen leaves on fire.

"Like *you* tended to forget to tell me why you came following me up the trail!"

She leaned toward him, her body trembling. She was ferocious, wild with the anger she'd been holding in all day as they rode.

"*Half* the treasure!" she cried. "You'll get half the treasure when you have killed me and taken the other half, too."

"Don't be ridiculous."

"It wouldn't surprise me," she insisted. "You must be crazy. Crazy with greed. You are already very rich!"

Fiery anger burned him inside and out. The back of his head felt as if it would burst.

He clenched his fists, crushed his hands that still wanted to reach for her. Wanted to drag her off that horse, pull her across his saddle, shake some sense into her beautiful head . . .

But he would never let her see anything from him but coldness. Never again.

"I may be rich in land and cattle and horses," he said, calmly, "but those are also my father's. I need cash money."

"Well, you will not get it on the Mesa Rica. I will never give up one coin to you!"

His cold control snapped.

"Who is the one who has been shouting that we are meant to find the treasure, the two of us, together, recipients of songs and visions

from the All-Father?" he roared. "Am I to help
and have no reward?"

"Your reward will be peace and the saving
of The People—*your* people! I will need all of
the treasure for that. Have you no heart?"

That cut him so that he turned away, swung
El Lobo's head around.

"You have no treasure," he barked, cruelly,
wanting only to hurt her as she had hurt him.
"And you probably never will have. It'd be a
miracle if we ever found it."

She came lunging after him like an aveng-
ing fury.

"There is no *we* to find it! I am going on from
here without you. Get away from me, get away
from the Mesa Rica. Go home! *I never want to
see your face again.*"

By the time Fay rode into the scattering
of rough-barked new buildings—bunkhouse,
two-room cabin main house, and lean-to
barn—that Old Man Waters so grandly
called headquarters, he was wishing he
hadn't spooked and left the cattle. The
boys would hooraw him pretty good about
that.

And they did, at first. But when he was
squatting around the cookfire eating with
them, telling what he'd seen on the trail, all
their attention went to their scalps. Everyone
of 'em had seen the charred remains of last
year's ranch buildings, just down the river
a piece. None of those ranch hands had
survived.

"There'd be a bigger bunch of Injuns if it was a raid on this ranch and they wouldn't be leading no packhorses," Taffy said. "They're headed someplace else."

"Ain't no place else up here," somebody said.

"No, they'll attack us for sure," Jed Beeler whined, "but why'd they send a girl along?"

"That ain't *even* the best question," Lowell said. "Why's the young hidalgo riding with them? Them Comanch' could be hunting a good place for winter camp or a buffalo herd, but he's got no use for either of them things."

"He's got no more use for Anglo ranchers than the Injuns do."

They all drew closer to the fire, tin supper plates balanced on their knees, and looked around their little circle.

"It's dark as the inside of a cow's belly around here," Jed said. "Do you reckon . . ."

The drumming of hoofbeats stopped the rest of his words in his throat. Everybody put down their plates and got away from the fire, hands on the butts of their guns.

"Hello, *el rancho*!" a voice shouted. "*Me llamo Jaime, El Comanchero!*"

"Come on in!" Taffy called.

Jaime rode in and got down, Cookie got him a plate, and everybody went back to their suppers, glad for the distraction and for some news.

"I have some information for *Señor* Waters," Jaime said, after bolting half of what was on his plate. "Is he around?"

"Nope," Taffy said. "He's gone with a couple of diggers he's hired to look for the Mesa Rica treasure again."

"Perdition!" Jaime said. "I'll have to ride after him. *Mañana*, at daylight, I'll go."

"Must be important," Taffy probed, gently.

"*Sí*."

And that was all they could get out of the Comanchero, although several of them tried. So they fell back into speculation about the trio Fay had seen.

"Montoya?" Jaime said. "Don Rafael? You are sure?"

"I know 'im when I see 'im," Fay said.

Jaime threw back his head and laughed.

"My friend Pedro, he is wanting to kill him for interfering between him and his woman," he said. "He swears he will catch the young don out without no vaqueros to back him and put a knife in his heart!"

He paused to pick up his tin cup of coffee and take in some of it.

"And now," he went on, still laughing, "instead of vaqueros, Montoya has Comanches riding with him! I wonder what Pedro would think of that? Would he risk losing his scalp to get his revenge?"

Everybody laughed and made jokes about Pedro and his courage. Everybody except Fay.

When the noise had died down, he said, "What all has Pedro got to sell right now? Got any whiskey?"

"Two wagonloads," Jaime said, nodding and then scooping up a big spoonful of beans. "Just rolled in on the Santa Fe Trail."

"It's sad, ain't it, that them wagons is so far from here?" Taffy said. "We ain't got a drop on this place for a drink."

That was not far from the truth, Fay thought. His stash was nearly gone.

"No, and that tightfisted Old Man Waters won't even buy us none for Christmas," Joey said. "You boys just wait and see."

Fay's hands shook at the thought of the whole, long winter with no whiskey.

Then, suddenly, he knew what to do. He would bribe the cook's helper to ride like hell to Chaparito, this very night, find Pedro, and tell him that Montoya was in the hills. In exchange for two barrels of that whiskey. The boy could be back by sundown tomorrow and Cookie wouldn't care. Not if he got his share of the red-eye.

It wouldn't be necessary for the boy to mention to Pedro that Rafael Montoya wasn't riding alone.

Fay breathed out a great whoosh of air and started listening again to the talk.

"What we *oughtta* do is ambush them three out there on the trail this very night in case they are lookin' over this new ranch with an eye to a raid," Tony said. "Put a stop to it before it starts."

Fay's breath tied his lungs in a knot again.

"You never seen 'em, Tony," he said. "You never seen that Comanche warrior's eyes. Nor the way Don Rafael Montoya had a rifle in his hand, its muzzle tracking steady ahead of a coyote running hell-bent for leather, before another man could turn loose of his reins."

"Yeah," Lowell taunted Tony, as if he had seen all that for himself. "You and what army gonna ambush 'em, Tone?"

Jaime nodded and said, "Two of the riders is Comanche, and, from what Fay has said about the girl and her horse, she is Pretty Sky, Windrider's daughter. I saw her on that mare at the rendezvous."

Fay muttered, "Don't wanta mess with the War Chief's daughter. That's right."

Pretty Sky. Her name was Pretty Sky.

He smiled. It sounded too peaceful for that stormy look on her face.

Then Taffy took over and laid down the law.

"Them Comanche'll lift yore hair in a heartbeat if you try sneakin' up on them. And Montoya's the prime rifle shot east of the Rockies. You all know that."

He stopped and looked around at all of them the way he always did when he wanted to make sure they knew who the foreman was. Then he went on.

"I'm the foreman here and I say we send Fay with Jaime to find Mr. Waters and tell him all what's going on."

He paused, to let Jaime have one more chance to tell them why he had ridden up here

looking for their boss, but the Comanchero
didn't say a word.

Taffy sighed.

"Dead cowhands don't turn out much
work," he continued. "You boys best crawl
into yore soogans and sleep in yore beds,
'stead of snoozin' it up six feet under."

Sky knelt in the middle of the parfleches
she'd taken from her pack and hastily threw
several strips of jerky, a scant handful of hackberry balls, and two pieces of pemmican onto
each of three sycamore leaves that had not yet
turned entirely brown and brittle.

"The food is ready," she called, mindful to
keep her voice soft so it wouldn't carry out of
camp in spite of the fact that she wanted to
scream at them both.

Of course, Rafael was still there, now that
she'd told him to go.

Just as he had refused to come when she'd
begged him at the rendezvous.

Bossy, treacherous, controlling, *men*!

From the moment they'd decided not to
risk going on against the coyote's warning—
in spite of the fact that High Wolf's scouting
foray turned up no danger and the fact that
they had not a moment to lose in searching for
the treasure—they had taken over her expedi-
tion, *her quest*, and made every decision as if
she were not even there. They never asked her
opinion, they never heard it when she volun-
teered it, and they never argued one time.

Oh, no. Not the blood brothers.

Instead, they agreed on everything, hardly even needing to use any words.

No fire, in case whatever danger the coyote had predicted by running across their trail would see it and find them.

No hobbles and no loose horses grazing, in case they had to ride out in a hurry.

No unpacking and no undressing and no bedrobes, for the same reason. They couldn't afford to lose any of their coverings if snow should come early. Tonight, each would wrap up in one blanket and sleep on a bed of dry leaves.

She slapped the fold-over flaps of the parfleches closed and threw all of them into their places in her pack. Packs must be ready to load all night long.

Well, then, they could just do without breakfast, begorrah! That's what her mother would say.

She threw a fierce glare at High Wolf and then one at Rafael. Neither looked up, neither moved. Fine. They would learn, soon, that they would starve before she would carry their suppers to them.

If they were still with her when she found the treasure, they probably would try to divide it all up between them and not give her a coin. Well, *that* was where she would make herself into a force to be reckoned with!

She fought to keep her fury up, her anger hot. If she ever let it die down, *she* would die.

She would fall to pieces, shattered by the awful hurt that stabbed through her every time she thought of Rafael's cold announcement, *"I have need of cash money. I will take half."*

Without her frenzy, she would remember last night in his arms.

High Wolf put down the tack he'd been mending in the last of the light and came to get his food. Soon Rafael laid aside his rifle and followed him.

Sky got up and walked away into the lonesome time of day without tasting a bite of food. She couldn't eat. She would never eat again.

Because she had given her heart to a man who would take another man's word against hers.

This time yesterday she had been a foolish girl. Today she was a woman. A wise woman.

Who would not make the same mistake again.

Behind her, Rafael asked, "We can continue in the same direction tomorrow?"

"Yes," High Wolf said, talking around a bite of jerky. "If we heed Coyote's warning until Father Sun comes up in a new day, the danger is gone."

"Coyote is a Trickster," Sky snapped, rebelliously. She whirled on her heel to glare at them.

"We should have gone on as far as we could this sun."

She felt, rather than saw, the disgusted look that High Wolf shot at her.

"Coyote is known as a Trickster," he said, talking to Rafael. "And he has much medicine.

For knowing what's ahead and for changing shapes."

His tone proclaimed clearly that this was the beginning of a story. Why, Sky wondered, why had she never noticed before how much High Wolf loved the sound of his own voice?

"One time, long ago," he went on, "a man in our band called Red Jacket killed a coyote for no reason when he was out raiding for horses. A great twisting storm came down and picked up him and his horse, stood them on their heads, and finally set them down on top of a cliff far, far away. A cliff that had four steep sides, no grass and no water."

"What did he do?" asked Rafael.

"It took him three whole suns to get down."

The old story, and the way High Wolf told it, made bumps come up on Sky's arms. But she would never let him know that.

Sarcastically, she said, "And that very same thing surely would have happened to all three of us if we had gone on in the same direction after we saw Brother Coyote."

To her total surprise, Rafael answered as if there could be no doubt of that.

"Three whole suns would have been a much longer delay than an hour or two," he said.

"That is so," High Wolf said, solemnly.

Her fury burst into a great storm inside her.

"You sound like two silly boys! You are grown men, yet you sit around and believe old legends and tales instead of riding on and using the daylight to stop the Anglos' guns from firing at our warriors!"

"We are all here because *you* believe old legends and tales," Rafael said.

He was so calm, so cold, so utterly unfeeling that her heart split right in two.

She ran from them, crashed across the campsite and through the trees toward her horses, completely careless of the noise, wanting only to find Pabo and Far Girl and throw her arms around their necks.

She had to have warm, live flesh against hers, had to hold a friend near her heart. Never, ever, had she felt so alone.

Until, as the night fell fast and hard over the hills and the plains, as darkness devoured the earth and the sky, beneath the small, snuffling night sounds of the horses, she heard the hoofbeats.

Far away, but from the east, the direction they were traveling, and iron-shod.

Coyote and High Wolf and Rafael had been right.

Chapter 9

They were ready to ride east again by the time there was light enough to see.

Rafael stood beside El Lobo, tucking in the end of the latigo strap he had just jerked tight.

"Why don't you continue to lead the way?"

He heard High Wolf's voice, but the words didn't sink in.

"Montoya? Will you ride in the lead again?"

This time, he forced his ears to listen, his mind to work.

Yes. He would do anything not to ride behind Sky and let the sight of her torture him all day.

Even as he had the thought, he glanced at her, as he had surreptitiously done a dozen times since they all awoke. She was sitting still and beautiful atop Far Girl, her solemn face set straight ahead, the fringes on her saddle and her clothes swinging with every restless step of the mare, who was inspired by the cool morning and itching to go.

But his treacherous eyes saw her in the blue silk dress with the low, ruffled neckline, smiling up into his eyes.

While she listened to him pour out the feelings of his heart.

Fool that he was.

"I would like to lead," he said, and stuck a foot into his stirrup, stepped up onto the stallion. "But my father and I traveled on the south side of these hills from El Rancho del Cielo to La Mesa Rica. You might know this north way better than I."

"Go ahead," High Wolf said, making a sweeping gesture of one bare arm toward Rafael. "I will say so if you veer in the wrong direction."

Sky sent the eager mare pushing rudely in between them, lifted her into a trot, with the packhorse at her heels.

"Please feel free to follow *me!*" she called angrily back over her shoulder. "Or stay here and practice your good manners all day."

She turned her head and rode hard toward the sun.

Rafael yelled to El Lobo and went after her.

She urged the mare faster, but the deer path they were following was rough and overgrown.

He caught up and went crashing around her.

"I'm leading," he shouted, angrily, "and don't try to start another race."

"Why not?" she called back, flashing him a furious glance. "Afraid you'll lose again?"

Then their eyes met.

Just for an instant, his soul mate of the day before showed in her eyes.

His falsehearted soul mate.

"Get back," he said. "Ride in the middle."

And he charged ahead, into a position where he could not see her.

If he had one sliver of good sense in his body, he'd turn around and ride for the *rancho*. He should never have come.

But now she had made it a challenge, had told him to go home, so he was honor bound to stay.

The hooves of the horses coming along behind him beat a swift rhythm that echoed from the low, rocky hills. Good. They were right to hurry. For all three of their sakes, as well as for The People's, they must get this thing over with as quickly as possible.

If it even *was* possible. Windrider might be right, the treasure might not exist.

If he, Rafael, could have such bad judgment as to open his heart and speak his deepest feelings, for the first time in his life, to someone with no honor, he thought, bitterly, then he wasn't the one to decide the significance of his hallucinations in the fire.

The deer trail curved around the edge of a grove of evergreen trees, then took them straight into it. El Lobo long-trotted into the dark, night shadows that still lay between two tall, fat juniper trees, hanging with blue berries, crowding in on the trail from each side.

The horse made no hesitation, gave no sign of sensing danger, but the hairs on the back of Rafael's neck began to prickle.

A shivering crawled along the skin of his arms.

The weak, early sunlight cut through the tops of the trees and lay across the land ahead in a pale pink shape. Before he even cleared the trees, Rafael knew what it would look like, glimmering on the thin frost that clung to the blades of the blue grama grass. It would look exactly like the tip of a lance.

And it did.

He rode toward it, then into its weak warmth, and shifted in his saddle for a steep downhill slide before he saw it was there.

It was a sign. He *did* have a medicine spirit.

The feeling filled him, sure as any knowledge he had ever possessed.

Sure as he now knew that those really were visions that he had had seen in the fire.

The rough earth beneath his horse carried him down and down, gravel spewing from beneath El Lobo's stiffened legs, more rolling past from the other horses' descent behind him. But his thoughts lifted.

Now he knew. They would find the treasure.

His heart twisted like a trapped thing inside him. They would find it, but there would be no pleasure in it, now.

He set his jaw. Ysidora Pretty Sky could just stand aside while he took his half. He would get the upper hand on this whole arrangement with Marquez yet.

But he couldn't concentrate on thoughts of buying Beck's ranch and the power it would give him because a strong scattering of embers danced in his veins just from thinking her name. Well, that fiery, carnal desire was something that a man with his iron control could certainly tame. And he might as well start now.

He didn't even look at her when he twisted in his saddle and signed that they should angle north after they'd crossed the nearly dry creek.

Fay thought he'd missed the little pine grove that Boss Waters always used as a marker, but he spotted it just before he and Jaime rode over the ridge the wrong way. The sunlight filled that valley and, while he ran his eyes along its length, it picked up the gleam of a running stream and then the low glow of a cookfire.

"The boss has to have his coffee hot, no matter what time of day he rides in," Fay told Jaime. "One thing you can count on— hot coffee and plenty of it in a Charlie Waters camp. Just don't expect no whiskey."

"All my belly expects at this minute is *food*," Jaime said. "To give me strength to bargain with *Señor* Waters."

"Good luck," Fay said. "Sometimes he don't furnish but two meals a day."

They rode down toward the camp, with Fay whistling a scrap of a tune and calling from a little way out to say who they were.

"What's wrong?" demanded Water's irritable, hoarse voice. "What're *you* doin' here, Nickerson, instead of gathering cows?"

He couldn't wait for them to ride on in and tell him—fretful critter that he was, he walked on out to meet them, tin cup of coffee in his hand.

"Seen some riders," Fay drawled, as he swung down and led his horse toward the fire. "Thought you oughtta know."

"What riders?"

The boss signaled to one of his treasure hunters, Sullivan, to bring coffee for him and Jaime.

"*What* riders, Fay?"

It was all Fay could do to keep from grinning as Waters bustled back to squat beside him by the fire, practically leading Jaime by the hand in his hurry to get the story out of both of them.

"*What* riders, dammit?" he rasped.

Both the treasure hunting hands sat at the fire, too, their eyes and ears wide open.

Fay took a leisurely sip of coffee.

Then he said, "Don Rafael Montoya and a couple Comanches."

Stunned silence fell.

"Scouting for a raid on my ranch?" Waters asked, and glanced over his shoulder as if the three were right behind him. "Burn out the competition, huh?"

Fay shrugged. "Who knows?"

"I know something might shed some light," Jaime said. "Something real important to you, *Señor* Waters."

"All right, man, spit it out!"

Fay bit back his grin again as Jaime hemmed and hawed about the debt he owed *Señor* Waters and the poor trading season he had had this summer, his hope that this information might take the place of at least most of the money he owed.

Finally Waters snapped that he'd consider the deal.

And then Jaime took their breaths away, including Fay's, with his story. He dragged it out and blew it up big—how his partner, Pedro, was following Montoya looking to cut him since the ranchero had interfered in some trouble between him and his wife, how the auburn-haired girl that Fay had seen, who was Windrider's daughter, was talking about hunting the treasure of Mesa Rica and begging Don Rafael to help since he had had a vision about it.

Then Jaime paused, spit into the fire, and added that Windrider was planning to lead all the Plains Tribes on the warpath.

Nobody breathed and nobody moved.

Except Mr. Waters. He was scared, Fay could tell, but he was a tough, cool old coot.

"I been burnt out by the Injuns last year," he said, "and I don't aim to let it happen again. You, Raymond Dale, ride straight for Hatch's Ranch and don't stop 'til you get there."

He paused, frowning, and took a gulp of his coffee.

"Tell General Sykes he can stop this whole war before it starts by laying an ambush of soldiers at my new ranch. That's what's got Windrider riled and that's where he'll hit first."

Raymond Dale got up and left them.

Waters stared at Jaime for a good, long time.

"A vision," he mused. "Them Spaniards and you Mexicans and them Injuns got the second sight."

He stared at Jaime some more.

"Your debt to me is repaid, Jaime," he said, at last. "If you will do one more thing. Ride with Raymond Dale and tell Sykes from the horse's mouth about hearing them war plans. Don't mention the treasure or the vision, though."

"If you could supply me with some food for the ride, *Señor*," Jaime said, and stood up. "I would be happy to speak to the *general*."

Waters told Sullivan to pack food for two and then hollered for Raymond Dale to come back.

When he came into sight, leading his horse, Waters said, "After you and Jaime have talked to Sykes, you hightail it back up here and tell me what his answer is. Hunt us down—we could be anywhere on the side of the mesa by then."

"Yessir, Boss."

Then Waters turned to Fay.

"You stay here and help me and Sullivan trail them three treasure hunters," he said. "We'll let 'em find it—then we'll take it away from 'em!"

He smiled his rare smile and slapped his hands on his knees as he looked from Fay to Sullivan and back again.

"That'll be a hell of a lot better'n' diggin' and rollin' rocks and goin' into them snaky caves for ourselves, won't it, now, boys?"

Sky kept trying to drop back and put High Wolf in front of her, but he insisted that she take the protected position in the middle. So she had to ride right behind Rafael's packhorse all morning, had to watch his broad shoulders, his narrow waist and the solid, unmoving seat of his small buttocks in the saddle, had to see the sunlight shine in the club of his hair that showed beneath the brim of his hat. Just as she had done on the day he had caught her on the trail.

A lifetime ago. When she had been only a stupid girl.

The urge thrummed in her veins, clawed at her heart, surged in and out of her brain—the desire to dig in her heels and yell to the mare to run. She would run ahead into the hills and lose Rafael and High Wolf, she would run back to the camp of her people and stay with her parents and friends, she would run away and never see any of them again. Anything to be out of this trap, this prison between these two men.

"There it is!"

Rafael called out, then rode to a stop at the top of the hill.

Sky came out of the straggling trees and sent Far Girl off to one side, away from him. She lifted her eyes and looked off to where the morning light hit the high, broken side of the Mesa Rica. It shone there, turning the earth a shimmering red and gold.

From here, a person barely could tell that the top of the mountain was flat. This end of it, shaped like the crescent moon, was one huge, stony crag after another, interspersed with brushy, narrow valleys that jutted in between the cliffs like pointing fingers. In the center of the mesa, the half circle swept deep into its side with smaller rock crags sitting on the valley floor and trees scattered in layers all up and down it.

There were caves, she knew, and somewhere, the hot, healing springs. There were canyons and cracks in the walls.

How, *how* would she ever find the right place, the one that fitted the song and held the treasure? Such a search could take the rest of her life.

Rafael lifted his arm and pointed forward. They started down the side of the hill they were on.

But before they had reached the bottom, a strange, scary feeling crept over Sky.

Something, no, someone, was behind them.

The knowledge hit her like the diving eagle in Hukiyani's song.

Somebody human was watching them.

"We have a visitor," she said, calling softly to the men without turning her head or changing her position. "He is watching us now."

Rafael looked to both sides and slowly scanned everything in front of him as he rode. She knew that High Wolf was doing the same behind her.

"I see and hear nothing," High Wolf called, in that infuriating tone that meant nothing could be there if he didn't hear or see it. "But I will go back to look. Ride on."

Rafael did so, and Sky followed him, although every nerve in her body was screaming for her to go with High Wolf and look for herself. She took his packhorse from him and prayed that he would find whoever it was that was making her skin tingle.

The mesa was crawling with Anglos looking for the treasure, Don Diego and Rafael had said. Some of them were so greedy for gold they would kill without even thinking, most of them would shoot any Indian, especially a Comanche, on sight.

Just ahead the way turned treeless and completely exposed.

She shivered.

What would happen to her people if she died?

A terrible bitterness shook her. Rafael wouldn't save them. He only wanted the treasure for himself.

His arrogant seat as he rode ahead of her was an irritation to her eyes, his silence grated on her skin like an unpleasant sound. He seemed to feel that only High Wolf was worthy to converse with him, since she was such a liar.

At last, High Wolf came back, appearing suddenly like a deer or an elk at the edge of the last grove of trees.

"Nothing," he said, and rode along between them as they trotted out onto the plain that stretched toward the mesa. "I searched both sides of our trail for a long way back. No one has been there."

"She's overwrought," Rafael said, in a condescending tone. "She'll feel better when she has rested."

"You can talk directly to me!" Sky cried. "And we are *not* stopping to rest early today, no matter what coyote or ghost you two may see on the trail!"

Rafael and High Wolf exchanged a glance and a nod.

"*We?*" Rafael said, slanting a look at her over his shoulder. "Who just said that someone's lurking on our trail?"

"He may be gone now," she said, stubbornly, "but someone was there, watching us."

"I looked. I listened. I saw and heard nothing," High Wolf said, impatiently, pushing his mount to pick up the pace. "What did you see or hear?"

Sky hesitated, turned around in her saddle and looked, as if to try one more time to find proof.

"Nothing," she admitted glumly. "But I know someone was there."

Rafael and High Wolf exchanged that superior look again.

Sky kicked Far Girl out ahead at a gallop.

The feeling came back again, more insistent than ever, after they had ridden into the side of the mesa. It had faded while they rode across the open plain at its foot.

Probably because their pursuer had to wait, Sky thought, since that place gave him no cover. But here, in the rocky canyons of the mesa's north side, he could hide anywhere.

"He's back again," she said, when they had crossed a shallow stream and were climbing into the arms of the big, flattopped mountain. "Someone's following us, I know it!"

"You're imagining things again," High Wolf said, gruffly, leading his pack horse around a bed of prickly pear that clung bravely to the little bit of soil scattered there between the rocks.

Rafael asked, "Have you seen or heard anything this time?"

"No! I just have a feeling!"

"Try to have a feeling of where the treasure is, instead," he said, and she wanted to strangle him.

"You believed Brother Coyote!" she cried. "But you won't believe me!"

"I have much medicine," High Wolf said. "And so does Brother Coyote. I saw and heard nothing and he is not out here running across our trail."

Sky's palms broke out in sweat.

"I, too, have much medicine," she said, "and I am going to put you both on top of a mountain so high it will take you three *moons* to get down!"

She dropped back, stood in one stirrup and leaned toward Pabo, pretending to adjust the rope on the pack on her back. She motioned for High Wolf to go ahead of her as they rounded a bend and began dropping into a ravine filled with tall, thin aspens, their leaves waving in the breeze like great bunches of yellow feathers.

When the rump of High Wolf's packhorse had disappeared, and the rustling of the leaves drowned out the soft plops of its hooves, Sky leapt down, led her horses deeper into the woods, tethered them to a tree trunk, and began slipping up the mountainside. She darted among the rocks and trees, glad that her elkskin clothing would blend with both the yellow leaves and the tan earth, until she was high enough to see down on their trail. She threw herself flat on her belly and searched the way they had come.

Father Sun took a step or two downward. The aspens' leaves melted from yellow to gold. They whispered secrets to her as fast as they could move.

But they told her nothing of anyone following their trail, and she heard no other noise, except the calls of the birds. She looked at the place where they had crossed the stream and come into the hills, then sent her gaze zigzagging back and forth across the path they had taken after that.

The follower was sneaking along in the thickening tree cover, no doubt, being careful not to get too close to their horses, who might whinny a greeting to his.

She saw no one. No one and no movement that did not belong.

"Sky!"

The sound froze her for one breath, then she turned her head tightly and looked over her shoulder.

High Wolf. She should've known.

"What are you *doing*?" he demanded, making fierce gestures for her to come with him.

"This is strange behavior for someone who refuses to stop and rest early, someone who got into a fit of temper last night because we observed Coyote's warning!" Rafael said, thoughtfully.

She whipped her head around. He was approaching from her other side, giving her that sardonic look of his.

She wanted to fly in his face, push him back down the hill.

"Why did both of you come after me?" she cried. "Just so you could outnumber me? Ever since you two met, you've been doing that very well!"

"We both came in case you had blundered off the side of the hill," Rafael said, with an infuriating tilt of his brow, "and we had to haul you and your horses up out of a canyon."

"Or in case you had gotten lost and turned around and started riding away in the wrong direction," High Wolf said.

Sky leapt to her feet, glaring from one of them to the other.

"Or in case an enemy, *who has been following all morning*, had sneaked up behind us and snatched me away!"

"He'd give you back soon enough if you spoke the same language," Rafael said, bitterly, and took a step closer to her.

His spicy, masculine scent drifted into her nostrils, brought memories flooding back.

She took a step away, only to come up against an aspen trunk at her back.

"What do you mean?" she snapped at him.

"You could tell enough lies in the first five minutes to tie his brain in a knot. He'd be so confused he'd forget why he captured you."

He came one step closer still, the anger in his eyes hot enough to burn her.

But his voice remained cool and deadly calm.

"We're in the Mesa Rica, now, Sky. You could already be searching for the treasure."

She tried, but she couldn't look away from him. All the memories that were tormenting her were there in front of her, reflected in his eyes.

Her heart beat so hard against the cage of her ribs that she thought they would break.

Finally, after what seemed a full moon had passed, High Wolf spoke.

"No woman of mine will be roaming around the Mesa Rica alone," he said, gruffly. "Pretty Sky, do not leave me again."

She made no reply.

Rafael's gaze held her pinned to the tree trunk for a few more heartbeats, then he swept his eyes away from her, turned and started downhill.

"If you're in as much of a hurry as you seem, get down there to your horses and let's get on the trail," he barked. "Get this treasure hunt over with."

High Wolf took Sky by the arm.

"Don't go off by yourself again," he warned.

Sky ignored him as they started after Rafael.

"I'll prove it yet!" she called to his stiff back. "Maybe right now. Whoever is following us has probably stolen all our horses."

But when they reached the bottom of the ravine again, the horses, including hers, stood exactly where they had left them, like a living confirmation that the men were right in insisting that no danger dogged their trail.

Sometime in the middle of that night, Sky came fully awake out of a restless sleep. She opened her eyes to a world washed in moonlight. Sister Moon, yellow and almost full, rode high in the west.

Inside her body, Sky's flesh trembled, waiting. Outside, her skin tightened to hold her muscles still. She lay on her robe, listening.

Because whatever had waked her was like a warning voice calling her name.

A night bird whistled a high-pitched call. The wind picked up from the north and blew a cold breath into the little valley. The smell of faraway pines, and beneath it, the scent of snow, swelled into her nose.

Someone, sleeping across the dying fire from her, sighed and then gave a great snore. She listened for a long time, but no sound came from her other companion.

Finally she raised up onto one elbow and looked.

The sleeper was High Wolf, rolled up in his robes on the east side of the firepit.

The place on the south side of it was empty.

Rafael was gone.

Chapter 10

Sky flung herself out of the bedrobes and flew across the campsite. It was true. Only Rafael's blankets lay there, their folds and wrinkles carelessly catching the moonlight.

She whirled and ran down the slope toward the grassy spot where they'd left the hobbled horses, straining her eyes to adjust to the shapes thrown onto the ground by the shadows of high, rocky cliff at her back, trying to make sense of the chaos churning in her head. The only thought she could get hold of was if his horses were there, he surely hadn't left for good.

Sky stopped at the edge of the shadows. El Lobo and Rafael's packhorse grazed alongside the others.

Shakily, she reached behind her for the trunk of a pine tree and leaned back against it, willing the shaking inside her to stop. Where *was* he?

Why did she care? If he would go home as she had told him to do, there would be no dividing the treasure.

And there would be no more torment of riding with him.

Why was she panicking like this?

She closed her eyes and took a long, trembling breath in through her nose, air heavy with the smell of the pine and the horses. The image of his face, so close to hers this afternoon, appeared on the black of her eyelids. She forced her eyes to open.

El Lobo lifted his head into the beam of moonlight that fell across him and pricked his ears, gazing away from the mesa through the dark. He spoke once, softly, deep in his throat. A greeting.

So. Rafael was out there. The stallion would not stay so relaxed if it were anyone else.

Sky looked in that same direction, away from camp. Toward the open mouth of this little cove tucked into the mesa's rough side. The way thay had come in.

A wild, angry thought took hold of her.

What if he had gone to meet whoever had been following them? What if he had known who it was all along, had planned for a servant or a friend to follow and help him take the whole treasure, once they had found it?

Her heart jumped into her throat. That would explain why he had refused to believe her when she said someone was watching and following them!

She started walking toward the place El Lobo had pointed out, keeping to the shadows, feeling with her bare feet for rocks and gravel and pinecones, trying to stay on grass. If he didn't hear her, she could creep up and catch them talking and plotting!

But in the next instant, she came to herself. Her idea was an insane one, a middle-of-the-night conviction born of her desperation. Rafael was much bigger and stronger than she—he would need no help to take the treasure from her. And he hadn't known, any more than she had, that High Wolf would join them.

But she didn't stop and turn around. She kept working her way toward the spot El Lobo had shown her. She moved along the edge of a narrow band of aspens which the breeze shook and rattled over her head. It picked up even more, blew her hair across her face. A cloud drifted over the moon.

Sky's heart boomed in her chest like thunder. But she didn't slow—her eyes could see in the dark by now and her toes knew how to feel for good footing. She moved faster.

An aspen branch hung down in her way. She reached out to brush it back. And held it.

She saw him.

Rafael was coming toward her up this side of the narrow, grassy finger of a valley, staying, as she was doing, in the shadows of the trees. Once in a while, though, the mellow moonlight caught and reflected off his bare shoulders. He wore no shirt—only the tight, black breeches and his knee-high boots.

Desire broke her open, swelled up through her body like a hot spring gushing in the desert. It made her body weep.

And brought tears of fury stinging to her eyes.

She wanted to *touch* him! By Sister Moon riding above them, she needed to feel his skin, the shape of his bones, his hard muscles, his sweet flesh beneath the tips of her fingers!

She needed to run forward and throw herself into his arms.

Sweat broke out in her palms.

Her hand crushed the leaves on the aspen limb to powder. She *craved* the feel of him.

The thought ran through her veins; she jerked her hand downward, clutching the branch of the tree like a drowning person. Its stripped leaves fell like flakes of rain on her face and her bare feet.

"Who's there?"

The low-voiced demand was so hard with menace that her hands started to tremble.

"Rafael, it's Sky," she called quickly. The words came out soft and strangled.

She turned cold as winter inside. He was armed, without doubt. He could have shot at the noise the minute she made it.

And whoever was following them might be watching, too. She had rushed out into the night without even her knife as a weapon.

The All-Father help her! She'd have to get a grip on herself or she'd never *live* to find the treasure!

"Sky?"

She stepped out where he could see her.

He was carrying the rifle, balanced low and loose in one hand, with an easy authority that made her suddenly weak.

Not only because she'd been dangerously foolish.

Because the way he moved drew her to him like a rope dropped down around her heart. It had been there since the very first moment she'd seen him. A rope woven of wet rawhide, too strong to break.

Her hands clenched into fists.

She *wouldn't* want him. She would not!

Never again. Because she meant nothing to him, not even enough for him to let her explain about her promise to High Wolf.

"What are you doing out here?" She demanded, in a voice she didn't even recognize as hers.

He took another swift stride to meet her, pulled her back into the protective darkness of the trees.

"What are *you* doing? If you know someone is following us, why have you run off by yourself again?"

"I haven't *run off* at all," she said, with as much dignity as she could muster with his hands on her shoulders and his hipbone touching hers. "And I asked you first."

"Looking for whoever is trailing us."

She pushed his hand away.

"Don't make fun of me any *more!*" she cried, struggling to keep from being loud enough for the watcher to hear her. "I am so sick of that!"

She whirled away from him, ran out into the patchy moonlight. It didn't matter if some enemy did see her. Nothing mattered.

He came up behind her, caught her arm in his hot, hard grip and spun her around.

His hand burned her like a brand.

"I'm not making fun of you!" he said. "Listen to me! I began thinking about what you said about sensing someone on our trail and I decided there was truth to it."

"Oh, you *did*?" she cried, pulling with all her strength in a futile attempt to get loose. "Well, thank you so much, *Señor*, for your trust! Have you decided now that I am not a liar?"

He went still. Sky stopped struggling.

Over their heads, the aspen leaves barely whispered. The moonlight drifted down to touch their faces.

"You lied to me, all right," he said, in voice gone heavy and raw with hurt. "You lied to me twice."

"No! Only once! About . . . whether I had ever been with a man."

"*Only that*," he said, sarcastically, "and about whether you were promised to marry. Not very important lies at all."

Frustration overcame her.

"Now you listen to me!" she said. "I've tried to tell you—I was no longer promised to High Wolf in my heart."

"But he did not know that."

"*I* knew it!"

"*I* didn't!"

"What does what High Wolf knows have to do with what happened between you and me?"

"Everything. As long as he and Windrider, who also gave him his word, and your band think you'll marry him, you're not free of the promise."

His fingers closed more firmly on her arm.

"Custom and parents can confuse what's in one's heart," he said, hotly, "they can overcome it—I know that from my own life. You weren't free, Sky."

"I *was*!"

"No. You came into my arms and my bed without telling me that you were promised to another man!"

His grip tightened. He shook her a little.

"Think about it, Sky. Doesn't that seem like lying to you?"

"Turn me loose!"

He dropped his hand to his side.

"I asked you straight out if you were to be married and you said, *No*," he persisted. "You cannot be trusted, Sky."

"I can be trusted to say what is in my heart!"

"In your changeable heart!"

"It is not changeable! I am *nasupetipu*, a faithful person!"

A shaft of moonlight fell across his mouth, turned his sensuous lips from copper to gold.

His eyes burned down at her from the darkness.

"You let me open my heart to you, Sky!"

The pain in his voice went so deep that she felt it to her bones. She closed her heart against it. He had done his share of hurting her, too.

"I talked to you as I never have done to any other person. Because I thought you cared for me."

She took a step toward him.

"I thought *you* cared for *me!*" she cried, her voice cracking. "And for my people. But you care only for more money and land for yourself!"

He made a rough sound of denial.

She hurried on.

"High Wolf came and you didn't even say one word about being with me," she blurted, her voice breaking completely, "after such a night that we became part of each other! I . . ."

He grabbed her by both shoulders and jerked her to him, bent and stopped her words with his mouth. His lips, hard and straight, ground against hers, as if he'd love to destroy her.

Then, with a suddenness that stunned her, they went soft and sweet.

She resisted, kept hers closed tight. But he wouldn't accept that.

The tip of his tongue trailed across the seam of her lips, traced the shape of her mouth, tantalized her by commanding her to open it, transfixed her.

With desire.

An incoherent moan came from someplace deep within him.

She lifted her hands and ran them up the bulging muscles of his arms, from elbow to shoulder.

He dropped his free arm around her, lifted her feet from the ground, pulled her closer. His skin was cool, chilled by the hint of winter in the wandering wind, yet as soon as it touched hers, the flame he had lit became a raging fire inside her.

Her treacherous mouth betrayed her, then, opening to his like a blossom to a honey-bee, her tongue rushing to meet his with no thought and no shame. He tasted of moonlight and wind, of cedar and aspen leaves.

He tasted as he had before; he tasted like Rafael.

Without him, she would starve.

With him, she would never get enough.

He groaned and slid his hand beneath her blouse at the waist, splayed his palm and rubbed it over her back in a circling motion that created heat like a flint against a stone. Insatiable desire flared, pulled them even closer.

Then broke them apart.

At the same time, they each stepped back, hands falling away from each other as if suddenly burned.

But still their eyes met in the moonlight, they met and clung desperately.

Finally she forced her swollen lips to move.

"You do believe that I'm right about somebody following us?" she managed to ask.

"Yes."

"*Why*, if you said all day I was wrong? Why, if I can't be trusted?"

"I couldn't sleep for thinking about how you instinctively know things," he said. "You knew when I had both my visions and you knew exactly where to find me on that creek when I fired at the bear or whatever it was that night."

She laughed.

"I knew where to find you because you were making as much noise as a herd of buffalo!"

He grinned. "I was only trying to scare the wild animal away."

"Of course," she said, teasing him, and for one precious moment their old closeness was alive again. "I should've known that's what you were doing!"

"It worked, didn't it?" he teased.

Then he sobered. He'd felt it, too, she could tell—that instant when all the loneliness was gone from the world.

"Did you see or hear anything out here?" she said.

"No."

He spoke abruptly and looked, suddenly, as arrogant as he had when he took the silver from Pedro that day.

He said, "We need to get back to camp."

Without another word, Sky turned away.

It was over. Her aloneness was back to stay. Never, ever, again would they have the companionship they had once had because Rafael would never trust her.

He held the aspen branches aside with the rifle and, with his other hand hovering at the small of her back, took her through the trees, into the leaves whispering and murmuring into the night, and then out into the silent shadows, heading them back toward the camp. Where High Wolf was sleeping.

"Your spirit tells you many things, Sky," he said, then, low in her ear. "If you say someone is following us, then I say so, too."

Sky's throat tightened and her eyes filled with tears.

That declaration of his trust melted her heart.

But he didn't trust her about anything else. Only about this enemy trailing them.

High Wolf stirred when they came back into camp, then he sat straight up to look at them, pulling his blanket tighter across his body as he stared.

In the language of the *Nermernuh*, he muttered something unintelligible, then, like a cut tree falling, he lay back down.

"Get some sleep," Rafael said, as he walked her to her bedrobes. "So far, whoever it is, is just following us. Probably another treasure hunter who thinks we might have a map."

Sky shivered.

"Crawl in and get warm," he said, brusquely. "I'll keep watch."

Sky lay down in her bed but for a long, long time she couldn't get warm.

Not without Rafael's arm around her.

The next morning, Rafael sat for a long time just outside of camp in the trees. He felt as if he had taken root and grown there, felt as if he could never move again.

He'd thought about Sky until his brain was sore and his heart lay in pieces.

After such a night that we became part of each other!

At midnight, out there in the moonlight, she had said that with such sincerity that he had believed it.

God knew that he *needed* for it to be true. Without Sky, what anchor was there for his new self to hold on to?

He stayed still while the gray of first light changed to pink and then to the full rosy dawn of northern New Mexico. Faithfully, he watched every color fade into the next one.

Because Sky was awake now and bustling about the camp and he couldn't look at her without wanting to touch her.

He couldn't even hear her voice without a wild hungering to hold her close.

"I'm putting these hackberry balls onto the sticks to roast and then I'm going to rub my horses down while the water boils," she said, to High Wolf, her smoky tones soft and strong in the clear morning air.

High Wolf's only answer was a disdainful snort.

Then there was silence. Rafael turned his head just in time to glimpse the back of her elkskin dress, sleeve fringes swinging, disappearing into the aspens on her way to the horses.

She moved with the natural grace of a deer, he thought. Everything about her was natural and free as the mesa and the trees.

Including her use of the truth.

That awful thought pulled him off the stump and onto his feet. He couldn't sit around and think about her. He couldn't stand it.

He walked out of the trees and into the camp.

"Well, Spanish," High Wolf growled, when he saw him, "I saw you walking out all night with my woman."

He was obviously furious. Good. Maybe he'd jump him and they could have a fight that'd make them both feel a lot better.

"So," Rafael said, with what he hoped was an infuriating coolness, "You were sleeping with your eyes open, hmm?"

High Wolf hunched on his haunches beside the newly blazing fire, idly playing with one of the several long sticks which lay balanced on some stones, holding the berry balls on their sharp points over the fire. His narrow eyes never left Rafael.

"I thought at first I had a bad dream," he went on, in that same surly tone, "but then I knew it was real. Do not walk beneath the moon again with my woman."

Rafael's blood leapt. A fight would feel wonderful.

"I thought there was some question about whether or not she *is* your woman," he said, in a baiting tone.

He kept his gaze on High Wolf while he walked to his saddle and slid the rifle into its scabbard. His pistol and belt lay with his packs, but he didn't pick them up. High Wolf was unarmed.

Yes. That was what he needed. A good, hard fight that would hold his attention so he couldn't think about anything else.

He strolled over to the fire.

High Wolf stood and faced him.

"She *was* my woman, without question," he said, and jabbed the stick he held into the air with a gesture fierce and quick as an attack with a lance. The berry ball was gone—the point of the stick was sharpened like the end of an awl.

Rafael resisted the urge to step back from it. He stepped forward instead, to show he was not afraid and could not be intimidated.

What a pleasure it would be to wipe that hateful expression off High Wolf's face!

"When you came onto this trail, High Wolf," he said, quietly, "Sky said she had decided to take back her promise to you."

"She doesn't mean it when she says such things. Always she has been hasty and thoughtless—everyone in our band knows that. And she tries to take too much into her own hands. Her father will insist that she keep her promise to me."

Everything about that speech made Rafael fighting mad.

"She may play things a little fast and loose sometimes," Rafael said. "She may be hasty, but you can't call her thoughtless. She follows her heart."

High Wolf went pale as the early morning, but he managed a sinister smile.

"You're saying she followed her heart to you last night?"

"She followed me out of camp when she saw I was gone. I went to look for whoever's been trailing us."

High Wolf snarled.

"Ahhh!" he said, almost strangling on the word. "So now you tell her that you believe her imaginings so that she will come to you! Liar!"

"I've decided that I do believe her!"

"Then you believe a worthless tale! Pretty Sky is daydreaming enemies now in addition to a nonexistent treasure. Instead of all that foolishness, her thoughts should be filled with thoughts of me and of our marriage—of my lodge to keep and hides to scrape and food to prepare!"

It took all the strength Rafael could muster to keep from slamming his fist into that smug face. He didn't, because he wanted the stupid dolt to hear him.

"You have *no right*, none whatsoever, to try to change her!" he roared. "You don't deserve her because you don't understand one thing about her—she *knows* things, you idiot! Think about it! She can sense truths that she has no other way of knowing!"

"*I* can sense that you must leave us," High Wolf said, his voice very low and trembling with rage. "Get out of this camp, Montoya, and go back to your *rancho*. I need time alone with her to teach her to behave like a wife."

A strange, cold hand clutched at Rafael's gut. He would never leave Sky alone with High Wolf. Never.

He met High Wolf's furious eyes and shook his head slowly. He smiled at him.

"You don't want me to go. You need me too much."

"I need you too much!" High Wolf snarled, like one of his namesakes. "Yes! I need to cut your heart out! I need to take your scalp!"

"You need me to watch your back for you. This mesa's crawling with Anglos who'd shoot a Comanche on sight, and you know it. No telling how many are in the bunch that's already on our trail."

"No one is following us!" High Wolf shouted. "I have looked and listened—even Sky has seen no one!"

Rafael said, "They are there."

"*Who*? And why would they follow and not attack when dark came? Why, if they are so many, did they not raid this camp and take our horses and our hair?"

He brandished the sharp stick, flashed a terrible, hateful grin.

"If they are there, then why are you not guarding Sky from them at this moment?"

"They're following to let us find the treasure," Rafael said. "I thought of it while I was keeping watch last night. Sky begged me to help her hunt for the treasure while I was sitting my horse in the middle of a swarm of Comancheros and their customers."

"Why would she beg *you*? Not because you have gone to the mesa before with Don Diego—our band has been there, too."

"Because I had a vision about the treasure during the Council," Rafael said, bluntly, knowing, suddenly, as he spoke, that that would make High Wolf more jealous than ever.

He was right. High Wolf's angry face became a mask of envious disbelief.

"Sky somehow knew that I'd had a vision," Rafael went on. "I didn't tell her. And she knew what it was about."

"But *I* have had no vision of the treasure! And I am shaman of Windrider's band of the *Nermernuh*!"

"Also, while we rode to this mesa, I had another strong insight," Rafael said, feeling his lips lift at the corners when High Wolf's face went even more pale. "We're getting close to the treasure. I'll find it."

High Wolf's skin turned ashen.

"It is not right," he said, slowly, "for you to have so much *puha* when I am the one who is medicine man. And it is not right for you to walk out of camp with my woman."

He opened the palm of his left hand and tapped the long stick against it, gently, watching Rafael through narrowed eyes.

"But I won't kill you now. I'll see if your medicine is strong enough to find a treasure which is only legend."

He smiled a thin smile.

"I should warn you," he said, "strong medicine or no, I will kill you. You camped one night alone with my woman and walked alone with her another night."

"Well, High Wolf," Rafael drawled, "*I* should warn *you* that you'd better go home and get that whole damn band of Windrider's to help you if you decide to try to kill me."

"And *I* should warn *you* again," said High Wolf, mocking Rafael's sardonic tone, "that Pretty Sky does at each moment whatever her feelings tell her. She cares nothing for you, but only for your vision to lead her to the treasure that does not exist."

That stabbed Rafael right in the heart.

High Wolf paused to look at him, to judge the effect. Rafael let him see nothing.

"The treasure does exist," Rafael said, smiling a little more, needling him.

High Wolf shrugged.

"I do not think so. But Pretty Sky must see for herself, so after that I can change her. And I must see your medicine at work—if, indeed, you have any medicine."

Cold anger filled Rafael and he embraced it.

He broadened his smile.

"You couldn't change Sky in a million years," he said, then his words slowed to a drawl. "As for trying to kill me," he said, staring into the hard, narrowed eyes, "give it your best try, High Wolf. You pick the time and the place."

Chapter 11

The creeping feeling up the back of Sky's neck came over her again, stronger than ever, as she knelt beside the firepit to cover it with dirt. She glanced toward Rafael, busy loading his packhorse at the very edge of the trees.

"Our friend is with us again," she said.

High Wolf, riding into the clearing at just that moment with both his horses packed and ready to go, spoke loudly, glancing first at her and then at Rafael.

"The Spaniard can hear. Nevertheless, it is good you warn him when I come."

Puzzled, Sky frowned at him. He'd been prickly as a cactus all morning—he must not have been as deeply asleep as he'd acted when she and Rafael returned to camp last night.

"But not at all necessary," Rafael said, calmly, and for a moment Sky thought he, too, had misunderstood her warning.

However, he pulled El Lobo around so that he could look across the saddle he was centering and cinching to search the surrounding aspens for a movement or a flash of color that didn't belong. He was relaxed and unobtrusive about it, but that was what he was doing.

He *did* believe her!

Then, in that same, cool voice, he said, "You, yourself, warn me of your arrival quite nicely, High Wolf, with all your noise."

She looked at them. What were they talking about? Surely they weren't about to get into a fight.

"*A-i-eeee!*"

The long-drawn, keening cry wiped out High Wolf's answer. It froze Sky's knees to the ground.

It came from her left, a little behind her. She turned her upper body just in time to see a shrieking, blurred form hurling itself out of the woods.

Toward Rafael.

The only part of it she could see clearly was the blade of a knife held high, flashing in the sunlight.

Aimed at Rafael's back.

He whirled around.

It was aimed at his heart.

Instinct pulled her to her feet and set them running.

High Wolf would intervene before she could get there—he was closer, and mounted, and armed. Rafael wore his pistol.

They would not need her help.

But she could not stop.

All High Wolf would have to do was reach out and strike the knife from the wild man's hand, ride one step and bring his rifle crashing down . . .

From the corner of her eye she glimpsed

High Wolf moving forward as if he'd had the same thoughts. Then he stopped.

He sat still, safe on his horse, and watched.

All the while Sky's numb body was moving toward Rafael, which seemed longer than a whole season but was less than a heartbeat, High Wolf sat there and watched. In front of her, Rafael's hand grabbed for his pistol, but the loosely woven cinch caught his fingers.

He tried to jerk them loose.

Sky threw herself at the attacker one instant before El Lobo let out a panicked squeal and reared, rising over her like a kicking, tottering mountain. She missed.

Both men disappeared from her view as the ground reached up, grabbed her shoulder, and pulled her, helplessly rolling, beneath the towering, screaming stallion. Vaguely, she got a glancing sight of the heavy black saddle flying high into the air and she thought that at least Rafael had pulled his hand loose, then all she could see and think of were the huge-muscled hind legs waiting for her to roll into them, planted there like trees, yet trembling like leaves in a tornado wind. The terrible, piercing cries kept on coming, torn from deep in El Lobo's body.

His forefeet came striking, down and down through the air, searching for whatever had brought him into this fog of terrible fear. Sky's mind scrambled to save herself, but her body couldn't begin to respond.

Her eyes strained to see a way of escape, her mouth opened to shout for someone to help.

But no sound came out—she didn't have air to breathe, much less to yell.

Her arms and legs, her entire body, all numb, all in the grip of another power, she squeezed her eyes closed against the blinding dust and prayed that the first hoof to hit her would free her spirit.

Something crashed to the ground right beside her, shook Mother Earth so hard that Sky's flesh moved on her bones. She was going to find out, this very moment, what it was like to die.

She was dead.

But she could still hear.

"Swine!" a strange voice spit, in Spanish. "You will . . ."

The next sound was a grunt, a deep-seated sound of pain and then another and another incoherent noise in that same rough voice. A sharp crack broke the ground beside her ear and the stallion snorted and whinnied high again.

Rafael's voice gasped out, "El Lobo, El Lobo," in a soothing tone.

Then he made a startled sound of pain.

Something wet slapped Sky across the face.

Her eyes flew open.

El Lobo was slinging his head, globs of white froth flying from his lips in all directions. His reins stretched taut, down from his flecked black muzzle to pull his nose toward the ground.

Sky's shocked gaze rolled down the length of them.

To Rafael's hard, brown hand.

His arm jerked, as he smashed that same elbow into his opponent. The stallion protested with another fling of his powerful neck.

But now all four of his deadly feet stayed on the ground.

Her mind began trying to work again.

How had Rafael had time to get his fingers out of the cinch, hold off his attacker, and grab hold of the flying, lashing reins?

He had spun the stallion on his hindquarters to bring his forefeet down on the earth instead of on Sky. And all the while he was trying to keep himself from being stabbed.

Something moved, in the corner of her vision.

High Wolf. *Now*, now that Rafael was down on the ground, holding his adversary off with one hand in a life-and-death struggle, with his two-handed enemy on top of him, knife flashing and darting in every direction, High Wolf moved.

He leaned out of the saddle and took El Lobo's reins at the bit.

Rafael's eyes cut toward him for the briefest of instants, then they touched Sky and were gone, back to the man who was trying to kill him. He brought the side of his newly freed hand down on the back of his adversary's neck.

The man took the blow as if he were made of wood.

The knife waved closer to Rafael's face.

El Lobo jumped sideways as High Wolf pulled on his mouth and, finally, Sky's instincts succeeded in telling her body to move. She covered her head with her arms, drew her body up into a ball, and tumbled, over and over, out from beneath the horse and away.

She got to her hands and knees. Then the dizziness clutched her. It made her go completely still.

She closed her eyes, took a long, deep breath, and fought down the queasiness in her stomach.

She scrabbled to her feet.

Sweat ran down into her eyes, but she wiped it away with her sleeve and rushed toward Rafael. At least, with El Lobo out of the way, there was no more danger of the fighting men being trampled.

But there was no hope of her getting into the fray.

The men lunged toward her through a fogging cloud of dust, locked in a deadly embrace that took them both flat again with a terrifying thump. They rolled and plunged, smashing and kicking, straining, always straining, to stab the knife downward or to hold it away.

They rolled onto the dirt-covered firepit and off the other side.

After an eternity, the knife shot up and out of the melee, arced through the bright morning air, end over end, with its wicked blade shining. It landed, stuck in the ground, at her feet.

The dust swirled harder, then started to settle.

So did Sky's heart.

Rafael was on top, on his knees, straddling the man who had rushed him, pounding his face with both fists. His attacker made a desperate, strangling noise that sounded vaguely like a word, and Rafael stopped.

"Who are you?" he demanded. "Why did you jump me?"

Sky stared. She knew the man, yet she didn't.

His features obscured by dirt and blood, his clothes full of dust, it was hard to tell anything about him. He grabbed the end of his serape and used it to wipe his eyes.

His pink-and-brown-striped serape.

She realized who he was the instant before he spoke.

"Pedro," he mumbled, finally, stiffly, because his bottom lip was cut.

Of course. She could see him now, dropping his wife's silver combs, one by one, into Rafael's hand, his face black with hatred.

"What Pedro?" Rafael shouted hoarsely. "Pedro of where?"

"Pedro the Whiskey Trader, of Chaparito!"

"Ah!"

Rafael sat back on his haunches, still astride the man, and pushed his loose hair behind his ears. His tieback had vanished in the fray.

He scowled fiercely, as if the name meant something to him, but Sky could tell it did not. He had thought the man so low and mean the first time they met that he had not bothered to look at his face or remember his name.

"Tell me, Pedro," he said, in a quiet voice

full of danger. "Why have you made this futile effort to stab me in the back?"

"Because you have shamed me!" Pedro said, glaring his hate up into Rafael's hard face. "With my wife."

Rafael looked so completely bewildered that Sky felt an hysterical chuckle bubbling up in her throat.

"I never met your wife."

"You *did*!" Pedro hissed. "You caused her to leave me. At the rendezvous."

"The rendezvous!"

"You forced me to give back her combs. She took them and went to live with her sister. She won't come home and cook for me no more."

The last word came out as a gasp and he seemed to sag deeper into the ground. The long speech had taken the last of Pedro's strength.

Except for the hatred glimmering in his eyes.

Recognition filled Rafael's face and he leapt to his feet with a disgusted kick of the dirt toward Pedro.

"God in Heaven, man, you surely haven't followed me all this way!"

He frowned at the man, thinking.

"I know you didn't. Nobody was behind me when I left El Rancho del Cielo. And if this is the best you can do for a sneak attack, you're no tracker, I'd bet good money on that."

Pedro lay silent, staring up at Rafael through slitted eyes.

"I followed you."

"You couldn't follow your own nose across your wife's kitchen."

Quick as a snake striking, Pedro was on his knees, lunging for Rafael's legs, trying to take him down again.

Rafael sidestepped the attack, reached out with one powerful arm, grabbed a fistful of Pedro's serape and shirt, and hauled him to his feet.

"How did you know where I was?"

Pedro answered with a venomous glance.

Rafael slapped him, open-handed, across the face.

"Answer my question, dammit!"

Pedro spit at him.

"I heard you and the girl talking at the rendezvous!"

Rafael dragged Pedro's face right up to his own.

"That didn't tell you enough," he said, in a low, calm tone that made Sky's skin crawl. "This is a big mesa and you found me fast. How did you know I was here?"

"Waters's boys," the man mumbled. "They sent the cook's helper to tell me."

Sky's insides contracted into one tight knot. *Waters. Waters, the man she must persuade to take her bargain. Waters knew they were here.*

Only three of them, deep into a country that none of them knew very well. A country that held the treasure that would save her people.

No telling how many men worked for Waters. All of them wanted the treasure, too.

She and Rafael would have to search fast.

But Rafael was shaking his head, scowling at Pedro as if he didn't believe him.

"Why would anybody ride so far just to bring you that bit of news?"

"To trade it for some whiskey. Waters, he is a cheap man to work for. One of his hands who saw you not too far from the Río Gallinas, he loves my whiskey very much."

"Why not just shoot me from ambush? You must've had plenty of chances."

Pedro's face filled with a new fury.

"I wanted you to look into my eyes, ranchero. Look and know who it was would take your life. And I wanted you to beg—in front of your Comanche *compañero*, who argues with you today, and in front of your woman."

Rafael jerked him closer, and shook him, hard, even though he still held him with only one hand.

"And is that what you want now, Pedro, *mi amigo*?"

"No, no!"

One of Pedro's eyes was rapidly swelling shut, but the other flared open in fear.

He raised one trembling hand toward the heavens.

"I have tried and I failed, *Señor*," he said. "No more."

Rafael's look was so terrible that Sky felt a shiver of fear. His hand went to the butt of the pistol he wore; the air stopped in her throat. He would kill the man, surely, right in front of her eyes!

From the look on Pedro's face, he believed it too.

Rafael said, in a voice as full of menace as

the look on his face. "Swear that you will never come near me again. If you do, I will kill you without giving you time for a prayer."

"I . . . swear it."

Rafael didn't move. His gaze didn't flicker.

"If you are ever tempted to go back on that vow, Pedro, remember that I am known throughout the New Mexico Territory and all of Comancheria as a man of my word."

"I . . . I know that, *Señor*."

"Is anybody with you? Waiting for you in the woods?"

"No. I wanted to kill you alone."

Rafael's eyes held Pedro impaled.

He said, "High Wolf. Give my horse to Sky. Ride into the woods at my back and get the poor animal that carried this piece of dirt in here."

To Sky's amazement, High Wolf did as he was told.

Rafael held Pedro's reins with one hand and, with the other, pulled out the battered gun that was in the man's saddle scabbard. Pedro painfully heaved himself onto his mount.

"Go tell your buddies at Waters's place not to mess with Montoya," Rafael said, pointing off the Mesa Rica with the worn-out gun. Remind them that I can shoot a fly from the ear of my favorite horse."

Then he shouted, "*Vamanos!*"

He slapped the shaggy pony on the rump and sent it charging into the trees, reins flying under and over its feet, Pedro clinging to the saddle horn with the last of his strength.

Sky watched him go with the last of hers.

She felt a sudden, fierce need to sit down, but her knees didn't have strength enough to bend.

Rafael turned toward her.

The look he gave her then held her on her feet.

He laid Pedro's gun down and strode across the campground to her.

"Sky! Did El Lobo hurt you?"

At the sound of his name, the stallion snuffled and nudged at her shoulder, as calm now as he had been excited before.

Rafael touched her cheek with his rough fingertips.

She felt a rise in her blood.

"No-o," she said, slowly, surprised, somehow, by the sound of her own voice.

Once again, her mind refused to work.

El Lobo stamped his foot.

"No," she said, at last. "You turned him just in time, Rafael. I'll never know how. I owe you my life."

The dark flame leapt in his eyes.

"No. I owe you mine," he said, simply.

She looked at him in disbelief.

"You threw yourself into danger to help me," he said, in a tone so full of wonder that it brought her tears. "Thank you, Sky."

"You are welcome," she whispered.

Rafael shook his head ruefully.

"I was wrong about our stalker not attacking," he said. "I'm glad he didn't come charging in in the middle of the night."

She heard his voice, but she couldn't listen to him.

He was alive, dirty and disheveled, bruised, but alive. He wasn't hurt.

She needed to touch him, but at this moment she could not lift her hand. They had come too close to lying here in the dust, dead. Or bleeding and broken.

He reached out and tucked a strand of hair behind her ear. She leaned her cheek into his palm.

"Then I suppose we're even," she said.

"No. You still owe me."

His words ran softly over her ears, like a stream of water. She hardly knew what they said. All she wanted was the sound of his voice, low and sure and sweetly alive.

"How do you say that?"

"You scared me more than Pedro did. Again and again, in my memory, I see you throwing yourself at that knife and falling under El Lobo."

He held up his free hand.

"Look. I'm still trembling."

She shook her head, watching his smile. Her cheek moved softly against his callused palm.

Little coals of new fire danced through her veins.

She placed her open palm flat against his. He closed his fingers around hers with a swift force that stopped her heart.

"You must never do that again, do you hear me?" he said. "I can take care of myself. I've been in rough spots before."

El Lobo jerked back on his reins. They ignored him.

"I don't know how you remember I rolled under El Lobo," she murmured, teasing him. "Pedro was keeping you far too busy for you to see me."

"I saw you," he said, huskily, and his eyes burned their way over her face. "Dear God, Sky, I . . ."

"What are you two doing? Waiting here to give Waters and his men time to find us?"

The question crashed through the air like a rock thrown.

Their hands still entwined in the air, they turned to look at High Wolf.

Sky stared. She had forgotten he was even there.

But he was. Sitting his horse like a disapproving father, shooting holes in both of them with his eyes.

"We can wait here for Waters and his men to find us or we can get on the trail back to the camp of our people," he declared, his voice harsh as a crow's cry.

The sound of it sent new strength surging through Sky.

"Or we can search this mesa as fast as we can," she said, "and watch our backs. Unless this medicine man warrior of the *Nermernuh* is too afraid of a few whiskey-drinking Anglos."

His face turned into a thundercloud.

"This warrior is not afraid," he said, the words grating like sand on a rock. "But he can count. We are only three."

His tone dropped to one of derision.

"And one of those is a woman."

"A woman who was not afraid to stand at my back."

Rafael shot the words at High Wolf like bullets.

High Wolf's eyes flared bright. He knew exactly what Rafael meant.

"I was not *afraid*," he said.

Sky shivered.

High Wolf now *hated* Rafael because she had been alone with him in the moonlight.

Rafael reached down and took El Lobo's reins from her limp fingers.

Sky stood where she was while the horse walked around her, making a chuckling sound deep in his throat at being taken by his master.

"I do thank you, though," Rafael said, "for taking the horse out of the way of the fight, High Wolf."

"You must know I did that only to protect my woman. She was beneath his hooves."

Sky opened her mouth to protest again being called his woman. How, *how* would she ever convince him that she truly would not marry him?

But some terrible, errant thought, something about Pedro, was nagging at her until she couldn't.

"Rafael," she said, finally, and her lips barely would move, they had gone so stiff with fear. "Think about this—remember what Pedro said. He overheard me begging you to come with me to the Mesa Rica."

"Yes."

He stopped the horse, stood still, and looked at her, his hand in El Lobo's mane.

"So Pedro heard me say Windrider was calling for war!" she cried, louder. "That he was sending for all the Plains Tribes! Rafael! You know their first raid will be on Waters's new ranch and now he will be forewarned!"

He shot her a sharp, sideways glance. It said he had already thought of that.

Sorrow and guilt and a terrible, lung-crushing urgency came down over her body like a slide of rocks off a mountain.

"Oh! It's all my fault!" she cried, and panicked tears filled her voice and her eyes. "I should have been more careful! Oh, Rafael, I was trying to save my people and I've killed them instead!"

"No, you haven't," he said, in a comforting tone and reached for her hand.

"I could bite off my tongue! Pedro is on his way to Waters now. When Windrider comes to their ranch, the Anglos will be on guard!"

"Windrider will have many more men than Waters," he said. He began leading her toward her horses.

She was in such a turmoil inside that she could barely stumble along.

"When I ran after you and begged you to come with me, I was only following my heart the way I always do," she said, her eyes searching Rafael's face for comfort. "But I was *wrong*! I should've stopped to think!"

High Wolf spoke up, handing down his judgment from the back of his horse.

"That is true. And, Spanish, you should never have let Pedro leave us alive."

"If he heard us talking at the rendezvous, so did other people," Rafael said, shortly. "And how many had he already told before he ever came to the Mesa Rica?"

"Oh, no!" Sky cried. "That only makes it worse! This is all my fault!"

"Yes, it is," High Wolf said. "But you can make up for it. Forget looking for this treasure that you've imagined and go to warn your father of the danger that's real. I'll take you to him."

Sky stopped in her tracks. Rafael stopped, too, and El Lobo danced restlessly to one side.

A terrible feeling gnawed at her.

A feeling she could never remember having before.

Uncertainty.

She reached for the sure instinct, the strong impulses that usually guided her, but found only a confusing whirlpool of contradictory emotions.

And her mind couldn't tell her. She couldn't think.

"Rafael, maybe I should!" she said, searching his face. "Perhaps High Wolf is right. Oh, my father will die because I did this . . ."

Her voice broke beneath the weight of the whole, awful responsibility.

"I should've been more careful," she admitted, and the words were strange on her tongue.

Careful was not a word she often used. "I should've stopped to think, as you've been telling me!"

"No, no!" Rafael said, and, suddenly, his voice sounded as raw and anguished as hers. As if her pain was causing him pain.

"Don't doubt yourself, Sky," he begged, his grip tightening around her arm. "Windrider has fought in many raids and wars, and he'll send scouts ahead—he *knows* the Anglos may be waiting, ready to fight—that's true of every enemy."

"I know, but . . ."

"Besides, Waters doesn't have more than twenty or thirty men. Windrider will have ten times that many—or more, by the time the word reaches all the Plains Tribes."

"Come with me, Sky," High Wolf said. "Let's go."

She wheeled around and looked at him.

"That's the answer! *You* go, High Wolf! You go and warn my father while Rafael and I stay and find the treasure!"

He stared at her from eyes like chips of stone.

"I am not leaving you here alone with this man, this Spaniard! Windrider sent me here to protect you."

"Don't be ridiculous! Rafael won't hurt me!"

She pulled free of Rafael's hand and ran to High Wolf.

"Go, High Wolf! You can carry the warning alone!"

"No. My duty is to do as Windrider asked

me. You must give up this foolish treasure hunt, Sky, and make up for your mistake."

He glared down at her.

"If you hadn't stood in the middle of camp begging this Spaniard for help at the top of your lungs, instead of behaving as a woman should and leaving war in the hands of your father and me and your brother and the other men, you wouldn't have betrayed your people."

"She didn't betray anybody," Rafael growled, striding toward them with El Lobo in hand.

Sky threw a look at him over her shoulder.

"I didn't mean to, but I did!" she cried.

She turned back to High Wolf.

"*Go*, High Wolf, please! Only Rafael and I can find the treasure and stop the war."

He did not move.

"Come with me," he said. "The warning will stop it."

"No! It'll only cause it to start someplace else. The treasure will stop the whole war!"

High Wolf gave a nasty laugh. His narrowed eyes switched from Sky to Rafael.

"Do you agree with such a stupid plan, Montoya?"

"Yes," Rafael said. "You'd better be on your way to Windrider."

"I am not going anywhere that the two of you do not go!"

Sky said, "High Wolf, because of your jealousy, you're playing with the lives of our people! You're supposed to be their healer, their shaman."

High Wolf jerked his back up straight, taking great offense.

"I do not intend to argue with you about this anymore," he said, with his strictest dignity. "Sky, you know that our warriors will die in ambush at Waters's *rancho* and that it is your fault. You can save them. Will you take that responsibility?"

Sky put her hand over her heart.

It was tearing itself to shreds, darting one way and then the other, caught, always caught, on the question of which action would be best for her people. She looked at High Wolf and then at Rafael.

She couldn't think, she couldn't breathe. She was in agony.

For once in her life, she, Ysidora Pretty Sky, was of a double mind. She did not know what to do.

"It's true," she said, her throat almost too full to let the words out. "Pedro is on his way to warn Waters right now. He *will* set an ambush."

"Well, then," Rafael drawled. "As the brave wise woman said just a little while ago—we'd better be watching our backs while we search the mesa as fast as we can."

He smiled at her and went to lead El Lobo to his saddle.

For one long, shocked moment, Sky looked after him.

He was advising her to follow her heart.

After all the times he had told her to stop and think—not to be so impetuous, not to believe that the treasure existed, not to hope that the treasure would stop the war—he was urging her to follow her dream.

And she would.

She followed at a run to get her horses.

Chapter 12

When the lone rider appeared from in amongst the chokecherry thickets that grew along the foot of the mesa and wandered toward them at a crooked trot, weaving and swaying in the saddle, Mr. Waters held up his hand and started slowing his horse. Fay and Sullivan did the same.

"Maybe he's shot," Waters said. "We better hold up and find out—no sense goin' ridin' hell-bent into trouble."

The rider came on, nearly falling clear off of the shaggy cayuse a time or two. Fay watched him closely—there was something mighty familiar about him.

Finally he stumbled up to the three of them and stopped.

He had lost his hat somewhere and his bruised, bloodied face was streaming sweat from the hot sun. His clothes were torn and dirty, he kept dabbing at his face with the end of his serape.

A pink-and-brown-striped serape.

A terrible, sinking feeling came over Fay.

Of course. His gaze darted back to the battered face.

Pedro. Dammit all to hell.

213

Fay squeezed his horse, trying to ease in between the Comanchero and the boss.

He needed like sin to signal to him somehow not to say nothing in front of Waters about the deal for the whiskey.

But another glance at the Comanchero's face blasted that hope all to hell. Pedro was in no shape to think fast enough to pick up on a signal or hear a quiet word dropped in his ear. Pedro was one beat-up human.

Fay let his horse drop back, silently cussing his luck.

Pedro just sat there, slumped on top of his horse, squeezing his saddle horn with both hands like it was a sack of gold dust.

"What's happened to you?" Waters demanded. "Who are you?"

"Comanchero they call Pedro the Whiskey Peddler," Sullivan piped up, like he was singing in a choir.

Stupid blabbermouth couldn't even figure out nobody was talking to him.

"Well, Pedro, I don't use the stuff myself," Waters announced, sanctimonious bastard that he was, "and I won't have it on my place. But that's beside the point. What nest of hornets did you just run into?"

Pedro slowly turned his head toward the voice. His one eye that was still open passed by the boss, then returned and focused on Waters.

"Montoya!" he said, and then let his swollen lips fall closed as if they hurt too bad to talk more.

Good. Maybe he wouldn't put out the effort to mention the whiskey deal.

"Montoya, eh?" the boss said, and his piggy little blue eyes lit up. "He somewhere just up ahead?"

Pedro nodded and mumbled, "In that first valley, one with the aspens thick as grass."

The boss tensed like he was going to ride on that very instant. Fay's hopes rose.

So did his memories. She was just up there ahead, the girl! Soon he'd see her again, the Indian princess riding through her own country, yellow aspens against the blue sky making it more beautiful than heaven.

But Waters didn't ride on right now. No. Waters always had to poke his nose into everything.

"What'd you do to Montoya?" he demanded. "He catch you trying to read his treasure map?"

"*He* try to come between me and my woman."

Pedro squinted his one good eye all around at the three of them and tried to swallow.

Then his swollen lips parted and he said, "At the rendezvous."

Waters gave a brisk nod. "Aha! I already talked to your friend about what you two overheard. You think Montoya's getting anywhere close to the treasure yet?"

Pedro started to shake his head no, then clasped it with both hands to hold it still.

"No treasure. I know nothing. Only that Montoya has much magic to control such a horse while evading my knife. He has much magic."

Waters gave a noncommittal grunt.

Pedro let out a pathetic sound. "I know nothing more. I have ridden very hard and fast, many hours to get to Montoya. Now he has badly hurt me. I cannot sit in the sun and talk."

"Ride straight on west from here," Waters said, "and it won't be too long 'til you come to my headquarters. You can rest up there for a little while."

Fay's heart thudded, hard and fast. It was over! He was safe! Waters would never know about the whiskey and Fay and the boys would have a much more bearable winter because of it.

But then, even after Pedro had kicked his horse into starting to walk west, the boss, nosy bastard that he was, kept on digging.

"Hey!" he called after him. "How'd you know where to find Montoya, anyhow?"

Fay's desperate, dry tongue blurted out, "Reckon he must've followed him from El Cielo, Boss."

But Pedro yelled back to him, in spite of the fact he could barely open his mouth.

"Your boys, they sent me a message," he said. "A trade. My enemy for some of my whiskey."

Charlie Waters turned in his saddle and looked from Fay to Sullivan, his narrow blue eyes burning like he would pistol-whip them both if he could spare the time.

"You boys had better listen to me," he said, through gritted teeth, "and listen good. You work for me, you go by my rules. When we get back to headquarters I'm confiscating that whiskey and sending it to Santa Fe to sell."

Fay's sick feeling came back, strong enough to knock him off his horse. He'd have a long winter with no whiskey, after all.

Waters shifted his seat and glared at them harder.

"I ain't heerd one piddling thing about no whiskey, Boss," Sullivan said, and cut his lying eyes at Fay. "You know as well as I do who's the drunkard around here."

"Well, let me just tell you this," Waters snapped, as he got his horse moving again. "Now that I know you'll go behind my back and break my rules. You boys got one way and one way only to keep your jobs with me and to ever get another one riding for any ranch in this territory."

"I tell you, I ain't guilty," Sullivan said, and threw a hot look at Fay, who threw it right back at him.

Waters rode a little ahead of them, but they had no trouble hearing what he said.

"You two had better sneak around real easy now. You gotta keep from scaring Montoya and his friends and keep from losing them at the same time. I aim to have that treasure and they know where it is."

"We'll find it," Sullivan assured him.

"*They* will," Waters corrected him. "And we'll take it away from them."

"How about taking the girl, too?" Sullivan snickered. "Or are we supposed to treat her like one of the men?"

"I could give a damn about any of them," Waters snapped. "As long as we get the treasure."

"That girl'd cut your heart out and throw it to the dogs, Sullivan," Fay said, in a voice full of venom. "That woman's a she-cat on horseback as you will find out if you try to mess with her."

"Well," Waters called back over his shoulder. "Sounds like you got a pretty good look at her, Fay."

"Yeah," Sullivan taunted. "I think old Fay's done gone and fallen in love."

"No," Fay blurted, "but I got a good enough look to know that Sullivan's not worth the fringe on one of her sleeves."

And neither are you, Charlie Waters, rich and powerful bastard that you are. Neither one of you has enough gumption to know that all wild, free things oughtta stay wild and free.

A shot fired from somewhere behind them.

"Damn, what was that?" Sullivan exclaimed.

They turned to look.

Off in the distance, Pedro had stopped and was pointing back at them, another rider, on a tall, rangy roan, was starting to try to catch up.

"Thank God!" Waters exclaimed. "Raymond Dale. Wonder what he found out?"

Eager beaver Waters rode back to meet his messenger.

Fay glared at Sullivan.

Sullivan tried to meet his eyes and actually succeeded.

"I'd tell you what I think of you," Fay said. "But they'd be fightin' words and he'd fire us both on the spot. Later, I will."

"Anytime," Sullivan said, with such bravado that it was all Fay could do to keep from dragging him off his horse on the spot.

Together Waters and Raymond Dale rode back up to them.

"Don't worry about your scalps anymore, boys," the boss sang out, "unless these two Comanches up ahead git ahold of you. When we get back with the treasure, a company of soldiers'll be waiting for Windrider at my new ranch."

He led them all toward the mesa then, at a long, hard trot, and Fay kept on holding his horse in with theirs. But he didn't know how he even had the strength to squeeze him with his legs. He was sick—sick clean through. He would quit this blathering, cheap, greedy little tinhorn boss in a minute if he had anywhere else to go.

And if he didn't have a chance to see that auburn-haired girl ride through Comanche country one more time.

Rafael made sure that High Wolf didn't ride at his back anymore. It wasn't hard to do, since the medicine man had begun striking out ahead every chance he got, hurrying, as if trying to say with his actions that the treasure wasn't here, nor there, nor anywhere.

When they rode into the fourth of the wind-carved valleys they searched in the mesa's north side that afternoon, High Wolf sent his horses edging against Sky's and pushed in front of her.

"If you're in such a hurry, go home!" she called to him. "I am not going to overlook the treasure because you are rushing me!"

He didn't bother to answer, only rode dog-gedly halfway in, and began scanning the ground and rocks in the same cursory, care-less, useless manner that he had had all day, a pretense of a search that would have found nothing that wasn't lying on top of the ground.

Rafael couldn't resist taunting him.

"Think the *Conquistadores* may have left some tracks?" he called.

Suddenly, directly in front of him, Sky stopped her horses.

He brought his to a halt, sending El Lobo skidding a bit to keep from bumping into the rump of her packhorse.

Sky's face was lifted to the east side of the valley, high up, where the afternoon sun had turned its rough, carved rock surface into a wall of gold.

She whipped her horse sideways, angled her head to get a different view.

"The spyglass!" she called, reaching across Pabo's loaded back to hold out her hand to Rafael.

She didn't spare him so much as a glance; her eyes clung to those rocks as if she could see the treasure itself.

He lifted the leather strap from the horn of his saddle and laid it in her palm. Her hand was shaking.

Her face was filled with a light brighter than the sun that lit the mesa.

"Rafael," she cried. "I see a sign!"

Her voice soared like an eagle.

Rafael's heart plummeted.

What if nothing was there? What if her hope was giving her hallucinations?

His blood chilled.

What if he had done wrong in encouraging her?

She gasped and kept looking through the glass as she urged Far Girl forward.

He shaded his eyes with his hand and tried to see whatever it was that drew her.

The cliff's face glittered back at him.

"Look!" she cried. "It's the lodge made of flaming rainbows!"

With a scrabbling of hooves on the hard ground, she backed Far Girl up and held the spyglass out to him.

He took it and threw it to his face.

Red and gold arches burned against the pink of the cliff.

Maybe they were flaming rainbows.

Maybe they were shadows and sunlight in the crevices.

"See them?" she cried.

The fire blazing inside her was going to burn her up.

But he couldn't be the one to put it out.

He was the one who'd thrown fuel on it.

"Yes," he said.

Sky stood up in her stirrups to look for the best way to get to that bluff. Her whole body leaned toward it as if she could make it close enough to touch through the sheer force of her will.

She gave another cry of victory.

"Ay, ay!" she cried. "Look, Rafael—the rocks run back racing."

He set the glass where she pointed.

Sure enough. A double row of rocks, big rocks, flowed down from and around the foot of the pink cliff.

"You are *poo?sa?*," High Wolf called, riding back toward her. "*Loco*," he translated, with a sharp glance at Rafael to show that he was included in the judgment. "Rocks do not run."

Sky ignored him.

"All we have to do is follow the rocks around the end of this valley," she said, and finally tore her eyes from the miracle she'd found to turn and look back at Rafael. "We'll find the trees that are like arrows on its other side."

The pure faith in her voice made Rafael's hair stand on end.

She pulled her mare's head around and started out of the valley.

"On its other side, in the next canyon, you will find only the healing springs," High Wolf proclaimed, following her. "Our people, and many other people, have gone there for years and never found any other treasure."

Sky kept going.

"Sky," Rafael said, "maybe . . ."

"We're going to find it," she said, without hearing him at all. "I know it. I just know it! We'll find the treasure during this next sun and we'll have Waters back across the Gallinas before my father can gather all the warriors!"

She turned her dirty, sweat-streaked face to him, as she passed, her eyes blazing with victory.

A dull ache began, deep inside him. She did care for him, he knew that now. She had risked her life to try to save his.

And what had he done for her in return?

Encouraged her in this quest that could kill her boundless spirit.

Triumphantly, she said, "We both saw the flaming rainbows. Grandmother Hukiyani gave me the song and the All-Father gave you the visions. You and I, Rafael! We'll stop the whole war before it even starts—two or three suns from now!"

She had such heart.

A hard lump formed in his throat.

How could so much raw passion, so much fierceness, exist in such a slender body? She vibrated with it.

His arms ached to reach across that narrow space and pull her to him. His heart *hurt*, he yearned so much to tell her that everything she wanted to happen would happen just as she had predicted.

And he wanted her to look at him that way because she wanted *him*.

As she had done on that one magic night.

A terrible fear stabbed through him.

Never, ever, in all of his twenty-eight years, had he wanted anything so much as he wanted Sky to be safe and happy.

It terrified him.

He couldn't even try to make that happen, not for long, anyway. She would have to leave him and he would leave her when this hunt was over.

Unless he went with her.

He slammed his mind closed on the thought. "We may need a little bit longer than two or three suns to do all that, *Señorita* Sky," he said, and he rode out beside her.

High Wolf snorted, "Much longer!"

Rafael dropped back, to let him catch up and not be behind him.

Sky rode down out of the valley, leading her packhorse, scanning the land in every direction. Singing.

Father Sun's rays are traveling to find his heart in the Earth Mother's breast.
The rocks run back racing, the trees turn into arrows that fly.

The joyous, confident sound lifted Rafael's heart, poured encouragement into his veins, took away his weariness.

It even inspired the horses to go on—all of them, even High Wolf's two, began to pick up their feet higher, began to move faster. El Lobo threw up his head and let out a loud call, Far Girl lifted into a lope.

Tears stung Rafael's eyes. Once again Sky was bold and full of heart, not doubting herself anymore.

The Eagle dives through the wind to strike flame from the coals of the fire.
He'yay, He'yo, He'yo, yoyo!

"You are a fool!" High Wolf scolded her, pushing his tired horse to come up between them. "What if someone should hear you?"

"It wouldn't matter, would it, High Wolf?" Sky said, laughing back at him. "According to you, the treasure does not exist."

"It does not," he said, solemnly, and Sky and Rafael laughed together.

"Then what does it matter if I sing? Besides, it was Pedro who was following us and now he is gone. No one is watching or listening. We are free until Waters's men can find us and that will not be today!"

She twisted around in her saddle and smiled at Rafael, her dark eyes sparkling.

"Before they can find us, we will have the treasure and be gone!"

She turned around, looked ahead and then wheeled her horse to a stop.

"There!" she cried, and pointed to the southeast, toward the next cut back into the mesa. It ran deeper, was much more far-reaching back into the mountain's heart than any they had been in so far.

"There they are!"

High Wolf pulled his mount up short.

Rafael rode El Lobo to one side, trying to see.

The slant of the light across the land was just beginning to change. Dusk was being born, so sunlight touched the tops of rocks and trees, shadows took the ravines and the valleys.

Rafael glanced at Sky, fixed the angle of her gaze, looked again at that spot. A cluster of junipers grew a good distance away from where they sat, halfway up the eastern side of the mesa's endless canyon.

The sky was empty, there was no eagle diving.

No arrows.

No particular ray of light traveled to Earth Mother's heart.

The blood died in Rafael's veins. Poor Sky. She wanted to see another guiding mark from the song so much that she had imagined it. He put his heels to El Lobo and rode up close beside her.

"We need to make camp soon, Sky," he said, softly. "*Mañana*. Tomorrow is another day. We will search some more then."

"Right there," she murmured, without turning her head or moving her gaze. "Don't you see them, Rafael? It's the trees turned into arrows."

He looked at the junipers again.

They grew tall and thin instead of fat like some trees of their kind, perhaps because they grew so close together. And they all had tops that closely resembled each other.

Roughly triangular, pointed tops.

"Arrows," Sky whispered. "Arrows close together in a quiver."

Rafael stared at them some more, his heart racing.

"*Es verdad!*" he said.

A great joy rolled up in him, like the happiness in her voice when she sang. It was true, all of it—the visions and the song—all of it was true!

He had been right to encourage her to follow her heart to the treasure instead of going home to give warning!

And he had been right to risk everything, his father's love and his *rancho* to have such an astounding adventure!

He and Sky turned to each other and laughed, laughed for pure happiness.

"Let's camp in them tonight," he said, already starting to ride toward the arrow trees. "There looks to be a stream coming down the mountain there, and the wall of that valley will protect us from the wind."

Sky turned such a look of blinding brilliance on him that he wanted to sing, too.

"We're doing it right, aren't we, Rafael? Didn't I tell you that we can do anything together?"

"What are you talking about?" High Wolf called to her.

But she ignored him.

"*Miaru!*" she shouted to Far Girl and set the tired mare into a long trot again.

The long-forgotten command to go, spoken in the language of his birth, of his earliest days which now were only shadows among his memories, brought that crazy thought back into Rafael's head again. Maybe, when the treasure was found, he would not go back to the *rancho*.

Maybe he would ride the wild Comanche ways with Ysidora Pretty Sky.

But it was too much, too startling to think about, and Rafael put his heels to El Lobo and passed Far Girl and Sky, heading for the magical trees, letting his mind roam free.

He smooched to El Lobo. The quick, autumn darkness was coming and the way up to the juniper grove would be rough. He'd better put his energy into memorizing it now while he could see.

He managed to keep at bay every thought except that one until they were there.

They rode up the creek, trickling down through its half-empty bed and into the arrow-pointed trees just as the sun dropped all the way down. The coolness of the coming night and the little moisture it held in the air already were bringing out the junipers' sweet, pungent aroma.

"At last!" Sky barely breathed the words as she slid down off Far Girl. "Tomorrow, tomorrow, we will find the treasure!"

Rafael stood in his stirrup and swung down from El Lobo while High Wolf raised a fog of dust around them by galloping in fast.

Finally it cleared, blown ahead of the rising night breeze.

"Rafael!"

Her cry carried such a sudden alarm that he whipped around to El Lobo's other side so he could see her.

She was staring out over the way they had come, clinging to the leathers of her stirrup, stiff as the wall of the mesa where they stood.

"Look! At the end of the rainbow cliff."

He did, and for one, heartbreaking instant, he saw what had thrown such fear into her.

At the end of the cliff they had just ridden around, on the racing rocks, stood a silhouette.

The unmistakable shape of a man, wearing a wide-brimmed cowboy hat, not a sombrero, showing clear against the last of the light.

Chapter 13

Sky's fingers lost their grip on the stirrup leather, her knees gave way. She leaned against Far Girl's sweaty, heaving side and stared at that spot on the mesa. Night was coming on fast. The man was gone.

But not far and not for long.

She could not bear it.

Her legs thrummed, her head swam from putting her feet on the ground and losing the motion of the horse. Her joy and excitement turned into an angry frustration that drained away her strength.

"I didn't think Pedro could get to Waters's ranch before tomorrow!" she cried, hoarsely. "Oh, I could just cut my tongue out for talking about the treasure where he could hear me!"

"Make up for it by going to warn Windrider," High Wolf said, quickly. "We can start at dawn."

"No!" she said, lifting her head to glare at him across her saddle. "Don't you understand? We're almost there—we're about to find the treasure!"

She half turned to try to see Rafael.

"We've got to move on," she said, her voice rough with discouragement. "Don't unsaddle.

We don't want that Anglo to know about these trees."

Behind her, a pack thudded to the ground.

"You're not able to move on," Rafael said. "And neither are these horses—think about them. Eat and then we'll talk about our Anglo *amigo*."

"No," she whispered, but he didn't hear her. Or he pretended not to.

She turned and pressed her forehead to the lathered hide of the horse and closed her eyes, barely breathing in and out, willing the strength to gather in her muscles again so she could remount. It flowed out the bottoms of her moccasins and away from her into Earth Mother, instead.

He was right. She was losing her mind—she couldn't ride Far Girl to death!

"I'll start the fire," Rafael said. "Do we have any more of that cornmeal?"

"Yes," she murmured.

"Then I'll give you something hot to eat soon."

It was wonderful to think about that.

Sky turned her head and let her cheek rest against Far Girl, hardly feeling or smelling the mare's heavy sweat. She tried to think.

If they couldn't ride out again—and they couldn't, because the horses were totally spent—all was lost. The Anglo would follow them from this precious sign of the arrow trees to the treasure itself.

Her exhausted emotions stirred.

The next sign would come to her at daybreak. It would be the eagle diving. Or Father Sun's rays pointing to the exact place in the Earth Mother's breast where the treasure was waiting for her.

The thought roused her hope, her determination. They had to get the Anglos off their trail.

Tomorrow they would find the treasure.

"The food is in this pack," High Wolf said, speaking to Rafael in his derisive tone that she hated, "if you mean what you say about doing woman's work."

Something else thumped to the ground.

"I'll cook," Rafael answered, sounding completely unperturbed. "While you water and hobble the horses."

The bustling, busy sounds of a camp being made brought sudden tears to her eyes. If she didn't look, she could almost imagine she was with the band and her mother and father.

But she wasn't. And she might never be again.

Windrider might be killed at Waters's ranch.

They had to escape from the Anglo.

So they could find the treasure and bribe that stubborn rancher back into New Mexico.

Sky placed both palms against Far Girl, and stiffened her arms. She turned around.

The rising evening breeze stiffened her wet cheeks until her lips could barely move.

She muttered, "If that Anglo follows us . . ."

Her voice broke.

Immediately, Rafael appeared in front of her.

"It is taboo," he said, "to speak of Anglos on an empty stomach."

His hands took her shoulders gently and moved her to one side. "Let me have your saddle," he said, "and High Wolf your horse."

His voice soothed her; she wanted to sway toward him. She wanted to lean against him; she could remember exactly how his body felt to hers. Her lids drifted down.

She didn't care what was happening then, all she could do was listen for him to speak again.

But her saddle and bridle went down with a thump and a swish of her fringes and High Wolf grunted a command. The horses took muffled steps as he walked them all away.

And, without another word, Rafael's arm came around her shoulders.

The unexpectedness of it, the *power* of it, brought a tremulous sigh from her lips. She leaned her forehead into the broad, comforting rock of his chest.

"Come over here and sit," he said, and she began to walk along beside him as if she had no will at all of her own. "You can advise me on building the fire."

"Can you build a fire?" she teased, feebly. "Your servants are not here."

He teased her in return.

"You *know* I can build a fire—with your help."

Drained as her emotions were, his sensual tone sent a tingling thrill down her spine.

But he was leaving her. His arm vanished from her shoulders and the night wind wrapped around them in its place. She shivered.

"Sit here on this robe while I grab some wood," he said, and let her gently down into the softness of her bed. "Soon you will have hot food and some of my chocolate."

Soon she would have hot food in her, she thought drowsily, and she didn't have to do a thing. She didn't even have to move. She *couldn't* move.

But something was wrong. She had to think. She couldn't let herself drift off to sleep. Something was not right, here.

It hit her when he set the kindling afire.

"We should make a cold camp!" she cried. "The Anglo . . ."

"The Anglo has seen us ride into these trees and start to unsaddle. The fire will tell him nothing more than he already knows."

"It will give him light to shoot by."

"He didn't ride all this way to shoot at us."

Her tired mind wrestled with that.

"At least, not before we find the treasure," she finally agreed. "Oh, Rafael! Here we are, on the edge of finding it with him and no telling how many others watching everything we do! Do you think it was my singing that brought him?"

She dropped her face into her hands.

"If I could ever learn to keep my mouth shut! First, Pedro overhears that we'll take the warpath, and now this!"

"Nobody heard you singing," he said, firmly. "You were hardly louder than our horses.

He was probably already out here looking for the treasure."

"Why *can't* I learn to think before I speak— or sing?"

He gave a dry chuckle.

"Sky, you're going overboard on all this guilt, this responsibility."

Somehow, just hearing that lightened her burden. She chuckled, too, then she sighed.

"I guess I am going to extremes, from faith to doubt," she said. "But aren't you the one who's been telling me to stop and think?"

He laughed.

"I think what we need around here may be a judicious mix of thinking and following our instincts," he said.

Sky laughed, too.

"I suppose," she said, drowsily. "You might try to make some progress in thinking less and following your instincts more . . ."

He interrupted firmly. "After you eat. No more talking until then."

He stood up and left the fire. The shadows swallowed him up but she could hear him rummaging in the packs. Her lids drifted closed again.

"Sky," he said.

She woke to find him sitting on his haunches in front of her, a wooden bowl of steaming mesh held in one hand, a tin cup of hot chocolate in the other.

"Eat and drink," he said, "and you can start talking again."

High Wolf's sour voice sounded suddenly from near the fire.

"If she is awake, she will talk, whether you say she should or not."

Sky didn't care what he said. The warm steam was rising into her face, the fragrance of the food was bringing saliva into her mouth.

But Rafael didn't give it to her. He set down the cup and she saw he also held a white piece of cloth.

She tried to focus on it in the faint light from the fire. His handkerchief?

"Before you eat, you might want to wash the horse lather off your face."

Sky laughed, looked up into his eyes.

"Even my mother and grandmother couldn't take better care of me," she said. "Thank you, Rafael."

"Soon he will be building tipis and scraping hides," High Wolf taunted.

Sky finished washing up and leaned forward to look at him. He sat by the fire with a bowl in his hands, he took a bite.

"Do not eat Rafael's food," she said, sternly, as she dropped the handkerchief, took the bowl from Rafael and picked up the horn spoon that was in it. "Because you aren't grateful that he cooked it for you. Did you feed the fire?"

"Yes," he growled, and took another large bite, glaring at Rafael as if he'd like to throw something at him, instead.

Rafael ignored him and so did Sky. She began to eat, then, and the marvelous warmth and strength in the food spread into every part of her body.

"Thank you, Rafael," she murmured.

"*De nada*, Ysidora Pretty Sky," he said.

She cleaned her bowl, drained her cup.

"I have eaten," she said, finally. "Now we can talk. How shall we get rid of the Anglos?"

"Raid their camp," High Wolf said, sarcastically. "You, Pretty Sky, are always bragging that you, a woman, have counted coup on your enemy. You can add to your honors during this night."

"They might add to theirs," Rafael drawled. "We have no idea how many they are."

"Are you afraid to ride against them, Spanish?"

"If they are more than twenty, I am," Rafael said, wryly.

Sky laughed.

High Wolf growled.

"*You* should be afraid of raiding the camp of only *one* Anglo," he said. "*I* have stolen horses from many, many soldiers who slept with them tethered to their hands. You are too clumsy to do such a thing."

"Your opinion means nothing to me," Rafael said to him, coolly. "But at first light you'll be forced to change it. I'm not too clumsy to lure these Anglos away into another part of the mesa."

"Yes!" Sky cried. "What a good idea! Trick them, Rafael, get them away from these trees so that we can find the next sign for the treasure."

"Ha!" High Wolf said, and swallowed the

last of his meal in one huge gulp. "These trees are close to nothing but the Mesa Rica. Which holds no treasure."

He tossed his bowl and spoon on the ground in Rafael's direction, as if to say that he could wash them since he was doing woman's work.

Rafael ignored him.

High Wolf said, "I will trick the Anglos for you, Pretty Sky. Then you can be free to see for yourself that there is no treasure here."

"If there isn't," Rafael snapped, "then the Anglos can follow us all they want and find nothing. Why would you ride hard to lure them away?"

"For Pretty Sky," High Wolf said. "They worry her, upset her."

"You are *muy generoso*," Rafael drawled, but his tone was low and dangerous. "I told you. I will lead the Anglos into a trap. When the sun stands mid-sky tomorrow, meet me at the healing springs. Do you know where?"

"I know," High Wolf snapped. "And now I know your plan. A man can lose himself and his enemies separately in the Canyon of the Springs."

He stared at Rafael, then, his face hardening in the glow from the fire.

"You think you are so wise. But you will be dead before Father Sun rides down his trail again," he predicted. "The Anglos will take you. Or you will lose yourself in the canyon before you lose them."

The awful words hit Sky's heart like cold stones.

Rafael set his bowl down, fast, and, for an instant Sky thought he would leap at High Wolf, but he held his hands flat on his thighs.

"You would like that, I know," he said, in a tone that ought to freeze High Wolf's tongue, "but you will be disappointed. If you want me dead, you'll have to make good on your threat and try to kill me yourself."

He got up abruptly.

"Take care of Sky," he said, "and meet me at noon."

Rafael went out into the blackness to get his blankets.

The wind strengthened, darted into the camp, picked up the dust and swirled it around the fire. It repeated Rafael's words, although Sky didn't want to hear them. So. It had come to what she'd feared the moment she'd recognized High Wolf's flute the morning that she lay in Rafael's arms.

Not only might the Anglos kill them all, High Wolf might kill Rafael!

She looked at High Wolf, sitting silent, staring into the flames.

Finally he raised his head and looked back at her.

"I do not accept orders from the Spaniard," he said, softly. "But I will take care of you, Pretty Sky. You are my woman."

She said nothing.

Enough trouble was lurking out there in the dark, beyond this camp and in it. She would not stir up more this night.

* * *

Faraway shouts pulled at her, annoyed her, shouts so faint they contained no words. But she needed to know what they were about.

Sky opened her eyes to gray light and black shapes of tree limbs barely moving in the wind overhead.

For one lonely, shifting moment she did not know where she was.

The shouts faded away. Then came the indistinct noise of horses, several horses running, in the distance.

She sat up. Rafael! That must be Rafael—he was planning to ride out and lure the Anglos away.

No.

She blinked. Rafael stood in front of her, beside the embers of the fire, his head to one side, listening.

Sky turned and listened, too, but the last, dim sound was gone.

"Damn that sneaking High Wolf!" he said. "Damn him!"

Sky tried to think.

"Maybe he's here somewhere . . ."

But she could see plainly that High Wolf's blankets were gone.

"No maybe," Rafael said, abruptly, striding across camp to look for the horses. "He's gone to lure the Anglos away."

Sky scrambled to her feet and flung herself after him.

"Damned show-off!" Rafael said.

Three hobbled horses—El Lobo, Far Girl, and Pabo—grazed there.

"He took my horse!" he roared.

"To have three so the tracks and the dust would look like we're with him," Sky said, trying to make her sleep-laden mind work. "But he didn't take El Lobo."

"I would've killed him if he had!"

Rafael whirled and looked out toward the rocks where they had seen the Anglo.

"I heard more than three horses," he said, and the anger in his voice took on a trace of pleasure. "They've gone after him. It worked. My idea worked."

He turned back, fast, and looked at her, all anger again.

"I'll kill him, anyway. He just couldn't stand for me to tell him what to do, for me to take the lead and have a thought about how to get us out of this situation! Damn him!"

"Now, Rafael, this is for the best," she said, and, stumbling a little, she went to him, rubbing the last of the sleep from her eyes. "Listen to me. You whipped Pedro and then you said to High Wolf that I have more courage than he. I told him that we didn't need him, that you were the only one who can help me find the treasure."

"Why would he care about *that*? He doesn't believe it exists, anyway!"

"I know, I know," she soothed. "But you took my side about looking for it and we found the signs that we both believe in. You understood how I felt and you took care of me last night."

"So what?" he yelled. "High Wolf called *me* a coward, too."

"But you are too strong for that to bother you," she said. "He is not that strong."

Then she asked, her voice breaking a little, "When did he first say he would kill you?"

"After he'd seen us coming into camp together in the moonlight," he said, abruptly, and closed his mouth.

He would tell her no more than that.

But she had to ask. "When is he planning to try such a thing?"

He shrugged. "Who knows? I'll kill him first—the very next time I see him."

"We have to fight the Anglos, not each other, no matter how angry we get," she said quickly. "Try to understand that his pride is hurting and this is the best way for him to heal it."

He grunted, angrily.

"*He'll* be the one to lose himself and never come out of there again. I've ridden some of that canyon with my father. How well does High Wolf know it?"

"Fairly well. We camped by the springs a few times on our way north to cut lodge poles."

The thought of those journeys, like the sounds of the camp last night, ripped a large, homesick hole in her heart.

Her people were in terrible danger and she had made it even worse. Fear came awake in her veins and screamed like a panther.

"Forget about High Wolf right now," she urged, and darted to her horses to lead them to camp so she could saddle and pack. "He took the Anglos with him. He's given us our chance to find the next sign to the treasure without being followed—we mustn't waste it."

She led the horses forward, one arm around each of their necks. All her limbs trembled with the weight of the responsibility she carried.

"We must start looking for the eagle that dives," she urged, and the hard beat of her heart drummed all through her body.

She broke into a run. Thanks be to the Great Spirit, the Anglos were gone. This sun, this very sun, they would find the treasure.

Rafael dropped back from staring over the rim of the ledge and looked at Sky for the thousandth time.

She still lay on her stomach at the end of the rocky outcropping, propped up on her elbows, keeping the spyglass at her eye constantly moving, scanning the heavens and the valley below. With her long, lithe body stretched tight as a guitar string.

Wishing, hoping, willing the eagle of the song to appear.

High-strung to the edge of tears.

He wouldn't be surprised if she leapt right off the ledge and tried to fly in circles, expecting it to come diving through the air to meet her.

He couldn't stand it a minute longer, this wanting to help her and not knowing how.

This being alone with her, wanting to touch her and not knowing if he could trust her with his heart. Because if he ever touched her again, that heart would belong to her.

Maybe High Wolf had been right in saying that all she cared about was the treasure.

She certainly had given no sign all morning that she had so much as a thought for Rafael.

Every word she'd spoken all day had had something to do with hunting the treasure. Except when she'd tried to calm his initial anger. And that had been meant to soothe him and get him started on the treasure hunt again.

"Come on," he said. "Let's go down below and see if there're any caves. We may be looking for an eagle-shaped rock or a shadow. A shadow might look like it's diving through the air."

"No!"

She raised one moccasined foot and kicked the mesa wall behind her.

"We won't see an eagle diving inside a cave!"

Her voice broke with the weight of her wanting and his temper snapped.

"What the hell do you expect from me, Sky? I can't *make* an eagle and throw it out there for you to find!"

She whipped her head around to look at him, her eyes blazing through the shadows thrown by the mountain at their backs.

"I'm so sorry to be so much bother to you!"

Her voice, her whole body trembled.

"I thought you believed in this, wanted this, as much as I do!" she cried. "If you don't care any more than that about finding the treasure, you can just leave here and go home . . ."

Her wide, brown eyes flew away from his, looked past his shoulder. She raised the spyglass and stared.

"Rafael!"

She dropped the glass, passed it into his hand.

"They've got him!" she breathed, just as he lifted it and saw what she meant.

"Oh, Rafael, they've caught High Wolf!"

His mouth went dry.

Directly below them, horses and riders moved briskly across the open side of the brush-dotted valley which cut a great semicircle into the mesa's north side. Three riders, five horses.

Even as his mind tried to deny it, he knew that the one in the middle was High Wolf.

No mistake. His naked torso flashed between the blue shirts of the others, the black-and-white spots of his mount gleamed like a beacon against the Anglos' dark, solid-colored horses.

Behind High Wolf came his own buckskin packhorse and Rafael's solid white one.

His anger with the man boiled up in him again, came out in savage irony.

"And he thought *we* were angry when he told us there was no treasure!"

Sky's shocked gasp made him wish he could bite off his tongue.

"They'll torture him!" she cried, clapping her hands to her face. "And he doesn't speak English, so he can't convince them he doesn't believe in the treasure, much less know where it is!"

She stared at the moving men and horses below.

"We'll have to get him out!" Rafael snapped, furious with High Wolf for dragging her into the danger that was sure to follow, for sneaking off and leaving them in the first place.

To his surprise, she smiled as she turned to him, her tear-wet eyes glowing.

"You are wonderful, Rafael!" she said. "High Wolf is waiting to kill you, but your first thought is to rescue him!"

And that made him furious with himself for thinking Sky cared about nothing but the treasure, just on High Wolf's jealous word. She was sincerely worried about the obnoxious medicine man.

She also cared about him, Rafael.

But what could it ever come to?

He had to turn away from the dazzling light in the look she gave him.

The parade passed on, starting to go out of their sight, traveling west.

Chapter 14

Sky thought she would be an old woman before they could gather their water bags, scramble off the ledge and back down the slope to the horses, unburden the packhorse and hide her, and strip their own saddles of everything but jerky, water, and weapons. But when they rode down and out across the mouth of the Canyon of the Springs, the Anglos' dust still floated in the air.

"They could go into any of these valleys," Rafael shouted, as they lifted the horses into a lope and began to follow the wind-spun cloud. "Watch ahead as far as you can."

Sky's voice felt trapped in her throat, but she managed to nod.

Rafael shot her a sharp look.

"Come down to a trot when we sight them. If they see us, we'll turn tail and run. Do you hear me? We head south and run for cover into the side of the mesa."

"No!" she protested. "You said we'd get him out. We can do it—there are three of us and only two of them!"

"They may be going to meet some others. Listen to me—I don't want to have to try to rescue you, too!"

"You *won't!*" she yelled back at him.

"I mean it, Sky, let me go ahead. You *hang back!*"

He put his heels to El Lobo, then, and galloped on ahead, as sure of her obedience as he had been of Pedro's to give him the combs that day so long ago.

She set her jaw and urged Far Girl to keep up with the stallion.

Father Sun beat down on her back as hot as if this was the middle of the summer season instead of *Yubamua*, the fall month, and the wind whirled dust into her face. Rafael rode ahead, taking the lead, ready to tell her what to do and when to do it.

But she couldn't feel frustrated or angry with him.

All she could feel was wonder and gratitude that, in spite of their enmity, he wanted to free High Wolf. And a fearful excitement about what lay ahead.

Soon the dust cloud turned at an angle toward the mesa. Rafael had guessed it.

Probably, they had a camp there. And they wanted to question High Wolf now, in a place not too far from the arrow-shaped tree camp that might have been on the trail of the treasure.

She stayed on Rafael's heels and wouldn't drop back until he did. Then they both slowed—galloping horses made a noise that carried a long way.

Time collapsed again. Father Sun didn't move a handsbreadth down the heavens, but

Sky lived for what seemed to be many seasons while they walked the horses on the flat and then walked them, slowly, carefully, up into the narrow, aspen-lined valley that the Anglos had chosen.

They concealed them in the trees and crept to within hearing distance of the strange, rough voices.

"I don't like this at all, Sullivan," one man said, and it took a moment for the English to make sense in Sky's ears. "We've got ourselves in a hell of a fix. He's liable to bust loose and take our hair."

"Shut up. Lash him 'tween these trees here and we'll find out where that treasure is. We're two against one."

"Yeah, but the one's a Comanche warrior!"

"Tell you what, Fay," the other man drawled. "You must be scared of your own shadow."

"Ain't *my* hands shakin' like these aspen leaves," the other one said.

"Well," the one called Sullivan said, "you might bring your rope here, too, just to make sure."

Then the flat sound of a slap, flesh against flesh, rang out. Sullivan spoke again.

"What d'you know about that treasure, Injun?"

Silence, except for boots crunching through fallen leaves.

Rafael quirked one black brow at Sky and signaled with a downward slice of his hand for her to stay where she was.

No. I'm going with you, she mouthed back,

and gave him her fiercest look.

The slapping sound came again while Rafael stared furiously at her.

Finally, he gave a short nod of consent and they moved forward silently into a windswept world of yellow and golden aspens. He was perfectly silent, crouching, rifle in one hand, pistol in the other.

Sky shifted her bow on her shoulder and pulled her skinning knife from its beaded sheath. She caught a glimpse of blue cloth straight ahead, stopped, and dropped to the ground. Rafael was already down.

"We oughtta try some Spanish," Sullivan said. "Most Comanches know a few words of it."

The wind blew harder through the chattering leaves. It made wonderful cover, so Sky and Rafael moved closer to the Anglos and High Wolf.

"You some kind of Indian expert, Sullivan? Scalp locks and Spanish, huh?"

Sky brushed away the two or three loose twigs showing in the mix of colored leaves on the ground and carefully stretched out to her full length, lying on her stomach. She could see four dirty boots beneath dusty cloth legs of breeches and, just between the two pairs of them, High Wolf's beaded moccasins, their long heel fringes swirled out gracefully onto the bed of fallen leaves.

One Anglo man took a step backward and then she could see all of High Wolf.

Her palms went wet with sweat and her lips

parted, pushed by a cry, frantic to get out. She clamped them shut and held it in.

High Wolf stood spread-eagled, tied by his wrists and his waist between two trees. Tied with two long lariat ropes, wound around and around the trees and his body.

Worse yet, his long, braided scalp lock stretched from the side of his head to the trunk of one tree. A folding pocket knife driven through it held it fast.

She dropped her skinning knife and pressed her wet hands into the leaves, fighting panic.

So that's what the remark about Spanish and scalp locks had meant! One Anglo knew the *Nermernuh* believed a man's hair was an extension of his spirit!

That desecration was hurting High Wolf more than the ropes that burned his arms and his body. It made Sky desperate to free him.

She glanced at Rafael, lying an arm's length away. His eyes, narrowed to slits, were fixed unmoving on High Wolf.

One Anglo stepped forward and kicked High Wolf in the side.

"If you don't want us to cut off that scalp lock and take your whole scalp, too," he said, in passable Spanish, "tell us where that treasure is."

"And the girl," the other man said, in English. "How come you don't have her or neither of her horses with you? Is she riding with Montoya? Ask him that, Sullivan."

"For God's sake!" the other man yelled, spinning around to face him. "Will you shut up about that girl? It's the treasure the boss is after!"

He turned back to High Wolf.

"Where's the *gold*, Injun?"

High Wolf said nothing. He stared up into the yellow leaves toward the sky, holding his face and his body perfectly still.

Then his lips parted and in a high, reverent voice he began singing his death song.

"Dammit!"

The Anglo, Sullivan, who had kicked him, hit him in the mouth. Blood trickled down his chin, but it did not stop his song.

"Damn you! I'll . . ."

A horse burst into view through the leaves, and a new voice broke in.

" 'Damn you' is exactly the words I would choose," a raspy voice yelled.

Another horse pushed into view behind the first one. The man who rode it was younger than the other one, and much taller.

He didn't speak, but the little one started to yell over High Wolf's song.

"You! Fay! Sullivan! What the *hell* do you think you're doing? You lost what little minds you had?"

He waved one arm in the air, brought his fist crashing down on his leg.

"Well, Mr. Waters, no," said the man who had kicked High Wolf.

Mr. Waters!

Sky's fingers dug into the leaves, squeezed them into crumpling handfuls. Her eyes glued themselves to the slightly built man.

This was the stubborn Anglo who kept crossing the Gallinas!

This was the man she had to bribe when she found the treasure.

High Wolf continued his death song as if nobody else at all was there.

"We split up so two of us could follow *him*," Mr. Waters shouted and jabbed his finger at High Wolf, "and so two of us could look for the girl and Montoya. What do you two buttheads do? *Catch* him instead of follow him—now you've fixed it so we'll never know what they know about the treasure!"

He spit in disgust.

"Does *follow* sound like *catch* to you?"

He climbed down from his horse, his face flushing redder by the minute.

For an instant, excitement sped Sky's breathing. He was the ranch owner. These men worked for him. And he was furious with them. Perhaps he'd make them untie High Wolf!

She threw a hopeful look at Rafael.

He didn't see it. He was inching forward to get closer and closer to High Wolf.

"All I can say is—you must be wearing your brains in your boots!" Waters shouted, waving both arms this time. "It's a good thing General Sykes is sending soldiers and cannons to be all over my ranch when Windrider gets there. If I left the defense up to you boys, you'd likely give the whole damn place to him!"

Sky's heart lurched into her throat, then it died inside her. She crushed the leaves to powder in her fists, dropped her head down onto them.

Her worst fear was true.

There'd be more danger, much more, than just a bunch of Anglo cowboys lurking in wait for her father and her brother and all the others when they rode onto Waters's ranch. There'd be soldiers and cannons and certain death.

This was all her fault.

Why, *why* couldn't she have controlled her runaway tongue that day after Council and made sure that she spoke to Rafael in private?

And why couldn't she have ridden out to warn Windrider yesterday, as High Wolf had urged, instead of clinging to her dream of the treasure?

She took several long, deep breaths.

High Wolf was in danger. High Wolf was in danger.

That's what she had to think about now. That, and nothing else.

She looked up. The three cowboys had gathered around their boss and were all talking at once.

Sky wiped her palms on her skirt, picked up her knife and she, too, began wriggling toward High Wolf. Rafael was standing, now, screened from the white men by a tree to one side of High Wolf.

With a last glance over her shoulder at Waters and his men, Sky got to her feet and darted the last short distance to join him, thankful that the wind was getting stronger in the noisy leaves.

High Wolf's blank gaze dropped and he saw them.

His eyes narrowed and he made an impatient gesture with one bound hand for them to get back. The rope that tied him drew blood from the skin of his wrist.

His gaze flicked to his captors and then back to them.

He changed the words of his death song. Changed the tune.

"Take Sky away from here, do it now," he sang.

In a whisper, she translated for Rafael.

"Far away," High Wolf sang. "Do it now."

More blood trickled from the corner of his mouth.

Rafael shook his head.

"I said I would kill you," he sang. "You are not bound to save me, your enemy. Take Sky away from here."

She whispered the words in Spanish for Rafael.

"I'm *not* leaving him," he muttered.

Sky smiled. "You said you would kill him, too," she whispered. "The next time you saw him."

He gave her a wry grin and a shrug, then flicked his sharp glance from the Anglos to High Wolf again.

"Before dark comes, my soul will be in the After-World," High Wolf sang. "I will tell them nothing of your treasure song. Go, now."

The Anglos were all talking at once now and none of them noticed Sky and Rafael.

High Wolf sang, "I will die with honor, as a warrior and not as a useless old man!"

Sky translated that, then slipped forward, fast, through the trees, reached out, and jerked loose the knife that held High Wolf's scalp lock. It fell to his shoulder.

One of the Anglos turned half around as Sky ducked back behind the tree.

"Go, now!" High Wolf sang, the terrible urgency of his voice sounding as if it would tear out his throat. He pulled at the ropes. "Take her away from here!"

Rafael nodded yes, stepped forward and grabbed Sky by the arm, then pulled her farther back into the trees, away from High Wolf.

"No! Don't!" Sky cried, just above a whisper. "We can't go!"

He clamped his hand over her mouth and dragged her farther back into the windblown leaves.

Her heart fell. He was deserting High Wolf, after all.

The Anglos' voices were rising higher and louder by the minute.

"If you idiots had to take an Injun and scare the others off from leading us to the treasure, you could at least have taken the girl!" Waters was yelling. "This brave and Montoya, then, they'd have done anything we asked to get Windrider's daughter back. They'd have led us right straight to the treasure, you fools!"

Another waterfall of cold fear ran over Sky. She went limp in Rafael's arms.

That strange, cold-eyed little man knew who

she was! He would like to have her as his captive!

"All right, enough of this!" Waters said. "Get a fire going here! Burning the location of the treasure out of this redskin is the only hope we've got, now."

Someone else said, "Fay, get some wood."

"Get some yourself, Sullivan!"

"Git the coffeepot, too," Waters ordered. "Might's well have some coffee while we're heating that iron."

Terrified for High Wolf again, Sky struggled.

Rafael squeezed her around the shoulders and placed his lips next to her ear.

"I only said we'd go to ease High Wolf's mind. Now, this is our chance. I'll get El Lobo and ride into them. You cut High Wolf's hands loose, give him the knife, then hide and use your bow to cover us."

She nodded.

He was gone and he was moving, fast. Sky crept back toward High Wolf, her blood leaping so high in her veins that it made her feet light as the drifting leaves.

High Wolf would not die this day.

And neither would she nor Rafael.

"What the *hell*!" one of the Anglos exclaimed, his voice sounding so close through the trees that she stopped stone-still and clutched her knife harder in alarm.

"Will you look at that? That sucker's pulled the knife outta that braid of his! And his hands is still tied!"

Sky smiled grimly and edged in closer.

"He's got magic!" another of them cried. "Big medicine!"

Good. Maybe they'd leave him alone now.

"Don't be stupid!" Mr. Waters's raspy voice said. "He jerked his head. You sissy-boys didn't drive that knife in good enough. Now, git out there and gather some wood!"

The strengthening wind came rippling in through the trees and whipped Sky's hair across her face. She sheathed her knife, tore a fringe from her sleeve, and gathered her hair in her other hand, tying it securely back out of her way.

From somewhere behind her she heard the faint noises of Rafael leading El Lobo in through the trees, but Waters and his men gave no sign that they heard him, too. Sky ran forward.

She moved more slowly than she wanted, but she had to take care not to let a limb catch the bow or the quiver full of arrows she wore on her back.

She stopped at the spot where she'd need to be to cut the rope from High Wolf's left hand. Her breath came harder as she parted the leaves and peered at the Anglos.

Rafael burst through the trees like a tornado.

Sky didn't even take the one, quick instant she wanted to see shock freeze the Anglos' faces. That was the time they were least likely to shoot at Rafael, the time he would need her least.

He fired his rifle, then his pistol, and someone

else fired in the next heartbeat while she darted to High Wolf and slashed, slashed again, at the rope that tied his hand, until it fell away.

Another gun fired, a different sound from Rafael's, and then another. And another.

She did not dare look to see if Rafael was hit. She slapped the handle of her knife into High Wolf's palm and met the quick, astonished look in his eyes, then pulled back into cover, grabbing an arrow from her quiver as she darted behind a tree.

While she was nocking the arrow she threw her shoulder against the tree's trunk and peered out through its leaves.

Rafael was out in the open clearing, exposed, reloading, using both hands, keeping El Lobo weaving and dodging with his knees, holding his big body low to the horse while he tried to stay between High Wolf and his captors. High Wolf had almost cut through the other rope.

Rafael's rifle had driven the Anglos into hiding. A gun flashed behind him, near a tree that still held a lot of green.

"Give up, Montoya!" somebody shouted. "We've got you outnumbered and you don't stand a chance!"

Sky jumped to one side to give her a better sight and pulled back on the string. Her arrow hit the shooter—she heard a scream—but before she could nock another arrow, more bullets came flying.

A bullet whined past High Wolf's head and he slammed himself to the ground.

"Hold your fire! Montoya's gun's jammed!

Let's take him alive—he's the one with the treasure vision!"

El Lobo whirled in a circle, his long tail flying out all around him.

Three of the Anglos rushed out of the trees in a blur of blue cloth and white skin and black hats. To try to pull Rafael down.

Sky screamed.

She launched herself out of the trees and into the clearing.

Straight into the arms of one of the Anglos who turned in mid-stride and caught her.

Screams rolled out of her throat, over and over again, sounding like someone else's, as she kicked and bit and scratched and hit, bucking her body up and down to shove the arrows on her back into his face. She tried to stab him with the end of her bow.

But his arms around her waist were like a trap.

Until El Lobo surged toward them, then veered away and Rafael's rifle butt came crashing down onto her captor's head. He fell as if he were dead, dragging her down with him.

"Don't fire! Hold your fire!" Mr. Waters screamed. "Get 'em alive; they can find the treasure!"

The hateful, clutching hands fell away from her, she scrabbled out from under the man, still holding her bow. High Wolf roared up from the ground and ran toward her.

The other three men, one with blood on his shirt, surged toward her, too, but Rafael whirled El Lobo around, went plunging right through them, then came back around, reaching for Sky, yelling at High Wolf, holding one hand down. And down.

He grasped her shoulder, picked her up and threw her across El Lobo's withers in front of him. As the stallion gathered his rear under him to get ready to charge away, she sensed High Wolf running, vaulting up onto El Lobo's rump.

She clung there, her face against the pumping, gray shoulder, but she did not see even a glimpse of the horse. Or one tree, one limb or one leaf on their way.

Because her vision was filled with the sight of Rafael's white shirt—the place at the back of his waist the size of her hand that was soaking in blood.

A white-hot flame burst into life inside her. He would not die. She would not let him die.

Then the triple-burdened stallion was crashing through more trees and into the copse where they'd left Far Girl and Rafael was letting Sky slide to the ground. She snatched the rein up and threw it at her mare's neck, slinging herself into the saddle just in time to go roaring out of the valley beside El Lobo.

Rafael's dark eyes flashed at her, to make sure she was coming.

Far Girl was running from the moment Sky got her seat and before they had left the thickest trees, the mare was moving as fast as the burdened El Lobo.

"Get ahead of us!" Rafael shouted, and although she shook her head no, he dropped back until she did.

"You're hurt!" she yelled, looking back over her shoulder. "I need to watch our backs . . ."

"They want you most of all!" he yelled at her with a fierce flash of his eyes. "Get in front!"

A horse whinnied, somewhere behind them, and then came the sounds of hooves.

Sky threw herself prone along Far Girl's neck and gave the mare her head. She would lead the way, then, and pick the fastest going for the stallion, because he had to carry the extra weight. She would not think about covering their backs nor about Rafael's wound—nor about the ambush of soldiers waiting for Windrider—until they were far enough ahead to stop for a moment.

Until then, she would pray to the All-Father that High Wolf had the strength left in his wrists to press on Rafael's wound and hold down the bleeding, which he would do if he could, jealous rival or not, because now he owed Rafael his life. And she would pray that both of them would be able to ride, and ride hard, for they had to be a long way to the east on their way to warn her people when Father Sun came up tomorrow.

A shot sounded from behind them.

She felt, rather than saw, El Lobo pick up speed, and Far Girl did, too. The ground sloped ahead, down through thinner brush and trees to the flatter land in front of the mesa. Rocks lay in thick spills in the low places; scattered trees grew along the higher ones.

Far Girl threaded her way among all the dangers, El Lobo at her heels, and when they hit the easier going, both horses gave a new burst of strength that Sky did not know they had. She led the way to the east and south, back toward the Canyon of the Springs.

The white flame in her belly consumed her. She had to find a place where she could see to Rafael's wound.

And she had to get them onto the trail to forewarn her father.

After they rounded the end of a large, stone bluff that jutted out from the mesa's wall like a giant's pointed finger, the one with the ledge where they'd been when they saw that High Wolf was captured, the sounds of shots and shouts behind them faded away.

Sky sat back and signaled Far Girl to slow. The gathering, rising wind lifted and swirled around them as the mare came down to a trot. Sky turned around in her saddle.

"Stop, now!" she called. "We have to bind that wound and then we'll get Pabo out of her hiding place for High Wolf to ride—we can be out onto the top of the mesa and headed east by dark."

High Wolf threw up his head and stared at her.

"The *top* of the mesa? Headed *east*?"

She stared back.

"Of course—you didn't understand the English!" she cried. "High Wolf, those Anglos are

Waters and his men and they said they'll have
soldiers waiting at the ranch for Windrider!"

For an instant, he said nothing.

"With their huge rolling guns!" she said.

Then, in an anguished, frantic voice she'd
never heard from him before, High Wolf called
back to her, over the sounds of the hooves.

"You were right, Pretty Sky. I should've left
you yesterday and gone to warn him."

El Lobo caught up with her.

"We'll all go," she said, "as soon as . . ."

High Wolf held his hand pressed over
Rafael's wound. A slow trickle of blood came
out between his fingers.

"As soon as we stop that bleeding!" she
exclaimed.

"It isn't so much . . ." Rafael said, but on the
last word he sucked in a great gulp of air
because High Wolf took his hand from the
wound.

The blood ran faster.

Sky's back went weak with dread and she
stood in her stirrups to reach out to him, but
High Wolf's hands moved like lightning. He
pulled Sky's knife, the weapon that had freed
him, from his waist, cut the thin fabric of
Rafael's sleeve, tore it free, and wrapped it
around his rescuer's waist in a quick flow of
movement.

"Make it tight," Sky said, "and we'll wash
it in the healing springs before we take to the
trail."

"Water," Rafael said. "I need a drink of
water."

High Wolf reached down for the water bag hanging from the saddle. He opened it, held it to Rafael's mouth, tilted it upward.

Rafael took a long, deep swallow.

He nodded his thanks.

Then he fell forward. High Wolf crossed his arms and caught him.

Chapter 15

Sky stopped Far Girl in her tracks.

"We have to lay him down!" she cried, frantic fears beating in her veins like trapped butterflies. She started to dismount.

"Sit in your saddle," High Wolf said, "and ride."

He shifted Rafael to one side so he could take the reins from his lifeless hands. He smooched El Lobo into a long, fast trot and Sky had no choice but to follow.

"He needs a poultice!" she shouted, sending Far Girl up to his side at a lope. "I have slippery elm bark and powdered maize in my pouch!"

"But you have no boiling water, now, do you?" he yelled back.

She didn't answer, only pushed Far Girl to get closer to El Lobo so she could try to see Rafael's face through the cloud of dust they were raising.

"High Wolf, listen to me! Rafael is hurt bad!"

He kept the stallion at the same swift pace.

"And our people are in much trouble. We can't go to them until we take care of him, so we must ride fast to the healing waters of the springs."

"Thank you."

She looked up at High Wolf.

The blood had dried on his face, but his lip was split and his cheek rising in a terrible bruise.

"Oh, High Wolf, are you hurt too much to lift all the packs? I'm sorry I can't leave Rafael to help you!"

He smiled thinly.

"The packs won't weigh any more than your Spanish friend."

He turned and left her.

"Be careful!" she called after him. "The Anglos are still out there!"

He answered with an uplifted hand, but he didn't look back at her. She turned to her task of cutting the rest of Rafael's shirt from him and making smaller pieces of the clean parts of it.

Rafael just lay there, unmoving and silent beside the pool, which talked and chattered, bubbling out constantly to run down the sloping wall. The land was so dry that most of it soaked in before it reached the gravelly creekbed below.

Sky knelt beside him, keeping her eyes on him while holding the cloth in the fresh, barely warm water. When it was as warm as it would get, she added her herbs to make a medicinal poultice.

Before she applied it, though, she soaked loose the wrapped bandage and the shirt glued to Rafael's skin by his blood. She held her breath while she peeled them away.

Thank God!

The bullet had only barely caught him, from front to back, just above his waist, but it had left torn flesh and muscle, and evidently, a broken vein. As she watched, more blood flowed out of the wound.

His skin felt cool to her fingertips, but it was covered with sweat—even the blustery wind didn't dry it. His face was pale.

She washed the wound, applied her poultice, and dug deep into her pouch for the blood-staunching herbs. The second poultice contained a mixture of them and the healing waters. It stopped the blood.

Soon the color in his face improved, his breathing steadied, and his body felt warmer to her touch.

His body.

Even though she had slept with her arms around him only one night, one single night out of all the ones she had lived during her eighteen summers, his body felt as familiar to her as her own. She knew the bare, bronze skin, every inch of it, the bulge and ripple of his muscles and the fascinating, narrow valley that ran down his spine.

She knew the shape of him. Wide, wide shoulders tapering to his narrow waist and down to the slim hips, then the long, long power of his saddleman's legs, encased in black breeches and fine leather boots.

The Spanish horseman.

And horseman of the *Nermernuh*.

A picture flashed through her mind, of him

on El Lobo, riding out into the middle of the armed Anglos with the courage of a cougar. Even with this wound, he could ride. She knew it.

He *had* to be able to ride! The lives of her people—his people, too—depended on it.

She began to talk to him.

After a time that seemed much longer than it must actually have been, judging by the movement of Father Sun in the heavens, he turned his face from side to side on his folded arm and muttered, "Sky. Pretty Sky."

Her anxious fingers flew to his now-warm skin, stroked him gently.

"Yes," she murmured. "Yes, Rafael. I'm here."

Thank goodness. He was all right. He was coming to himself, and back to her, and he was all right.

He turned over. She helped him ease all the way down with one hand, holding the poultice over his wound with the other.

His dark-lashed eyes opened.

"Didn't I tell you never to do that again?" he demanded.

Panic pounded at her. Was he out of his mind?

"Do what? I have to put the poultice on you!"

"Run out into the middle of a fight! *Damn* it, Sky, when will you ever learn?"

Relief poured through her like a river.

"I guess I already have learned," she said, and grinned at him. "When that Anglo caught me, I swore I'd be a complete coward for the rest of my life."

"Well, it's about time!" he growled, and let his half-glazed eyes roam over her face.

Then he grinned, too, to show that he was only teasing, and her heart turned over.

"I didn't know if I'd ever see you smile again," she said. "It makes me very happy."

The corners of his mouth turned up even more.

"*You* make *me* happy," he said, and shook his head slowly, side to side in disbelief. "I never saw a woman like you, Sky. You are your own brave self."

"My brave self is alive because you rode in on your stallion and got me out of a lot of trouble."

He gave a hoarse chuckle and started to sit up.

"No!" she cried. "Please don't!"

She put her hands on his shoulders and leaned over him to hold him down.

He sat up anyway, moving with more strength than she thought could be possible.

"Don't you dare start the bleeding again when I've worked so hard to stop it!"

"It's stopped?"

"Of course!" she said. "That's what I set out to do, isn't it?"

He chuckled.

"Ysidora Pretty Sky," he said, and entangled her gaze in his hot, dark one.

He lifted his hand to brush back her hair.

Then he scooted backward a little way and

she helped him, still holding the poultice in place, so he could lean against the sloping bank of earth next to the burbling spring.

"What's this?" he said, and glanced down at his bare torso. "Have you been tearing my clothes off me?"

"Yes," she said, sitting down cross-legged beside him. Close to him. "While you were defenseless."

He gave her a slow smile.

Her heart turned over.

"I'm sorry I missed that," he said. "Next time, no matter how many times I'm shot, I intend to stay conscious."

Her throat constricted with the fearful memory.

"You're not going to get shot again," she told him in a fierce whisper. "Not ever!"

She leaned closer to him, tears suddenly standing in her eyes.

"Listen to me! Don't! Rafael, I could not bear it."

"Well, then, you had better not run out into the middle of any more gun battles," he muttered hoarsely.

She could not have moved away from him then, because of the look that came over his face, not even if the Anglos had been creeping up behind her.

"Dear God, Sky, I thought you were dead when I saw you burst out of the trees and then that . . . Anglo caught you in his arms," he said, huskily. "I never felt such rage rise up in me!"

He ran his hand into her hair, then, and took a handful of it, shaking her a little, bringing her face nearer to his.

"Such fear, too," he admitted. "I was so afraid for you."

His lips were close, so close to hers.

"Don't you ever do anything like that again, do you hear me?" he whispered.

"I hear you . . ." she said.

His eyes were clear, not dazed at all.

He was all right. He really was going to be all right.

Her head went dizzy with joy.

And with the nearness to him.

With the sight of him and the smell, with the touch of him.

She felt a smile take over her face.

". . . but I'm not making any promises," she finished, in a whisper that matched his.

The old dark fire flamed up in his eyes.

"Good," he said, barely breathing now. "No matter what I say, I don't want you ever to change. Never. Not one thing about you. You are a fantastic, fascinating woman, Ysidora Pretty Sky."

The wind lifted the pine branch above them, then dropped it with a restless sigh.

A warbling bird called an afternoon message from someplace high on the canyon's wall.

The spring murmured in her ear.

She loved him.

The thought burst from her heart whole and complete, eclipsing the panic and the worry that raged there. It took over her world.

She loved Rafael Montoya and she would never love any other man.

She loved him.

"It is good neither of you is on guard," High Wolf's caustic voice said. "Or the Anglos would have all three of us tied to trees, singing our death songs!"

Sky started, her heart pounding in sudden panic.

She had forgotten High Wolf existed.

She turned to see him.

He stood behind her, feet planted apart. In the distance, tails whipping in the rising wind, stood the horses, ground-tied by their reins.

Then she realized what he had said.

"Did you see sign of the Anglos?"

He gave a short nod.

"We didn't kill any of them," he said. "All four of them are circling, looking for a sign, down by the mouth of the canyon. We have to move now."

He looked at Rafael.

"Are you able to ride?"

"All the way to sundown and beyond."

"Good."

He looked down and noticed the healing paste that Sky had mixed on a clean piece of cloth. He went to it, dipped his fingers in and wiped some on each of his wrists and on the wounds on his face.

"Let me do that for you!" she cried, running to him. "I'll poultice you, too, before we go."

He pushed her hands away.

"I can take care of myself," he said, and

turned to look from her to Rafael and back.

Then High Wolf lifted his gaze and looked off into the distance. He seemed to be listening intently.

The wind, steadily growing stronger, whipped his scalp lock across his battered face.

"I brought all the packs," he said, then, "but we'll be hindered by having only three horses for three people and all these supplies. Quick, we must open and remake them; some things we'll have to abandon."

But instead of going to the packs, he walked over to where Rafael was sitting against the bank of earth. Sky followed.

High Wolf squatted down so that his face was on a level with Rafael's.

The two men looked at each other.

Sky stared at High Wolf in surprise. It was considered rude by the *Nermernuh* to look another person directly in the eye, and High Wolf was always very polite, but he did it, now, as if to make sure that Rafael was listening.

"When the packs are redone," he said, "you and Sky hole up in the other side of this canyon until you heal a bit. I will ride alone to carry warning of the soldiers to Windrider."

Rafael cocked his head to one side and looked hard at him.

"What has made you decide this?"

Shocked, Sky went closer to listen.

"My medicine. When the signs came to Pretty Sky, the rainbow cliff and the arrow trees, I knew that she was right, but I wouldn't admit it. I forgive her, now, for running off irresponsibly into the hills with you, a stranger."

He didn't even glance at Sky, he kept his eyes fixed on Rafael's.

"You and Pretty Sky go and find the treasure and stop this war," he said. "My people are hungry. They need peace."

"Yes."

High Wolf continued as if Rafael had not spoken.

"Another reason I go is that when you took the Anglo bullet, Pretty Sky ran out into the gunfire to try to help you. Even later, as we rode away, she lost her mind, she could not think, she lost her color, she could not find her strength."

Sky's whole body went still. What was he leading up to? High Wolf *couldn't* have read her mind.

But he had.

"Ysidora Pretty Sky loves you," High Wolf said, flatly, "and not me."

He stood up, then, and raised his voice to a formal tone as if speaking to Council. He lifted his fist to Father Sun. He was taking an oath.

"I give her to you, Rafael Montoya. I give you Ysidora Pretty Sky. You are the one that she loves."

Sky froze to the spot where she stood, the whole inside of her body went cold as winter. Yet summer-hot embarrassment came flooding through her, too.

How *dare* High Wolf say such a thing? How did he even *know* it? She herself had known it only a few minutes.

And how dare he try to give me away as if I were a dog or a horse or a song or a saddle?

That might happen to all the other women she knew, but not to her. Her father and mother would not permit it, and neither would she. That was how she had come to choose High Wolf for herself.

She waited for Rafael to say that High Wolf had never been Sky's owner, to say that a man could not own a woman.

That a woman could not be bought or given away.

But Rafael said nothing.

"I am *not* yours to give!"

She tore her moccasins loose from the ground and pushed in between them, her blood roaring like thunder in her ears.

"I am not a piece of property to be given from one man to another! I belong to myself and my feelings belong to me! When they need to be spoken, I will speak them—I have a tongue in my mouth!"

She put her hands on her hips and glared furiously from one of them to the other, but tears of rage began to boil up in her eyes and she could not see.

"And this is what my tongue says," she cried, fighting with all her strength to keep her weeping from her voice, "I do not belong to any man. I do not love any man, and I will not marry any man!"

She swallowed hard.

"Not only have you tried to give me away like a buffalo robe, High Wolf," she said, and whipped around to face Rafael, "but you, Rafael, have not said one word, such as you did in Council—that a woman might have something wise to say! How can someone who can say wise things be given away like some parfleche?"

He looked at her.

Then he looked at High Wolf.

"Thank you," he said. "I will take care of her."

"You will not! I can take care of myself!"

Tiny ice crystals began to form around the roaring conflagration that used to be her heart.

No. Rafael had not answered her, because, of course, he agreed with High Wolf. Any man, *every* man, Comanche or Spanish or Comanche-raised-to-be-Spanish, believed that his woman was his possession.

The breath went out of her body. God, the All-Father had to help her.

Because she did love Rafael.

Chapter 16

High Wolf led their little parade deeper into the Canyon of the Springs and up a rocky cut that took them into the mesa at angle toward the sky, along a path that would hold no tracks. They rode over the top and down the other side far enough that they wouldn't be outlined for the Anglos against the moonlight. He slowed his horse and Sky rode up beside him.

The wind swirled the dust at their horses' feet, bent the few tufts of short grass toward them, then away. The faint light of Sister Moon made them look silver, but they were really blue-gray from the drought.

The drought.

A stillness fell on her mind in spite of the moving fingers of the wind, picking at her hair, lifting the fringes of her sleeves. The drought. The drought and the wind.

Then she knew, as surely as if the words had been spoken in her ear.

This wind carried the smell of moisture.

And with it, just once in a while before it shifted back to come from the south, it held the promise of the pine-covered mountains far to the north.

"High Wolf!" she said. "You must ride fast."

"Like the coming storm," he said, turning his head to smell the air. "We will see much snow. I was going to say it."

The freshening wind whipped his hair around his face. The braided scalp lock fell in front of his shoulder.

"From here you remember how to go to the hot springs?" he demanded.

"Yes. Where we camped when we came north the last time to cut lodge poles."

"Yes. Get him into one of the caves near the springs tonight—before the Anglos come this far."

She shivered. He was leaving her, at last.

With a blizzard coming.

"Thanks for bringing us this far, High Wolf," Rafael said, weakly, swaying in his saddle.

"*De nada*, Montoya," High Wolf said. "You saved my life."

"Ride safe."

"And you. Take care of Pretty Sky."

"I will."

High Wolf inclined his head toward Rafael.

"He will not be able to ride far for three or four suns," he said. "And by then the snow will be deep. The old ones say that the hot springs never freeze. With water and the caves you will be safe."

Suddenly Sky felt totally bereft. Alone, she would have to keep Rafael, at the moment barely able to sit up and ride, herself and two horses hidden from the Anglos and the coming storm.

It was hard to believe that, an hour ago, she had been furious with High Wolf for assuming he could give her away. And that, only one sun ago, she had been begging him to leave.

But she couldn't ask him to stay, even if he would. Windrider needed him far more than she.

The fate of The People rode with him.

"Are you sure you took enough of the food?" she asked. Her voice trembled.

"I have all I will need," he said, and gave an ironic little laugh. "All I can eat while riding night and day."

A gust of warm wind blew his words away. It had already switched to come out of the west.

To blow across the restless land, into the canyons and cuts and up onto the huge mesa.

"Hurry," Sky said. "I can do this. Go find my father ahead of the snow."

He turned in the saddle and sniffed the air.

"It may be another day away."

Then, to her surprise, he reached out and touched her hair once, like the brush of a bird's wing, as he reined Pabo away.

"Thank you for your horse."

"Be kind to her."

"I will."

Without another word and without looking back, he picked up into a trot again and rode away, angling down to the south and east, ready to climb up again and across the top of the mesa looking for the faraway place wherever it was that Windrider had chosen to make the new camp.

"The All-Father go with you," she whispered.

Then she turned her face to the way she and Rafael would go, a trail that led south and west, deeper into the mesa's side. She pulled Far Girl up beside El Lobo, looked to make sure Rafael's hands gripped the ropes of his pack.

"Can you ride at a trot? We have to hurry, the Ánglos may not sleep and a storm is coming."

"Neither of those things scares me half as much as you do," he said, his voice a bit unsteady. "That was quite a tongue-lashing you gave us back there. I can't believe you let High Wolf go without flogging the skin off his back!"

Then he gave her his low, delicious chuckle to show that he was only teasing.

Its dauntlessness tore at her heart.

And made her angry all over again.

"I hope you listened carefully to every word I lashed you with," she said, starting the horses off at a slow trot, "because I meant them."

"High Wolf meant his words, too. And he gave you to me."

"And you to me," she shot back. "He told me to get you into a cave near the hot springs down in this canyon. Be careful what you say or I'll put you in the hot springs near a cave."

He threw back his head and laughed.

But then he stopped abruptly, swaying dizzily, gallantly clamping his knees to the horse to hold on.

"Lean forward onto the pack," she urged.

"No," he said, and shifted his knees to get a better grip. "I just want you to know, Ysidora Pretty Sky, that I did not mean to insult you by accepting you as a gift. It was the only thing to do—conceding that you would never marry him can't be easy for a man like High Wolf."

All anger left her.

"You must admit," he went on, "that he was putting your feelings ahead of his own."

A stab of regret ran through her.

"That's true," she said. "I hadn't thought of it that way."

She glanced at him again, trying to see his face in the weak moonlight. He was riding only through the strength of his knees and his innate sense of balance. El Lobo was aware of that; he moved carefully beneath the double load of his master and the large pack of supplies.

Sky's heart came into her mouth. Hurry. She had to hurry.

The canyon widened at the next turn, and the wind swept more of the moonlight in. It washed the east side to the smoky yellow color of elkskin, as if changing the rock and earth into sheltering tipi walls to surround them.

A lodge where they could weather the storm.

If Rafael didn't pass out again and fall off his horse before she could get him into its shelter.

El Lobo trotted up closer beside Far Girl, then slowed, rolling his gleaming eye back at

Sky as if to ask what was wrong with Rafael. She took hold of his bridle and kept them moving down and down toward the faint sound of running water.

Rafael sat loose in the saddle, holding his reins on top of his bulky pack, not trying to talk any more. She leaned sideways to try to see if his wound was bleeding again, but she couldn't see it at all.

And they couldn't stop now. The rising wind was pushing them.

On the steeper places she stood in her stirrups to help balance him, torn between slowing the horses for fear he would fall and hurrying them for fear he would lose consciousness again. Finally they reached the bottom and turned straight to the south.

Sister Moon caught the sparkle of water, moving water, on the wall. Just below it, almost at the bottom, ran a long, dark line that must be the overhanging ledge she remembered. There was a cave beneath it.

A great, pent-up breath that she didn't know she was holding released itself from Sky's lungs. Soon she could get Rafael off the horse and let him rest. Soon he would regain his strength and talk to her and she wouldn't feel so alone.

She smooched to the horses.

It wouldn't be long until they were safe. It wouldn't be long until they were safe.

She hurried them faster, then, murmuring that comfort to the rhythm of their steps.

Sister Moon's full, yellow body was rising

higher, lifting on the wind to ride the night heavens. Clouds blew across her and away, then came back again.

At the north end of the ledge, Sky stopped the horses and leapt to the ground. Rafael muttered something incomprehensible, placed both hands on the bundle in front of him, and pushed himself to stand in the stirrup.

Then he collapsed into his seat again.

"Don't move, Rafael! Wait right there! Sit still!"

Her fingers slipped and shook on the rawhide ties, but after an age she got her thin blanket bedroll loose and ran to spread it on the sparse grassy cover of the earth just north of the ledge. No lying under its overhang or going into its cave tonight, not even to get out of the wind. Any wild animal could be hiding there and she wouldn't know it in the dark.

She led El Lobo to stand beside the blanket.

"Now," she said. "Get down now, Rafael, and I'll help you."

He stood in the stirrup, lifted his other leg over the pack behind his saddle, and half fell, half slid to the ground. Sky took as much of his weight as she could, her arms around his waist.

Terrified that he might have torn open his wound, she helped him onto the blanket.

"Lie still," she said, and knelt over him, lifted the edge of his jacket to look. The moss-packed bandage was still in place, and dry around the edges.

Her eyes filled with tears. Thank the All-Father.

His skin was cool to her touch, though. She had seen wounded men lose all their body's warmth and then die, even after their bleeding had stopped.

She had tied his coat around him by the sleeves to keep him from being chilled by the wind. Now she removed it so the warm wool could lie against his skin, put her other blanket over him, and dashed to do the necessary chores.

The packs and saddles she piled beside the blanket at the north end of the ledge; the horses she led to the large, shallow dish of rock which held the pool formed by the running water and left them hobbled to drink and graze. They couldn't go far.

Stopping only long enough on the way back to pull her water bag from her saddle, she returned to Rafael.

Taking off his boots was a bit of a struggle because she had to be so careful not to pull hard enough to hurt him, but she accomplished it. Then she took off her moccasins.

She lifted the top blanket and crawled into bed beside him. He lay on his good side, as she'd left him, facing the wall of the mesa.

Her buffalo robe was too heavy and loaded too deep in the pack. Being too warm might make him sicker, nearly as sick as being too cool, and the night was humid, hot for this time in the fall when the *Yubauhi Mua*, the Leveling-Toward-Winter Moon was coming.

No, her body heat would be just right to warm him.

Then she pulled the blanket up over her shoulder, scooted close, and wrapped her arms and legs around him. His body fitted perfectly into the curve of hers.

"Sky?" he muttered, and shifted his arm to lay it over hers. "The Anglos . . ."

"Shhh," she said, snuggling her face into the hollow between his shoulder blades, barely touching his skin with her lips. "We outran the Anglos. They don't know this place. We're safe here."

"Mmmhm," he agreed, and pushed his small, muscled buttocks more firmly into her lap. "Safe."

Desire tantalized her, came rushing through all her senses, but she pushed it away. He was wounded, exhausted, and she had used up every scrap of strength that she had.

Since she had slept, one entire sun and almost all of its night had passed. She had searched for the treasure and for High Wolf, had fought the Anglos and Rafael's injury, High Wolf's arrogance and the moon-shadowed trail through the night.

Since she had slept, she had fallen in love.

With a man who *was* different from other men, after all. A man who could see into other people's hearts.

"Sky?" he said, again, in that slow, satisfied way.

The way that said he already knew it was she.

And that he had been expecting her to come to him.

He closed his hand around hers and pressed her arm against his side. She could feel his skin gaining her warmth.

For a long time she lay awake with her fingers twined through his long, callused ones, hearing his heart beat deep within his hard body, remembering how he had looked at her when he told her that he never wanted her to change.

Watching the moon float among the ragged, scudding clouds.

He loved her, too.

He'd called her name in his sleep; he'd known she was there. He loved her, too.

A small, cool shiver went through her.

He did love her, she knew it, the same way she knew that the treasure was real.

And she loved him. She would love only him and no other man, and she would love him forever.

But could they live together? Would they go with her people or his?

Either was beyond imagining.

Could she actually be his wife and still be herself? Could she bear to live in only one place?

The very thoughts amazed her, sent a thousand pictures flying through her mind. She closed it against them.

This was enough. This moment, this peace, after all that they'd been through, was enough.

"Sky," he murmured.

She turned her face into his naked back, pressed her cheek to his warm skin, and slept.

Sky woke to high yellow sunlight, a south wind driving puffs of white clouds across brilliant blue heavens, a babbling waterfall, and an empty blanket beside her. At first she couldn't put all that together.

Then the memories raced through her.

Rafael! He was hurt.

She threw off her cover and sat up.

Her gaze swept the side of the canyon, found the horses grazing, the waterfall from the warm springs, its pool, the packs where she'd piled them, but disarranged. And smoke, curling out from beneath the long overhang of rock.

She got up and ran barefoot through the thin grass downslope to look.

Beneath the stone roof he sat cross-legged beside a fire, looking out over the shallow stream below, drinking from one of his tin cups. A cooking rack held a bubbling pot.

"Rafael!"

He turned and smiled, raised his hand to salute her with the cup.

"*Buenos días, Señorita!* Want some chocolate?"

She walked toward him, her heart lifting. He was all right. Truly he was.

"You are tougher than the hide of a buffalo bull," she said, and she could hear the happiness in her own voice. "How can you lose so much blood and still have so much strength?"

"I have a good medicine woman."

The low, rich timbre of his voice made a thrill run down her spine.

"And you no longer need servants at all, I see. Poor Tonio. What're you cooking?"

"My famous cornmeal mush. This time, I've added dried persimmons."

She laughed. "You're a natural cook—very inventive."

Her bare feet moved off the grass onto the worn earth beneath the ledge. It felt smooth as the satin of her Spanish dress. Silky as Rafael's hair.

"Sit," he said. "Have some."

His dark eyes twinkled into hers.

"Rafael, do you really feel this good? Has your wound bled any more?"

"Yes. No."

He gave her a long, grateful look.

"I'm very lucky. The bullet went all the way through and you knew how to stop the blood. Thank you, Sky."

She met his suddenly solemn gaze.

"*De nada.*"

He smiled and her arms went weak.

"I'm strong because I have been eating my own delicious cooking since early this morning. I thought you were going to sleep all day."

She managed to take her eyes from him long enough to pick up her bowl, fill it from the pot, and begin to eat.

"I almost did," she said, between hearty

bites. The warmth of the food flowed through her body, leaving the tastes of the corn and the fruit tangy on her tongue.

Rafael sipped his chocolate, his eyes on her face.

"Don't you like it?" he said.

"It's delicious," she said, laughing a little at his eagerness for praise. "Soon you'll be cooking whole feasts."

"Yes," he said, laughing, "whole feasts of cornmeal mush and chocolate, since I don't know how to make anything else."

She hardly knew what he answered, or what she said to him as they bantered back and forth. His bare torso caught the gleam of the fire, his eyes reflected it.

She wanted to reach out and touch him.

"I've seen no sign of the Anglos," he said, as she finished eating and took a drink of her chocolate. "Nor of snow. I think you and High Wolf were wrong."

"No. High Wolf may be right that it's a day away, but I'm thinking it'll come sooner."

He looked at her over the rim of the cup.

"It's too warm! The weather's beautiful! And we need to bathe in the springs."

His voice vibrated, low and warm, filled with sensual overtones.

The center of her sprang to life.

She set down her cup, pretended to frown.

"*We*? Are you telling me that I need a bath?"

"I wouldn't dare say *that* to the woman with the powerful tongue," he said, with his mischievous grin. "I say only that I feel grimy and sticky from dried blood, that I need someone to wash my back for me."

His grin widened. "And High Wolf gave you to me."

"He did *not!*"

She pretended to hit at him, he caught her wrist. Then he reached for the other one.

"Will you come willingly?"

"If not, then I won't come at all," she said, dropping her voice to a fierce little growl and narrowing her eyes.

"Ah! The dangerous *Señorita* Pretty Sky, scourge of Anglo rancheros and arrogant Comanche medicine men who dare to try to give her away! The very same who threatened to put me into a hot spring!"

"I can do it, too!"

Suddenly he was up, laughing, tugging her to her feet.

"Let's see if you can!"

She chased him out of the shadows and into the sunshine, her feet flying along with her heart at the thought he was actually able to do such a thing. He ran a bit awkwardly, and held his hand to his side, but he was still too fast for her to catch.

They ran up toward the waterfall that cascaded down from the springs high above in the canyon wall, past the grazing horses who threw up their heads to stare, to the edge of the pool that caught and held the warm water before it ran on down into the stream below.

On the edge of the natural rock bowl, he stopped.

"This is your chance!" he yelled above the noise of the water.

He set his feet firmly on the slippery stone and, when she ran to him, took her shoulders into his big hands.

"See if you can make good on your threat!"

She put her palms against his broad chest, marveling at the power under her hands. Even setting her heels against the rock and pushing with all her might, she couldn't budge him at all.

"It's not a fair contest!" she shouted up at him.

"Oh?" he chortled, grinning down at her. "Is the great Ysidora Pretty Sky, medicine woman, complaining?"

He put his hands on her upper arms, picked her up, and set her back from the water.

"Not at all! I mean it's not fair because you're wounded," she shouted, over the rush of the gentle waterfall. "I'm afraid I'll hurt you!"

He looked surprised for an instant, then threw back his head and bellowed with laughter. He pulled her toward him.

He put his lips to her ear because of the roar of the water.

"You're wrong," he said, and the old dark fire blazed up in his eyes. "It's not fair because you're still wearing your clothes."

"So are you."

"Only half of them."

Spray from the water gleamed in scattered drops all over his naked upper body. She reached up onto his shoulder and lifted one onto her fingertip, brought it to the tip of her tongue.

His eyes burned hotter, his gaze on her mouth.

"You see I wear only half my clothes," he murmured, "and you're a person who believes what's fair for a man is fair for a woman."

He caressed her arms, all the way down to the tips of her fingers, then back up them, this time to come down the sides of her body.

His hands stopped on each side of her waist, slipped beneath her loose blouse and slid up over her skin.

His eyes never let hers escape from their hot darkness.

"You tore my clothes off me," he said, huskily. "I intend to do the same to you."

She trembled. Never, never, should she have played this game with him.

She had to stop him.

Now that she knew she loved him, and that she would never love anyone else, all she wanted was to keep him with her forever. If he made love to her again, that wanting would consume her.

What would ever happen to them?

His hard hands moved slowly, ever more slowly, up and up, caressing her skin, thumbs circling, setting the center of her body on fire.

Making her mind dizzy. She tried not to feel, tried to think.

If . . . if he couldn't leave his home and come to ride with her over the plains, if . . . she couldn't live all her life in one place, then shouldn't she take all she could of him now?

To make memories?

He slid his hands up and cupped her breasts, squeezed them gently. His thumbs brushed across their begging tips.

Yes. Memories.

Live this moment to the fullest, this moment with her heart's companion, her kindred spirit. This moment when she couldn't remember what lonely meant.

Her back arched toward him, but his hands went away. They found the bottom of her blouse and pulled it over her head, brought it slipping down off her arms.

He stood back and looked at her, his gaze so hot that she barely felt the cool of the wind.

Every nerve in her body, every inch of her skin, tingled, waiting for his touch.

"Sky," he muttered. "You are the most beautiful woman in all the world."

His hands reached for her again.

Yes! This moment might be all they would ever have.

She walked past him, threw him a look over her shoulder. Then she stepped over the rim of the rock bowl and into the pool.

He threw her blouse away and came after her, reaching for her.

She darted into the waterfall and he followed.

"Aha!" she said, smiling up at him through the wonderful, warm water. "You are in the pool of the hot springs, *Señor*, and I have put you there!"

He thrust both his hands into her hair and turned her face up to his mouth.

"And I have put *you* in the bath, *Señorita* Medicine Woman!" he murmured against her lips. "Is that not so?"

She couldn't answer. She couldn't move, she couldn't breathe. She'd crumple onto the smooth stone beneath her feet if he weren't holding her up.

Playfully, he rubbed her hair, her back, her shoulders, teasing, as if he were scrubbing her clean.

But soon every touch turned to a slow, fierce caress, daringly deliberate—and exactly, entirely right.

Both his hands, both his big, magical hands, wise hands knew what she wanted next the moment before she quite knew it herself. They moved in loving circles over her ribs and slowly, slowly, up to her breasts.

They slid through the water pouring over them, their hard calluses coming through its slickness to rouse every inch of her skin, every drop of the blood in her veins.

She lifted her face for his kiss.

Chapter 17

But his mouth would only torment hers, barely brushing her pleading, parted lips. The tip of his tongue darted to meet her own beseeching one for no more than a heartbeat.

Then he was raining kisses, quick, light, possessive little kisses all over her face, upturned in the streaming waterfall, while his hands did away with her skirt, with his breeches. She was all his, his hands told her when they had thrown away the clothes and come back to her.

All his.

And he was hers, she answered, thrusting her fingers into his wet hair, standing on tiptoe to crush her cheek against his, grinding their cheekbones together beneath their sliding wet skins. Then her mouth found his and they were lost in each other, together again instead of alone.

Her tongue, his tongue found each other, met, danced away, came back again to entwine, to explore, to call up, from inside her, from inside him, all the flashing flames of desire. They whipped them into a blaze.

His mouth slid away from hers, but the conflagration raged hotter. His lips slipped down over her throat, down and down to her breast.

Instinctively she arched her body into the warm, running water, went up on tiptoe to make it easier for him. Every part of her body came alive as it never had been before, opened to him.

Rafael.

Her hands slid down the sides of his neck, its muscles flexing as he sucked the very strength from her body. They fell onto the breadth of his shoulders, clung there.

He cradled her hips in his palms, crushed her against him, lifted her up and fitted himself into her.

With a cry of delight, she brought him in, wrapped her arms and legs around him and moved with him in a rhythm old as the mountain they had run to for refuge. She buried her face in the hollow of his neck, in the clean wetness of his hair and bit the fragrant skin pulsing there until she tasted the copper sweetness of his blood.

Rafael.

She loved Rafael.

"Kiss me," he moaned, his lips against her ear, and she did.

Then, mouth on mouth and skin against skin, they threw themselves into pleasuring each other, holding on to each other until all the loneliness was gone.

Until they spiraled higher and higher into the limitless heavens like smoke from the fire they had built on the water.

*   *   *

When they walked slowly back to their bed through that blue, wind-whipped day, naked arms and hips touching at every step, ready to rest and let the sun dry their skins, Rafael leaned over and kissed her, long and deep.

When they untied the packs in the cave that ran back into the canyon's wall beneath the ledge where their fire was still burning, Sky redressed Rafael's wound, wrapping a clean strip of cloth tight around him. Then she spread out the buffalo robes, lay down on them, and lifted her arms to him.

At last, when Father Sun was slipping toward the earth again, and the wind was turning cold, Rafael raised up on one elbow and looked at her. Lazily, she smiled at him.

"I hate to trouble you, *Señorita*," he said, smiling back, "but I feel hungry enough to eat every bite of the buffalo who used to wear this robe. I would ask my servants to cook, but they are not here. I would do it—I have been told by someone whose opinion I treasure that my corn and persimmon mush is delicious— but I need to start bringing in some wood."

Sky laughed and laid her finger across his lips to stop the silly spate of words.

"So," she said. "You have decided that I'm right after all—that the snow is coming?"

He flashed his wry grin.

"This wind is starting to make me a believer," he said.

"You can't carry wood," she said, her fingers instinctively going to the fresh bandage and finding it dry. "I'll do it."

She sat up and reached for her dry buckskins, still folded from the pack. Then she whipped around to look out and see if the storm was coming soon.

Outside the broad cave opening that ran beneath the rock overhang, the sky was still that brilliant blue—that marvelous color so bright that it seemed to draw a person into its richness to fly away like an eagle.

She sighed in relief and jumped up to start throwing on her clothes.

"Oh, Rafael, you made me forget all about the weather!" she cried. "We have so much to do before the blizzard comes. It'll take a lot of firewood so we won't freeze."

When he didn't move, she turned to look at him. He lay exactly where she had left him, still propped on his elbow, his eyes devouring her.

"We won't freeze," he drawled, his voice barely louder than a husky whisper. "We proved that this morning, Ysidora Pretty Sky."

A trembling thrill ran through her, in spite of how sated she had felt only a few moments ago. She went to him, bent over, and kissed him as she tied on her skirt.

He ran his hand up under her blouse.

"Stop that!" she said, laughing. "You're the one who's crying hunger."

"I am," he said. He held her gaze with his dark eyes and refused to let it go.

"The *other* kind of hunger!"

She touched the high bone of his cheek.

"If you aren't afraid of freezing, then be afraid of starving," she said. "Go and learn to make dried meat stew instead of mush."

Still he wouldn't move. His eyes roamed up and down her body while she pulled her hair back and braided it quickly, then tied it with a blue ribbon from her pack.

"As long as I'm with you," he said, his voice low and rich inside the cave, "I'll neither freeze *nor* starve."

Sky melted to her knees beside him, her body wet again, suddenly, with wanting, and bent to kiss his cheek.

"I will not kiss your lips just now or I'll be back on the robes with you. Don't tempt me, Rafael. Remember, you won't be in your thick-walled hacienda when this blizzard comes."

He took her by the braid and kissed her mouth once, hard, and then got up and went to his things to look for more clothes. Sky watched him instead of going for wood.

She loved him so much that it hurt her heart.

Rafael got his way. While Sky cooked the dried beef stew and cleaned their wooden bowls, Rafael dragged in loop after loop full of wood in his rope from the back of El Lobo, who was completely insulted at being put to such work.

While they ate, Father Sun began to come and go behind the stringy, slate-colored clouds that blew across the bright sky. The wind began to shift more often, back and forth in every direction, its restlessness becoming almost a frenzy.

More and more, its breath was cold.

"We don't have long to wait," Sky said, as soon as they had filled themselves with hot food. "Far Girl and I will help you and El Lobo. The snow could blow for three or four suns and their nights."

They filled one end of the cave, just inside the long opening, to the ceiling over Rafael's head with dead branches, pinecones, and sticks for kindling. Finally, Sky glanced at the heavens and jumped down from Far Girl's back.

"Enough," she said. "Let's go see if there's room at the back of the cave if we need to bring the horses inside."

"I hope we don't," Rafael teased, "El Lobo is too much of a grouch for us to live with him through a blizzard."

Sky ran to pet the restive stallion.

"Oh, what a terrible thing to say about such a hard worker!"

She patted his neck and crooned to him as Rafael slipped the bridle off and turned him loose.

"You won't be a grouch if you don't have to drag in any more wood, will you, boy?" she called after him.

He answered her with a rumble deep in his throat, tossed his head as if only partly mollified, and kicked and bucked his way ahead of the storm toward the patches of grass that grew below the pool. Far Girl followed.

Sky piled more stones on the side of their fire next to the cave opening to protect it from the wind while Rafael put their tack away, then he lit a torch and they began to explore their new home.

"I'll let you go first," Sky teased. "In case there's a bear or a cougar living back here."

"Before we moved in, I told you there wasn't."

"You only looked in our room beneath the overhang! You didn't come through that opening, at all!"

She pointed to, then led the way to a low, arching doorway in the back wall, deep in their cave. There she stopped.

"I came in here but not beyond," he contradicted her, bending his head to go into another, smaller room. Suddenly the torch was the only light they had.

He put his arm around her.

She leaned into it.

"When I came in here the first time," he said, "I heard water running and felt a breeze from back in the hillside, so I know there's fresh air coming in from somewhere. This can be the bunkhouse for our four-legged friends."

"Good. *If* El Lobo doesn't stomp and kick the walls and scream that he is not a donkey and shouldn't be made to work like one."

They looked into each other's eyes, in the light from the torch and laughed, more than the joke was worth, just because they were laughing together. Over a shared memory made here, in this place that was only theirs.

When they went on exploring, they kept hold of each other. They didn't find the running water, even when they had turned sideways and slipped, hand in hand, through the next opening into yet another room, but they did see light and they found the source of the breeze. This was a tunnel, connected to another, that led back to the same overhanging ledge near the warm waterfall.

Sky ran, and Rafael followed her out to its mouth, which curved higher than the wide entrance where they had built their fire.

They stood there looking out over the rugged, storm-threatened land. Their canyon fell away sharply to the south and west, but they were high up toward the huge mesa's rim and could see across it into the ever-changing sky. Toward the north, both west and east, they could see forever.

The clouds had begun to gather and roll, moved by the wind which was never still. But, also, Father Sun blazed against the blue, disappearing only from time to time behind their racing, feathery shadows.

All the world was red and tan earth and gray rock, blue sky and white and gray clouds and yellow sun. The wind spun it all into a bright ball of entrancement.

Rafael looked far out across the undulating land.

"From this spot, that valley with those tall rocks catching the sunlight and the trees scattering down into its heart looks like our *rancho* from the hill behind our *casa*."

The sudden mention of his home startled Sky, sent a little thread of coolness into her veins.

But he dropped his hand from pointing and laid his arm across her shoulders. The touch fired her blood and warmed her with a feeling of comfort at the same time.

"I like to ride up there and look down at it all," he went on. "In the fall, it looks wild and rough, but in the spring, the flowers bloom and it's soft as a bed. The difference always amazes me."

She leaned her head back into his shoulder, thinking about that.

"I don't know what it'd be like to live in the same place," she said. "I always thought it'd be tiresome not to see some new place every day."

"The same place *is* new every day," he said. "The light, the weather, the season, something is always different."

"But not as different as this mesa is from the wide, rolling prairies and the desert from the Cross-Timbers," she said.

"My *rancho* is," he said. "It has grasslands and mountains, forests and desert."

"Of course it does," she said, and suddenly her voice hardened until she was only half teasing him. "It, too, used to be part of Comancheria."

Neither of them spoke for a moment, then, by an unspoken agreement, they left the conversation there and stepped out into the intermittent sunshine.

Far Girl and El Lobo alternately munched at a bite of grass and then lifted their noses into the wind and ran, their manes and tails whipping around them. Their shadows came and went on the ground as Father Sun winked in and out of the restless roving of the clouds.

They were beginning, far in the northern sky, to gather and roil.

Sky looked to judge the straight distance between this cave opening and their fire.

"Look, Rafael, we can bring the horses in here instead of into the little room behind ours!" she cried. "It's only a short way from our fire from the outside, or, if the snow's too thick, we can come to them through the tunnel."

He glanced in the other direction, toward the falls where they had bathed.

"Good idea," he said. "It isn't far to water them in the warm pool, either."

"That'll work as long as El Lobo doesn't think we're taking him out to drag in more wood!"

"Then he can stay in and be thirsty. At least, with him all the way over here, we don't have to listen to him!"

Laughing, they turned back into the cave. Rafael held the light out in front; Sky followed him.

They reached the juncture with their first tunnel but this time they turned the other way, heading deeper into the side of the mesa. As soon as the path slanted down and the light facing them began to grow stronger, the goose bumps began to rise on Rafael's arms.

It was the same feeling he'd had on the trail.

Within a few steps they saw the tall, arched opening, and, almost running to keep their balance, they dashed down and down and through it into a huge central room. It was filled with sunlight.

In the middle of the floor was a sinkhole, roughly round and filled with rubble and small rocks and travertine deposits. They reflected the sunlight in every direction, throwing it back at the ceiling and onto the walls in all the bright colors of the rainbow.

The rainbow. Rafael felt every inch of his body go numb.

This was the lodge made of rainbows.

It was largest around at the bottom, its walls sloped upward and in toward a small circle in the center of the ceiling. A hole. Like the smoke hole in a tipi.

Through it, the sunlight streamed. Thank God the clouds were not blocking out the sun at this instant, or he might not have recognized the place.

The sunlight strengthened as they watched, the colors grew deeper and brighter. The walls seemed to catch fire, the rocks in the floor glowed like coals.

The lodge made of flaming rainbows.

He heard Sky catch her breath. She knew it, too.

She stood as still as he did, watching the light. Neither of them spoke.

Rafael ran his eyes over the whole place again.

Rocks. There was nothing there but rocks and dust and bat droppings and . . .

He turned around. His gaze went to a spot at

the right of the high arch where they came in.

A jumble of stones that looked no different from any others around the circle.

But above it, and he heard Sky's quick intake of breath again as soon as he saw it, on the wall, there was a shadow. A shadow thrown by something growing down, slanting at an angle from the ceiling.

A shadow shaped like a bird. An eagle.

With its beak pointing straight down.

He extended the torch to Sky without turning to look at her.

"Hold this," he said, and she took it.

He walked to the pile of rocks and sat down on his haunches. With both hands, carefully, he picked up the top rock and set it onto the floor.

Dust flew up into his face, but he only blew it away and picked up the next one.

There was a nest of smaller rocks beneath those.

As soon as he moved the first handful of them, the sun caught the dull gleam of the gold.

Then the torchlight wavered onto it and Sky peered over his shoulder.

The incredulous gasp she made filled the stone room.

He scooped up a double handful, which was the most of them—round, cold coins of many different sizes with some other shapes mixed in. A jeweled cross about the size of his palm and a couple of small statues of saints sifted out of the money. His thumb moved, of its own volition, and rubbed the dust off a ruby set in the cross. The sunlight hit it and made it throw a flame like it was on fire.

"We've found it!" Sky said.

Her voice was light as a sigh, floating, full of wonder.

He could only nod.

Father Sun's rays are traveling. Father Sun's rays are traveling to find his heart in the Earth Mother's breast.

The song moved in the air, swirled around the room like a wisp of smoke, lighter even, somehow, than Sky's whisper. Because the song was a song and because it was sounding in his ears again in his grandfather's high, haunting voice.

"We've found it!" Sky said, again, in her usual husky voice now that the strength was coming back to her. "Oh, Rafael, we can stop the war!"

"And I can buy Beck's *rancho*."

"No!" she cried. "No, Rafael, surely not now!"

She squatted down beside him and held the torch directly over his hands.

"There isn't enough treasure to do both!" she cried, bending closer to see how much more was down in the nest of rocks. There wasn't much.

Her wide, brown gaze found his. Her auburn hair framed her face, the incandescent light in the cave made her look like an angel.

"Rafael, could you please let me have it all to bribe Waters?" she asked. "He's not a poor

man—I'm afraid it'll take more than this to
make him move back across the river."

His hands moved to give it to her.

To give her everything. His lips parted to
say, *yes*, yes, take it, Sky.

His heart ached to see her smile.

But he closed his eyes and hardened his
heart, clenched his hands around the treasure.

He had to think farther ahead than she was
willing to see.

It was possible that he himself was home-
less already and it was certain as the coming
storm that Windrider's band would be home-
less soon. Beck's *rancho* could prove to be a
precious refuge for them all.

But he couldn't tell Sky again that in a few
years her people would lose all of Comancheria.
And their way of life.

She wouldn't believe him, especially not
now, when her hopes were running rampant
in her eyes.

"I told you I was coming with you expecting
half the treasure," he said.

She sat back on her heels and stared at him,
holding the torch higher with a wavering
hand.

"*After* you had made think that you cared for
me! *After* you had made me care for you! *After*
we had lain in each other's arms. *That* is when
you said that you expected half the treasure!"

He looked down at what was in his hands.

"Half of this will move Waters if any of
it will," he replied, letting the coins spill
through his hands back down into their old

home. "This is the treasure of the legend, Sky. Owning half of what so many men have been looking for will make Waters special."

"But no more so than your *Señor* Beck with the other half!" she cried, and grabbed his arm with a hand that shook him, hard. "Waters will come back across the Gallinas again as soon as he finds out!"

She stood up, then, and held the torch so she could see his face.

"You *have* to give it to me, Rafael! You have to! Otherwise, all this searching and your getting shot and suffering and my putting my people in danger while begging you to help me has been for nothing! Half of this little bit of coins won't be enough to stop the war!"

He stood up, too, to try to look into her face, to talk sense to her.

But she glared at him with a fierce hurt in her eyes that formed a curtain he couldn't see through.

"How can you betray me like this after what we've had together?" she cried. "Rafael, how can you be so selfish? So *greedy*? You're as greedy as this Waters, who has other ranches, too! You already *have* an enormous *rancho*!"

Her huge, dark eyes burned with fury.

"An enormous *rancho* which used to be part of Comancheria, I tell you!"

Such anger as Rafael had not let himself feel for years surged through him. Nothing, *nothing* had taken over his emotions with such force since he had been a little boy.

Nothing except the love he had felt for her.

That realization terrified him.

He turned it into fury.

"My *father* already has a huge *rancho!*" he shouted. "I have no land that I can control completely. If I buy Beck's *rancho*, then your people can come there as a refuge!"

She stared at him, blinking in surprise, trying to make sense of what he had said.

"What do you mean?" she finally blurted.

"I mean that you might as well leave this treasure right where it is for all the good it's going to do as a bribe for Waters! I told you that at the rendezvous when you begged me to come with you. I've told you that since."

"You do not know one thing of which you speak!"

"I know a hell of a lot more than you do about the world and the way it works! Waters is only the first of thousands—*thousands*—of Anglos just like him. Greedy, land-hungry white men with nothing to lose."

He grabbed her by the shoulders, made the torchlight dance crazily all over her face.

"They're coming, Sky. They're going to pour across the Gallinas like the water pouring down from the mountains between its banks and there isn't enough old treasure anywhere in Comancheria or New Mexico Territory to stop them."

She stared at him, lips parted. Her hand shaking like the aspens in the wind.

"The Comanche way of life is fast disappearing," he said, brutally. "It can't last, not even if Windrider should fight this war and win it. You know that, Sky."

"I do not! I'll never admit that such a thing is true!"

"Then you're very foolish. Think how many of our people are already on reservations in Texas! At least if I had a *rancho* of my own, there would be some other refuge."

She drew herself up to her full height. Her hair brushed his chin. Then she stepped back from him, shrugged off his hands, held the torch like a weapon.

"We do not need your refuge," she said, her voice trembling with pride.

"You sure as hell needed my beef this past week," he roared. "And that was no disgrace. I myself may be needing someone to give me food. Don Diego may have disinherited me for coming after you."

"If that's true, then I'm sorry," she said, with an icy dignity he had never seen in her before. "But I can't give in to your plan. My people will *not* lose their range. Windrider was mistaken—we will *not* be squeezed from the face of Mother Earth."

Her voice broke, but she forced the words to keep coming out.

"I thought we cared for each other, you and I, but now I see the truth."

She took a step backward, away from him.

"I do not even know you, Rafael."

Chapter 18

The first stinging sheets of ice blew into the canyon just as Rafael returned to the room beneath the ledge. Their pinging noise started hitting his ears before he left the tunnel a few steps behind Sky.

She threw the torch into the fire and ran out into the storm, turning her face to the west. The wind blasted her hair out behind her, brought its strands back to whip around her face.

With every heartbeat, the sleet blew harder, thicker, faster.

He grabbed a blanket from the stack and ran out to her, tried to put it around her shoulders.

She shoved it back into his hands.

"We will be *tahkitemi?aru*, slip standing up, before this is over!" she shouted. "Get the horses!"

The words came at him like the icy pellets themselves. He threw the blanket over his arm, so as not to spook their mounts, and started toward El Lobo.

He and the mare had turned their rumps to the storm; the horses were moving toward him and toward the cave, the ice already sticking to their manes and tails, forelocks and ears. It

315

made a ghostly stripe down the middle of their backs and a medicine hat of white on each of their polls, painting them for battle.

He and Sky led them into the mouth of the tunnel nearest the warm water and the grass by that pool, where they had been together such a short time ago. They secured the horses without speaking and went back to their room, separately, to build up the fire.

Sky put water to boil, still without saying a word to him.

Rafael went to the wood, started breaking limbs to the right length.

She yelled at him over the roar of the wind.

"Don't tear that wound open now! It will be hard enough for you not to freeze without losing any more blood."

Warm words, but in a tone as cold as the storm.

He snapped a limb as big around as his wrist and stacked both the pieces before he saw how she was shaking.

He took up the blanket again and went back to the fire where she was working.

"Put this on and wear it or I'll lace you into it with the tie-strings off my saddle!"

"You just try that!"

But when he laid it around her shoulders this time she let it be.

He brought her buffalo robes and spread them out to warm by the fire, then squatted down on one of them beside her.

"It will be hard enough not to freeze if we huddle together in both of your buffalo robes," he said, into her ear while the wind roared out of the west like a stampede of wild cattle. "You might as well let go of some of that anger."

She whirled on him.

"Oh, yes! And let go of half the treasure, too! I'm not huddling in any robes with you. Go ahead and freeze, Rafael! *I* won't!"

He picked up a stick of wood, laid it on the fire.

Wait, he decided. Don't tell her what he had thought of just yet.

She moved the new stick of wood just a bit, placed it to suit herself beneath the pot of water.

The noise of the wind suddenly dropped. The pinging of the pellets stopped.

And the snow began.

Sky went from her knees to her haunches, then sat down, cross-legged, beside the fire.

Her shoulders slumped, she dropped her chin into her hands, placed her elbows on her knees.

"Sky," he said, as quietly as he could against the crack of the fire. "I've thought of a way for both of us to use all the treasure. A way that might bring peace and few more years for the old ways of the *Nermernuh*."

She turned her face and looked at him, not speaking.

"Listen to this," he said, and swallowed hard because his throat had gone dry.

She listened.

"Why don't we take all the treasure to the commander of the American soldiers at Fort

Biddle—that's their name for Hatch's Ranch—
and tell General Sykes he can claim it for his
country if he'll *force* Waters to move?"

Sky scowled at him, but she sat waiting.
Thinking.

"The general and his men are here to keep
peace between the New Mexicans and the
Comanche," he went on. "And his job would
be easier if the treasure was found and the
treasure hunters were gone. His government
could display what has been only legend for
three hundred long years and General Sykes
would be famous."

She stared at him for the longest time.

"And what about your *rancho*? What will
you do if Don Diego has truly disinherited
you?"

"The New Mexican government might give
me a grant of land," he said. "That's possible,
since I'm doing them this service."

She frowned and thought about it. Forever.

Finally, she nodded.

"I suppose we could try it. General Sykes
could forbid his men to ambush Windrider.
We'd be paying him for that instead of paying
Waters to leave."

"Yes, you could say that. I really think this
is our best chance, Sky."

"We'll take it, then. And if you don't get
your grant, you're welcome to come and live
with Windrider's band."

His heart caught in his throat. Would it come
to that?

And what if it didn't?

What if he did get a grant and live on it, come to love that one piece of land? Where would Sky be then?

"Well," she said, and fed another stick to the fire, "what'll we do now? We've found the treasure and decided what to do with it when the storm is over."

When the storm was over.

He couldn't bear to think about that.

"You agreed to my idea much faster than I ever thought you would," he said.

She shrugged.

"Everyone always says that I make up my mind too fast, that I'm too quick to act on my feelings."

"When your feelings are true, and yours are, because you *know* things, then you're right to do that."

She leaned forward and looked at him, her brown eyes so wide, huge pools as warm as the falls and the hot springs. Hot as the sun before the snow came.

"You're the only person who has admired me just the way I am since I became a woman," she blurted. "I guess that's why I love you, Rafael."

They stared at each other. The fire gave a giant hiss and the ice gave over almost entirely to snow, whirling in in a cloud through the mouth of the cave to challenge their fire.

Rafael reached out and laid another stick onto it.

He looked at her for a long, long time while the mixed ice and snow swirled and beat outside their cave.

Then he lifted his hands and took her face between them.

"That surprises me," he said, and he was shaking not from the cold.

"Why? Could you not hear what my body was saying to you this morning? And even on that first night we lay together?"

"Yes," he said, and let his mouth curve up in a grin. "But you were so angry when High Wolf gave you to me that it surprises me just the same."

She pretended to hit at him. He caught her hand.

"To answer your question," he drawled, "*this* is what we'll do now."

He lay back into the buffalo robe and pulled her down with him, wrapped her firmly in his arms while the canyon grew colder. Outside, the blankets were made all of snow instead of sleet and the blizzard began to rage.

Fay hobbled the horses inside the cave they'd finally found and went back to his job of piling in wood. He spit out a curse as the boss motioned for him to move faster.

The old bastard could see he was moving as fast as he could.

He was just mad as a hornet because he had a hole in his arm where Montoya's bullet went through it and a chunk out of his shoulder where the Comanche girl's arrow had caught him.

Fay tucked his face into his shoulder and grinned to himself. Funny that the boss would take two wounds and nobody else had any.

"Better start sayin' your prayers," he said, with a teasing glance at the old man. "Looks to me like the Great Spirit's trying to tell you something."

The other boys laughed, but not too hearty, since they all knew Waters was worse, much worse, to live with when he was riled.

What a deal to look forward to! No telling how many days and nights snowed in with the King of the Tightwads and Stupid Sullivan and Golden Boy Raymond Dale and no whiskey to be found.

Now *that* would be a real treasure to find!

"Better bring in another load or two before the snow covers all the deadfall completely," Waters ordered, in his raspy voice.

"Better git on these other boys' cases, too!" Fay shot back at him.

"No treasure's worth this kind of misery," Sullivan grumbled.

Then Waters said something none of them had ever thought they would hear him say and they all stopped where they stood to turn and stare at him.

"To hell with the treasure and the legend and the whole damn thing!" he said. "I'm waitin' now to put a bullet through Montoya's *head* and that Comanche girl's *heart*. That there arrowhead was probably poisoned and I'll never have full use of this arm again."

He touched both of his wounds and looked around at each of his men.

"The minute this snow quits we're gone from here a'huntin' the great Don Rafael and his squaw woman, have you yahoos got that? There's a twenty-dollar gold piece for whichever one of you makes that bitch and bastard pay!"

"Twenty whole dollars?" Fay said, and shook his head as he bent to go out of the cave. "For both?"

That was Charlie Waters to the core. Anybody else, wanting revenge that bad, would've made it a hundred.

The storm roared, blowing the snow so thick and hard that Sky and Rafael barely could tell day from night. It didn't matter, for the time all blended together like the white world did outside their cave.

Nothing was real except what was inside.

Even the horses that they fed mesquite beans inside the cave and held on lead ropes form the mouth of the tunnel stable to drink from the warm pool and paw for mouthfuls of grass seemed like illusions to Sky. Only she and Rafael were real, his body and hers, his words and hers, shared in confiding warmth inside their cocoon of soft, furry robes.

They talked of their childhoods, of their families, of their animals, and the land and the skies that they loved. And he told her that he loved her.

His body told her so over and over again.

And now, any time she said that he was welcome to ride and live with her band, he joined in and dreamed aloud of coming with her to roam the swath of the plains their treasure would make safe.

"When we ride into the Wolf Creek country, I'll go into the Antelope Hills," he murmured, as they were falling asleep on that third night in their own private world. "That sounds somehow familiar to me. Maybe that's where I was when I was taken from The People."

"I'll go with you," Sky said, nestling more securely into the crook of his arm. "Your Spanish will never convince those Kotsotekas that you're one of them."

He hugged her, hard, and pulled the big robe even higher up around their heads.

"But I won't need an interpreter!" he said, nuzzling his lips into her hair. "You're teaching me my old language again."

"So," she said, teasing him. "You don't need me. You don't want me to go?"

He pulled her even closer and threw one long leg over her. She wished the ever-colder air had not forced them to sleep in their clothes.

"I need you, Ysidora Pretty Sky," he growled, his lips brushing her ear, then kissing her neck, "I need you as I have never needed anyone else. Remember that."

Sky gathered those words and settled them carefully in her heart before sleep took her.

The next morning, Father Sun shone brightly enough to blind them. The silence rang loud enough to deafen them.

It woke them both at once. For one long

heartbeat, they lay, startled and still, looking into each other's eyes.

The outside world was real again.

Without a word, they got up and walked to the edge of the overhang.

The snow had drifted so deep that in places it would come to the horses' bellies. Everywhere, even on the highest places, it lay hock deep.

"Dear goodness," Sky breathed. "Oh, Rafael—what if High Wolf couldn't get through?"

"Then neither did the warriors. They haven't taken the warpath yet."

"But they will now! If my father had enough of them together before the storm hit, they'll be painting themselves right now and their horses, getting ready to ride. Right into the guns of the American Army!"

The panic in her voice was well justified. He hadn't told her, but all during the storm he had doubted that High Wolf could have been far enough ahead of it.

They had to hurry, to stop the ambush.

He had keep that in his mind every second so he wouldn't think about his time with her being over.

"Give me an empty parfleche," he said, turning back into the cave that had been their home. "I'll go get the treasure while you start packing."

Hurried as he was, though, he couldn't resist first walking up to the spot in front of the horses' tunnel and looking out across the snow-clad land to see the view that reminded him of home. Even with its contours buried beneath the white, it made him homesick.

What was Don Diego doing this morning? If Rafael rode up to the *casa* this minute, would he welcome him home or turn him away?

If he turned him away, how would he bear it? He was part of that land, his body and soul and spirit were all part of that *rancho*.

His sight blurred. He hefted the parfleches and ducked back into the cave.

By the time he returned with the treasure, Sky had the packs done and the horses waiting to be loaded. She was wrapping and tying her leggings.

She had tears in her eyes.

It was all he could do, but he succeeded in pretending that he didn't see.

"We'll divide the treasure between the horses," he said, briskly. "Half and half."

"Why?" she asked.

"In case of attack."

Sky was handing him the small bowl of hot, weak coffee she'd made from the last of their supply. Her fingers froze around it.

"Attack? Who is there to attack us now?"

"Think, Sky," he said, but he couldn't think, either, because he was looking into her eyes and remembering.

"The Anglos, of course," he finally said. "They were caught here, too, by the storm, unless they gave up the search for us a lot sooner than I think."

He looked down at the bowl.

"This is the last of the coffee? Have you had some?"

"Yes?"

He turned the bowl up and drained it. Before this ride was over, he'd need all the warmth he could get.

"You think they're still nearby?" she whispered.

She could barely speak, her lips had gone so stiff.

His heart twisted. But telling her the truth was the best way to protect her.

"If they found shelter," he said. "Keep watch and have your bow ready."

She rubbed charcoal across their cheekbones to cut down the glare, he gave her his extra hat for the same reason, he laid his rifle across his pommel, and they rode out into the white vastness.

He felt tears sting his eyes. The glittering landscape was almost too bright to bear. He squinted into it, swung his gaze and El Lobo's head to the north.

And put his mind on getting them safely through to Hatch's Ranch as fast as was possible in these conditions. North was the quickest way out of the canyon and the one they had to take, even though the Anglos had been following from that direction.

"Oh!" she cried. "I hope the snow is twice this deep at Windrider's camp. *Three times* this deep, so he won't lead the war party out yet! He is so stubborn!"

Her voice broke on that last word.

"So wonderful, too," she said, and the words came clearly to him across the snow. "I can't believe how much I love him. I really *miss* him!"

Rafael swallowed hard. He loved his father as much as she loved hers. And he belonged with him as much as she belonged with hers.

He tried to push that out of his mind, tried to concentrate on the journey.

"Keep your bow ready," he called to her, as she sent Far Girl pushing ahead, and she raised one hand in answer. "We'll go around the west end of the mesa's north crescent, then we'll strike southwest for Hatch's Ranch. It adjoins Don Diego's . . . my father's . . . holdings."

That thought, and the act of speaking his father's name, split open his heart as if it were a melon, ripe in the sun. An overwhelming flood of homesickness poured through him, bringing picture after picture to his mind.

His cattle had been out in this storm, including some mother cows trailing fall calves. Several hundred head must have still been in the grazing lands high in the Loma Parda.

Part of the horse herd was in the Mucha Que pasture when he left home. It had lots of junipers for windbreaks, but it had some sheer drop-offs, too.

The vaqueros would have to ride now for days, looking for animals hurt and in trouble, breaking ice on the ponds and rivers, hauling hay everywhere. Don Diego would know in general what to orders to give, but he had not

been active in running the *rancho* for three or
four winters.

Rafael loved that lifesaving work as much
as any in the cycle of seasons on the *rancho*.
Don Diego would, no doubt, not handle the
particulars of it as Rafael wanted them done.

And his health was not good. He might over-
do his strength.

Rafael's hand tightened on the rifle.

Don Diego might make himself sick this very
day, alone with the responsibilities, without his
son, whose life *he* had once saved.

His other hand tightened on the reins, his
legs aching to kick El Lobo into a run. A run
for home.

He urged the stallion on, pushed him to
catch up with Far Girl.

"I wonder how my parents and my cattle
have fared through the storm," he said, aloud,
calling across the quiet snow to Sky.

He was surprised to hear a tremble in his
voice. He tried to speak again without it.

"My father, no doubt, is riding out with
the vaqueros this morning to see to all the
animals."

The moment he heard himself speak, he
knew that he would never, ever be able to
ride away from home and go roaming through
Comancheria. Much as he would love that freedom, much as it called to his Comanche blood,
he was now, through and through, a ranchero.

Ranchero of one, specific place. El Rancho
del Cielo. The great, spreading stretch of plains
grassland and mountains, aspen woods and

piñon, ponderosa pine and spruce, wildflowers and sage that lay between the two *ríos*—Pecos and Gallinas.

Pray God in Heaven that he was still welcome there.

"You can stop and see about your *rancho* after we've talked with the general," she said. "Before you come with me to find our new camp."

The confident words hit his ears like bullets flying.

He whipped around in the saddle to look at her, an instinctive gesture, as if to protect himself.

She stared at him, her huge brown eyes searching his face.

"You can't leave your *rancho*," she said, slowly, and he could see that she was speaking each realization as it fell into her head. "You love that place too much. I saw you in front of the tunnel's mouth this morning, looking out across the view of the country that reminds you of your home."

Tears flooded her eyes then, and she lashed out at him in a thin, tight voice like the stroke of a whip to try to stop them.

"*My* father, no doubt, is worried about his *people*, for he has no cattle!"

Her eyes blazed, her beautiful face glowed with their fire. The fire of fury.

"You forget quickly that you are one of his people, Rafael," she said, and kicked Far Girl to go faster as if she wanted to run away from him.

The deep snow made that impossible.

"But then, unlike the rest of Windrider's people, you have no need to worry about starving or freezing without enough buffalo, or being rounded up and sent to a reservation, or throwing your body into the mouth of a white army's guns!"

Her voice, too, trembled then, with the same homesickness he had heard in his own, and with despair and sorrow. Despair and an awful regret.

Because she did love him. Her eyes, even full of fury, still told him so.

"I could never live in one place, the same place, all my life the way you do!"

She sent the bitter words slashing at him.

"And I do not understand how you, one of the *Nermernuh*, can do so, either."

He tried, but he could not tear his eyes from hers.

She was wild with anger, but she meant what she had just said.

The tears sprang into his eyes again and blinded him worse than the sun off the snow.

He would never be able to keep her and the *rancho*, too.

Sky rode through the snow, muttering encouragement to Far Girl, never speaking to Rafael nor lifting her head to acknowledge that he was still there. He had ridden out ahead of her, to let El Lobo's longer, stronger legs break the trail and she could not bear to look at him.

If she did, her terrible love for him would

kill her. It already had killed her soul the minute he'd said that about his *rancho* and she had
heard his boundless love for it in his voice.

How could she have been so lost in her
dreams that she didn't realize, back there in
the cave, how strong that bond ran between
him and his land?

She should have known then that he could
never leave it.

Her heart broke open and dripped out her
blood, drop by drop. She was surprised she
couldn't see the red spots staining the snow.

He would leave her, as soon as they'd finished this business with the treasure and the
army.

He would go back to El Rancho del Cielo
and stay there for the rest of his life.

He *didn't* belong with her, after all.

Once they parted, she would never see him
again.

Finally, after a time that seemed longer than
two lifetimes, but when Father Sun was only
halfway up in the heavens, they rode out of
the canyoned cranny in the mesa's wall and
onto the flat to the north. The snow was only
hoof-deep here, and Sky pushed past Rafael to
take the lead again for a while.

So she wouldn't have to see him and be
reminded.

So she could pretend she was only out a little
way from the camp of her band. She bore due
west and soon Far Girl rounded that end of the
mesa's horn-shaped north side and turned to
head southwest.

Toward the place that would take Rafael away from her.

Before they could even get lined out in that direction, though, Far Girl jumped sideways.

Then Sky heard the bullet come whining past her head.

Chapter 19

And another. And another.

One came very close and the other missed her by a good distance.

But it almost hit Rafael.

She whipped her bow off her shoulder, turned in her saddle while she drew an arrow and urged Far Girl to go faster. The shots had come from the tip of the pointed horn-shaped side of the mesa.

There. A glimpse of red cloth. And horses. And men. In a sparse grove of piñons.

There was no other cover in any direction.

And the snow lay too deep for the horses to run.

"Drop to the off side!"

She shrugged the blanket she wore around her shoulders off onto Far Girl's rump, ready to follow her own command.

But Rafael was ignoring it.

Her pounding blood congealed.

He *stood* in the stirrups, making himself an even better target, and lifted his rifle to his eye. Calmly, deliberately, with his body twisted to look behind him, he sighted in their attackers.

His bravery truly was that of a warrior!

He fired.

A scream of pain came tumbling to them over the snow, then Rafael was yelling. At her.

"Pass me! Get ahead of me, Sky, and keep going. No matter what happens, head southwest and don't stop."

Instead of doing what he said, she followed his example and turned, nocked the arrow and raised her bow to shoot, but she knew as she did it the enemy was so far away that she would only waste the arrow.

"Get around me, Sky, and do it now!"

His voice shook with fury and fear for her and he was pulling El Lobo down to a dangerously slow pace to give her a chance to go ahead of him, so she dropped the arrow back into her quiver and did as he said.

He fired again. That shot brought a hoarse yell and a curse.

And another shot whizzing by Sky's head in the very next breath.

Rafael shouted, "Get down!"

She stretched out along Far Girl's neck, screaming inside from frustration. There was nothing she could do. Nothing.

More and more shots rang out and came close, way too close, to them.

Both horses managed to move faster, making zigzagging lines of hoofprints through the snow. Sky stared down and back at Far Girl's trying to see El Lobo's trail following, desperate to see if Rafael was safe.

And then, strangely, all the shooting stopped. She raised up and turned to see that Rafael rode right behind her, unhurt, twisted in the saddle so he could watch their backs, rifle at the ready.

But the silence held.

"What happened?" Sky called. "Why did they stop?"

"I can't imagine!" he shouted back. "But let's not hang around here to try to find out!"

Everything fell quiet again except for the crunch and swoosh of the horses' legs, plowing through the snow. They were moving faster than she would ever have guessed they could, partly because the snow was thinner here on the exposed plain than in the protected canyon.

Then one, unintelligible word, and another, sounded loud and sharp, cracking out into the air from the piñons. They echoed off the rocks of the mesa and died.

But no more shots sounded.

The horses crunched through the snow.

Rafael's low voice called, "We're safe. Out of range and they're not coming out to chase us!"

His jubilance pulled her to him like an outstretched hand and she slowed the mare as he turned to face front.

In that first, shining moment their eyes met. In joy.

Joy that suddenly turned to a dark, fierce truth that came roaring to them through the brilliant cold air of the morning faster than the bullets of Waters and his men.

They were lost, anyway.

Fire leapt between them across the snow.

And her heart went right out of her body.

They were lost.

Waters's shots had not hurt them, had not killed them, but they were lost, anyway.

Because they loved each other more than life.

And they would part.

"Put them damn guns down, now," Fay said. "Careful, real careful, toss 'em to me. Slide 'em right on over here."

He dug his elbows into the sides of the old mackinaw he wore and held them there, trying to make his arms stop shaking. The muzzle of his old gun waved from Old Man Waters to Sullivan and back again, then steadied.

"Nickerson, have you lost your ever-lovin' *mind*?" Waters demanded. "I'll have you hanged for this."

"Yeah!" Sullivan growled. "I'll string you up myself, you sidewinder. Can't you see Montoya's done shot me? I gotta bind up this wound."

"Lay your gun down and you can use both hands," Fay said, in a voice he was proud to hear didn't have a tremor in it.

"The devil you say."

He smiled. He stared from Sullivan's pale, ugly face to Waters's pale, wrinkled one to Raymond Dale's pretty blue eyes.

"Don't trouble yourselves with plans all that far in the future," he said. "Best git what few brains you all got amongst you workin' on the best trail to take walkin' home!"

"Walk!" Sullivan gasped. "I need to ride! To a doctor!"

"You ain't bad enough to need no doctor," Fay said. "You're hardly even bleedin'."

"I knowed better than to hire you in the first place!" Waters rasped.

"Then you oughtn'ta done it."

Fay constantly swept his gun back and forth over them as he gathered the weapons he had forced them to throw at his feet. One by one, he stuffed them into his worn saddlebags.

"Somethin' else you oughtn'ta done, Waters," he said, "is to shoot at a woman."

" 'Specially not at no beautiful Comanche girl that Fay falls in love with," Sullivan sing-songed sarcastically.

Fay continued, unperturbed, "That girl's a wild, free thing who belongs in this country. This here country belongs to her. Nobody's blowin' her out of her saddle long's I can do somethin' about it."

Then he looked at each one of them, keeping the muzzle of his gun still moving constantly.

"Now, if you're lucky," he said, conversationally, "your mounts'll come when you whistle."

He swung up into his saddle and backed Red toward the trees where the other horses were tied.

He jerked their latigos loose, dropped their saddles, pulled their tie-reins loose, and pulled off their bridles, let all the tack fall to the ground.

"Course," he said, "you're a gonna need a mighty loud whistle."

He grinned, right into Waters's face.

"Have fun, boys, carryin' your gear back to the ranch!"

Then he slapped the old miser's gelding on the rump.

"Eeyah! Eeyah!"

The three horses scattered, crowhopping through the rocks and the trees and the snow down the side of the mesa.

Fay turned his mount and followed them.

Rafael rode on ahead of her, breaking the trail.

Breaking her heart.

It was a torment that went on for hour after hour and would go on forever. They stopped twice, to melt snow for the horses to drink and to rest them. They spoke very little, even then.

Words had no more power. Words couldn't come close to touching this pain.

So Sky simply bore it, following Rafael across the flat, then the more rolling plain all the way to the now-frozen, shallow Río Gallinas. They walked the horses across it without speaking.

And she followed him back up into the hills where he had found her that day that now seemed from another life. She pushed away the knowledge that she would lose him when Father Sun next rose up from behind Mother

Earth and let herself remember every moment of these days and nights they had spent together.

Then she simply watched him, memorizing for all time the shape of his shoulders, the carriage of his head. His seat on a horse.

So she could use them to warm her empty bed.

They pressed on, eating only jerky in the saddle, pushing straight for the fort all the rest of the day and through the dusk, into the night. West of the river, the snow lay across the land in a blanket that was thinner still, and they chanced a faster gait when they rode down out of the hills.

"How's Far Girl doing?"

Rafael turned in the saddle and glanced back at her.

"She has another half day in her," Sky said, having to clear her throat it had been so long since she'd spoken. "Keep going. Windrider may have taken the war trail when Father Sun came out this morning."

They had to stop the war. That was the reason they had ridden so far, taken such chances, the reason they now suffered all this pain.

Peace. That would be the good to come of it all.

And their love, Sky silently admitted, letting herself look at Rafael again. That love would exist even when they were apart.

Her heart twisted. At least, her love for him would endure.

And so would his love for her.

He loved her, but just not as much as he loved his *rancho*.

Sister Moon came out to shine on the snow, her rays glittering like showers of tears scattered over it. She was no longer full, a sliver had been sliced off one side of her, a piece the same shape as the Mesa Rica, but her light looked as strong as it had then.

Strong enough to blind her to the fact that it was night.

They stopped once more to rest.

"Hatch's headquarters are just over that low ridge," Rafael said, as the horses snuffled and blew clouds of steam out into the cold air. "We'll wake up the general."

"Maybe we should wait until morning. He might not agree to our bargain if he's angry."

"It'll be nearly sunrise when we get there."

He started El Lobo walking again.

"But no matter when, he'll agree. The treasure will be a coup for him. Besides, I've heard he thinks that The People are not being treated right."

Rafael's voice sounded so melodious, so dearly familiar and precious to her ears that tears came to her eyes, freezing on her lashes. She had to try to remember that, too—exactly the right sound to hear in her dreams.

Far Girl moved forward.

Peace. Stopping the war. That's what she must think about now, even though there would never be a stopping of the war that raged in her heart.

They rode up to the headquarters' buildings

at Hatch's as Sister Moon dropped lower and lower.

"*Hola, la casa!*" Rafael shouted, as they passed a fenced bunch of horses.

And then, in English, as if he had just remembered where he was, he repeated his call.

"Hello, the house! We are friends, riding in!"

Quietly, he said, "Whoa."

El Lobo stopped, so did Far Girl, and they all waited a stone's throw from the edge of the yard.

Sky leaned back in her saddle, placed her hand on the parfleche containing half of the gold. The lumps of the treasure on the inside and the smaller beads on the outside were all cold, so cold.

A terrible wave of doubt swept through her.

What if she was doing the wrong thing? She had it in her hands now, soon she would be giving it away.

In exchange for what? Empty promises?

And Rafael would be giving away his chance to buy his own place.

What if Don Diego had disinherited him? What if now he had no home and no land because he had risked them to help her?

A yellow rectangle fell across the snow.

The door to the house creaked all the way open, a soldier in a blue uniform filled its frame.

"Who's there?" he called.

"Rafael Romero Montoya y Teran, of El Rancho del Cielo!"

Somehow, the sound of his low, rich voice ran, lilting, into her veins. Quickly, she untied the bag holding the treasure to the back of her saddle, reached for the empty one hanging beneath it that had once contained jerky, and, while the guard demanded to know what they wanted and Rafael demanded to speak to the general, she moved some of the coins into the smaller parfleche. She scooped up a few more and threw them in, also.

When she glanced at the two men they were paying her no attention at all.

The guard went back into the house and shut the door.

Rafael rode El Lobo closer to the house, turned and motioned for her to follow.

She did, while she drew the parfleche containing the remainder of the treasure into her lap and prayed with all her heart that she was about to use it in the best way for her people.

Rafael stood in his stirrup and swung down.

The yellow light appeared again to fall across him, dusting his hair and his shoulders with gold as he took off his hat.

"The general's asleep," the soldier said. "I hate to disturb him. You could go to the barn . . ."

"You could go tell him we're here," Rafael interrupted, shooting the words over his shoulder like bullets as he came to Far Girl's side and help up his arms to help Sky down. "Or you could get out of the way because we're coming in."

His flat tone allowed no argument and by

the time he and Sky had climbed the low steps
to the door, the guard was standing aside.
They entered a huge, rambling room with an
iron stove in one corner.

"Have a seat," the guard said, pointing to
the several empty chairs around a worn oak
table, but looking, curiously, at Sky.

"Mr. Hatch is up and he has put the coffee
on. Help yourself while I tell him, also, that
you're here."

Sky took two steps in and stopped, trying
to get her bearings, trying to think. Trying to
adjust to the heat instead of the cold and the
stillness instead of the motion of Far Girl's
stride.

Rafael touched her arm.

The guard passed through, throwing another questioning glance at Sky on his way into
the interior of the house. Rafael and Sky
walked to the table and dropped the bags
of coins.

"This feels so strange to me," she murmured,
and loosened the blanket around her shoulders
as she turned to look up at Rafael. "Like it is
not real."

The room was hot, suddenly, unbearably hot
after the cold outside. Yet, inside, her body
was all ice.

"It's our only real chance," he said, frowning
down at her. "I truly believe that, Sky."

He turned away and went to the stove.

She stood there, uncertain whether she
wanted more to take off her blanket in the
heated room or burrow down into it for com-

fort. When Rafael came back with two tin mugs of steaming coffee, she left the blanket on and sat down to drink.

But she couldn't raise the cup to her lips. She could only wrap both hands around it to try to stop their trembling and stare at the treasure on the table.

Soon it would be gone and so would Rafael.

"Well! Hullo, there, neighbor! I reckon it's about time you came home!"

The loud, gruff voice brought Rafael to his feet and turned Sky around in her chair with the cup still clutched in her hands.

A grizzled, red-bearded man strode into the room with his hand outstretched. Rafael introduced him to her as Mr. Hatch.

"Glad to meet you, ma'am," he said, with the utmost politeness, but the look he gave her was as openly wondering as the soldier's.

Then he cast a curious, slightly disapproving eye on the parfleches in the middle of his table and slid a quick glance back at Sky, as if she were guilty of putting them there.

Then he dismissed her completely and turned back to Rafael.

"Don Diego's standing on his ear, worrying and waiting for you to come home," Mr. Hatch boomed. "He's sent word out in all directions for people to keep a lookout for you in case the blizzard caught you on the trail."

Sky listened, assimilated the English words.

Rafael's father had not disowned him. He still had claim to the huge *rancho* and he was welcome there.

He would leave her for sure.

But, then, she already knew that.

She lifted the cup to her half-frozen lips, made herself take a drink of the coffee.

The hot liquid melted the cold inside her, tantalized her throat and her stomach with faint hope. But her mind remained frozen, her mind and her heart. They both were exhausted, too numb to think or feel.

Until Rafael looked up and said, "General Sykes."

She set down her cup with a thump and turned around to look.

A tall man with dark hair and deep blue eyes strode into the room.

Immediately, he took control of it. Even dressed in ordinary clothes instead of the crisply pressed, gold-trimmed uniform and the shining boots he wore, that would have been true. He was accustomed to getting his way, he expected to be in command, and he was.

Sky could sense his power and it tightened her hands around her cup.

If he said yes to their proposal, he could stop the war before it started. Instinctively, she knew that.

But he might say no.

The set of his large, square jaw proclaimed to the world that he was not easily swayed.

He gave her one, brief glance as he reached the table and held out his hand to Rafael. But it was different from the looks from the guard and from Mr. Hatch. It lacked the curiosity.

It accepted her presence as a person.

"General Sykes, I would like to present you to *Señorita* Ysidora Pretty Sky," Rafael said, when they had greeted each other and had shaken hands. "Daughter of Windrider, War Chief of the Antelope Band of the *Nermernuh*."

"I'm glad to meet you!" the general boomed, and bowed over her hand.

He met her eyes in a brief, straight look.

And, to her surprise, he continued to speak to her instead of behaving as if she were another of the chairs, as Mr. Hatch had done.

"I have a great deal of respect for your father, Miss Pretty Sky," he said. "He's done a good job of leading his people in these hard times that are most unfair to them."

Astounded at hearing such talk from a white man, Sky looked at him again.

"Thank you," she said, in spite of the fact that her heart was thudding up into her throat.

She had to know. Now.

She pried her stiff lips apart once more.

"General Sykes," she said, and the English felt rusty to her tongue. "I must ask you one question, please. Have you sent troops across the Gallinas to protect Waters's ranch?"

Then she bit her tongue. She couldn't bear to hear his reply.

"No," he said, thoughtfully. "The blizzard has kept us snowed in."

Sudden tears flowed into her eyes.

Sky brushed her hair back from her face, dropped her hand to the table because she couldn't stop it from shaking, and held his gaze with hers. A sigh of relief escaped her.

"There is no need to send your men there, now," she said, quickly. "Windrider is fore-warned. He will not raid that ranch."

"I'm glad to hear that," the general boomed, in his low voice that reminded her in some way of Rafael's, although it wasn't as full of melody. "A lot of what has been happening in Comancheria is very wrong, to my way of thinking, and I always regret greatly when it leads to bloodshed."

"We are hoping that Windrider will not raid anyone, anywhere," Rafael said, smoothly, and pulled out the chair across the table from him for the general. "If you will help us, General Sykes, we may be able to avert a war."

"I'll be glad to listen."

"Shall I leave you?" asked Mr. Hatch.

"No, no, please stay," Rafael said, and suddenly, subtly, *he* was the one with the whole room in the palm of his hand.

Sky held her breath. If Rafael could present the plan in the right way, all of the pain of the treasure hunt would be worth it.

All three of the men sat down.

Rafael laid his hand on the parfleche he had brought in.

"General Sykes, this is the treasure of the Mesa Rica."

"Well! God help us all!" Mr. Hatch exclaimed.

General Sykes looked at the parfleche with dark blue eyes gone wide with surprise.

"We think this is the main thing that

drew Waters to settle across the Gallinas again," Rafael went on, "and that settlement is what has roused Windrider to call for war."

"That old legend has made crazy men out of a hundred half-sane ones, Waters most of all," the general said, lifting his piercing eyes to Rafael's face. "Are you telling me that that story was true all along?"

"True in that it does exist, but not nearly in the quantity that the stories would have it."

"Where'd you find it?"

"In a cave in the Mesa Rica. *Señorita* Ysidora Pretty Sky and I found it, and we propose handing it over to you if you are willing to meet our terms."

The general raised an eyebrow in surprise, then frowned terribly. Sky's heart dropped into her moccasins.

Rafael, though, was undaunted.

"If you'd spread the word that the treasure has been found and is in the hands of the United States Army," he said, "Waters might leave Comancheria, and the other treasure hunters certainly will. Even if you have to drive Waters out according to the provisions of the current agreement between the United States and the Comanches . . ."

He paused for the slightest moment to let that thought hang in the air, so the general would know that they were paying him to do what was already his duty, then Rafael finished laying out his bargain.

". . . obtaining the ancient treasure for your government and preventing a bloody Plains Tribes war would be quite beneficial to your career, General, would it not?"

Sky didn't hear a word of Mr. Hatch's surprised exclamations or Rafael's replies to him. Her ears had space only for General Sykes's answer.

To her astonishment, he smiled and looked from her to Rafael and back again.

"I applaud the two of you," he said, "not only for your discovery but for the astuteness of your thinking in putting it to use. Let me see what you have here."

That was an answer of flattery that was no answer at all, but Sky felt not one tremor of worry. Everything about the general bespoke sincerity, and her heart was already starting to beat fast, as if he had already agreed and their plan had succeeded.

She tried to make it slow down.

Rafael's hands moved to the skin bags, then stopped.

"Oh, and General Sykes, one other thing," he said. "I would ask you to put in a word with the government of the Territory of New Mexico concerning the application I intend to file for a land grant."

The general nodded, staring off into space as if he were thinking hard.

"Land grant," he said. "That'd be easy."

So Rafael opened the first bag and dumped the coins and crosses out onto the scarred table.

Sykes stared at the modest pile, lifted his arms and ran his fingers through it. He picked up the cross set with rubies, looked at it carefully.

"This gives all appearances of being the real thing," he said, and looked at Rafael.

"It is."

"This'll prevent a lot of long, cold marches and bloody battles," the general said, and held out his hand for Rafael to shake on the bargain. "I'll take it to my superiors and Waters will be back here, west of the Gallinas, before we have the next snow."

The tightness in Sky's muscles gave way. She slumped, her tired spine collapsing against the hard spindles of the chair.

The general fixed his blue gaze on her.

"I'm pleased to have this new weapon of an ancient treasure, *Señorita*," he said. "Thank you."

He turned back to Rafael.

"Montoya, if removing Waters will stop Windrider from taking the warpath, then he's stopped, but I don't know how long the peace can last."

A savage despair waiting just at the corner of Sky's mind to snap it up in one huge gulp, flashed to life, exhausted as she was.

Her victory, Rafael's victory, that they had fought for so hard was about to be snatched away!

She tried to close her ears, but the general's low, confident voice marched relentlessly on. If she believed him about stopping the war, she would have to believe him about this.

Every instinct in her told her he was a truthful man.

So she did not want him to say this.

But he did.

"There's such a demand for land, such an insatiable hunger for it, that this spring will bring another bunch of ranchers flocking up here like a plague of locusts," he said. "Someday there'll be too many of them for *anybody*, including the army, to keep out—especially since the politicians don't want us to. When that time comes, not even all of us and all the Indians in all the Plains Tribes will be able to stop them."

The bottomless chasm of hopelessness opened beneath Sky. She could feel herself falling.

Somebody had to dispute him! Somebody had to say it wasn't true. Somebody had to *make* it not be true!

Before she could open her mouth, Rafael spoke.

"No doubt about it," he said, calmly. "I know this is temporary just as well as you do."

He picked up the other parfleche by its bottom and poured its coins out onto the pile already there.

Like the Anglos would spill the blood of her people.

His people, too!

The traitor!

She leapt to her feet, knocking her chair over

as she snatched her blanket from the back of it.
It crashed all the way down as she ran across
the clay tiled floor, straining to see through her
furious tears how to get out the door.

Chapter 20

Rafael rose and reached for his hat and coat.

"Excuse me, *Señores*. The *Señorita* is exhausted from the ride. I must speak with her."

"Let me extend the hospitality of Fort Biddle," General Sykes said. "You can continue to your home and Don Diego when you have rested."

"Send him word that I am here and safe, *por favor*," Rafael said. "And *gracias*. I would be in your debt for rooms for me and *Señorita* Sky."

Then he stepped out into the freezing night to find her, his heart stampeding almost out of his chest.

God help him.

She didn't want to live in one place, she wanted to roam all that was left of Comancheria, yet he must persuade her to come live with him.

If he couldn't, how could *he* live?

He had known he couldn't leave her from the instant they had ridden into this place where he had thought they would part.

He jammed his hands into his sleeves and ran, boots crunching, out across the snow.

In the light of the dying moon he saw her, leading the horses to the racks of hay beside the fort's stables. She heard him coming, threw up her head, and turned to look.

"I'll let Far Girl eat and then I'm leaving!" she called.

Her rich, husky voice trembled with tension. She looked wild as a deer.

As if she would dart away and disappear forever at the slightest start.

He stopped in his tracks.

"Where will you go?"

"Where I belong! To my people!"

He grunted as if he'd been hit.

Now?

She'd never make it to any other shelter, that was one thing for sure. Both she and the mare had gone as far as they could go.

"Many times you don't feel that you belong entirely with your people," he reminded her, fighting to keep his tone calm. "You belong with me."

She dropped the reins and came toward him.

"Yet you will go back to your *rancho* at first light!" she called, bitterly.

He strode across the moonlit snow to meet her.

Neither stopped until they were close enough to touch. For a long time they looked at each other.

His blood was thundering. Beneath its roar, El Lobo's stamping feet and the jingle of his bit were the only sounds.

Rafael thought his heart would burst.

Quietly, he said, "Ysidora Pretty Sky. I love you."

Her enormous brown eyes filled with tears. She tried to blink them away, but they glittered on her lashes like the moonlight on the snow.

She lifted her chin proudly, swallowed hard as she tried not to cry.

"And I love you, Rafael."

She turned away abruptly and walked to her horse.

Rafael watched her, thinking the same thought over and over. *My heart will never beat again.*

She reached up, took something from her saddle, and came back to him with it jingling in her hand.

"I hope it is enough for you to buy that other *rancho*," she said. "I saved it out of the treasure in case Don Diego said that you are no longer his son. You know now that I told the truth when I said that I love you."

She held the gift out to him.

"I will love you forever, Rafael. Think of me when you ride over your land."

Rafael closed his hand around hers and the bag. He reached for her other hand.

"I am overcome," he said, and his voice came out in a low, rough whisper he had never heard before.

Perhaps because he had never spoken of such deep feelings in all of his life.

"I am overcome because you love me and because of the sacrifice you have made."

Tears filled his throat and, for a moment, he couldn't go on.

He swallowed so hard that it hurt.

"You have taught me to follow my feelings, to speak what I feel, Sky. At this moment I want to fall on my knees and beg. *Beg* you . . ."

His lips went so stiff they would hardly move.

"If you love me this much, then don't leave me. Come live on that *rancho* with me. Ride over it with me. Marry me, Sky!"

"No," she said, "I will not marry any man. I will not give any man such power over me."

Strength surged up in him, fired the determination in his blood. He would not accept that. He would not.

"*I* share power with you," he said. "You know that. In rescuing High Wolf, in finding the treasure, in deciding what to do with it."

"I lived too much in our dreams during the blizzard," she said, and her voice broke, at last. "Rafael, I thought you would come to live with my people. With *your* real people. To roam free with us."

She made a little hiccuping sob.

"And then I knew that you loved your *rancho* too much and that was hard enough . . . but . . . but then you agreed with General Sykes . . ."

She was fighting the tears now, as valiantly as she had fought the Anglos.

He could not help himself, he no longer thought of scaring her away, he reached out and grabbed both her shoulders in a fierce grip.

"My real people and you, *Mi Corazón*, soon will have no place to roam free. You heard the general say that the true treasure for the Anglos is land, more and more land, always more land."

"I know, but . . ."

"That greed cannot be stopped, not by you, not by me, not by the American Army or all the warriors of all the Plains Tribes. You must stop your dreaming and face the reality."

She shook her head back and forth, again and again, in one last desperate attempt to deny. Her dark eyes spilled over.

But he drove relentlessly on.

"They will cross the Gallinas by the thousands in the next few seasons, my Pretty Sky. It would be foolish for me to leave a *rancho* that will be mine and now this other one that you and I can buy with this part of the treasure you have saved."

He lifted one hand, touched her cheek.

"I would be leaving those *ranchos* for a freedom that cannot last," he said. "At least, if I have them, you and your family, your whole band, can come there when you must."

Suddenly Sky knew, deep in her heart of hearts, that what he said was true. She had known it ever since Windrider had said in Council that such an unthinkable thing could happen.

She had known it was true since that fateful Council on Don Diego's rancho, when Rafael had seen the vision in her father's fire.

That same magic day when she had first seen Rafael.

"In my heart, in Mr. Hatch's house, I called you a traitor," she whispered. "But you are not. You are a truth-teller."

He nodded. His sad, solemn face was so powerful it could splinter stone.

Yet even Rafael, this man of much *puha*, could not stop the Anglos when they came.

Her trembling lips could barely move.

"You would take us in, even if I do not marry you?"

His hard face stayed the same, but his dark eyes melted with love.

"Any day, any night, any season, any year."

Relief, then panic struck her.

"But, Rafael, what if I cannot bear to live in one place all the time, every season?"

Hope flared in his eyes like kindling thrown onto a flame.

"You can live in a tipi on the patio or in the cottonwood grove or camp down by the river," he said. "You can ride and roam the many thousands of acres of the *rancho* all day every day just so long as you sleep in my arms every night."

She stood still as midnight in the freezing cold dawn and let the warmth of his love flow through her. It washed her tears away.

"Now who is the dreamer?" she teased, and felt her mouth curve into a smile full of love. "What would your parents and all the proper Spanish say of such an arrangement? That I do not belong there."

"Who cares?"

He reached out and drew her close so he could take her into his arms.

"Oh, Sky," he said, into her hair. "It's not that we belong with our blood people or with the proper Spanish. That doesn't matter. We belong with each other."

They held each other tight and rocked back and forth in the snow.

Sky stood on tiptoe and laid her cheek against his.

He snuggled his face into her hair.

Into her ear, he said, "You have taught me the best way, my *notsa?ka?*, my sweetheart. We won't worry about living on one *rancho* or in all of Comancheria. You and I, Ysidora Pretty Sky, we'll live in our hearts."

Avon Romantic Treasures

Unforgettable, enthralling love stories,
sparkling with passion and adventure
from Romance's bestselling authors

COMANCHE WIND *by Genell Dellin*
>   76717-1/$4.50 US/$5.50 Can

THEN CAME YOU *by Lisa Kleypas*
>   77013-X/$4.50 US/$5.50 Can

VIRGIN STAR *by Jennifer Horsman*
>   76702-3/$4.50 US/$5.50 Can

MASTER OF MOONSPELL *by Deborah Camp*
>   76736-8/$4.50 US/$5.50 Can

SHADOW DANCE *by Anne Stuart*
>   76741-4/$4.50 US/$5.50 Can

FORTUNE'S FLAME *by Judith E. French*
>   76865-8/$4.50 US/$5.50 Can

FASCINATION *by Stella Cameron*
>   77074-1/$4.50 US/$5.50 Can

ANGEL EYES *by Suzannah Davis*
>   76822-4/$4.50 US/$5.50 Can

Avon Romances—
the best in exceptional authors and unforgettable novels!

FOREVER HIS Shelly Thacker
77035-0/$4.50 US/$5.50 Can

TOUCH ME WITH FIRE Nicole Jordan
77279-5/$4.50 US/$5.50 Can

OUTLAW HEART Samantha James
76936-0/$4.50 US/$5.50 Can

FLAME OF FURY Sharon Green
76827-5/$4.50 US/$5.50 Can

DARK CHAMPION Jo Beverley
76786-4/$4.50 US/$5.50 Can

BELOVED PRETENDER Joan Van Nuys
77207-8/$4.50 US/$5.50 Can

PASSIONATE SURRENDER Sheryl Sage
76684-1/$4.50 US/$5.50 Can

MASTER OF MY DREAMS Danelle Harmon
77227-2/$4.50 US/$5.50 Can

LORD OF THE NIGHT Cara Miles
76453-9/$4.50 US/$5.50 Can

WIND ACROSS TEXAS Donna Stephens
77273-6/$4.50 US/$5.50 Can